FISHING
THE DEVIL'S TRIANGLE
IN A
DRUG WAR

Capt. Cross Sea Bones

ABSOLUTELY AMAZING eBOOKS

Many thanks to you, SeaSwan, for transcribing this handwritten book. I couldn't have done it without you.

FISHING
THE DEVIL'S
TRIANGLE
IN A
DRUG WAR

INTRO

Into The Triangle

It's the dead and gone days before Doppler radar, in a place that only a few can enjoy and nature rules. Fishermen, smugglers, pirates, poachers and law enforcers take their chances.

It's my 30th birthday, and I'm fishing solo aboard the sixty-five-foot commercial vessel, "HELLCLONE II," bruce anchored in the mud over the northeast ridge of the eighteen fathom rock pile, inside the eastern apex of the Devil's Triangle. Not to be confused with the Bermuda Triangle.

In the still, moonlit and peaceful darkness I'm pulling large mutton snappers out of the coral heads with a hand line, using big chunks of bonito for bait.

Within the reflections cast upon the water by the deck lights, Spanish sardines and Sand Key pilchards are eating crab spawn. Beyond the artificial light in the deep blue crystal clear water, horse eye jacks and black fin tuna rush up from the depths to prey upon the pilchards and sardines. Causing the water to become streaked and glowing with pulsating multicolored bio-luminescence undulating behind the fish as they dart here and there in pursuit of their quarry.

Fishing the Devil's Triangle...

Rare moments in times past I have seen so much fire in the water, and its' fascinating beauty was always a hair raising omen of something foreboding and treacherous on the horizon.

The early morning is flashing lightning. The edge of darkness is laced with lavender, another hair raising omen. The dawn reveals red clouds capped with black and churning. The barometric pressure is falling.

Feeling the pressure change, the terns and the man-o-war birds begin to screech and squawk a raucous cry as they flee from their roosts in the rigging. I curse as northeasterly winds are gusting across a rising tide, peaking to its rip. Causing the gulf to become confused and standing. Its massive waves surging and crossing, their pinnacles cresting with white caps foaming. Off to the sow'west between the breakers that keep building, the jagged teeth of Pulaski Reef are showing. Shrieking winds at one hundred knots. Swinging athwart ships, taking the beating on her port beam ends. Crashing seas smashing in the engine room door, flooding the bilges and stalling the engine. Two hundred fathoms of scope out on four anchors tangling. The bruce anchor is clogged with ripped up coral heads and dragging. The ninety pound plow anchor is sheering the thick gray acidic mud of the gulf bottom. Riding the swells then sliding, the braced grapnel is bent and tumbling. Skipping through the froth with its chutes blown out, the sea anchor is useless.

Cutting rains slice though all the howling. The anemometer has broken. The compass is spinning. Atop the mast a brand new 'Old Glory' has been blown away. In a tattered blue patch there is one star left streaming. Reaching the base of the coral wall in fifteen fathoms and the anchors are ripping up the coral heads trying to fetch. Plunging into the trough thirty degrees to starboard, the anchors have hooked up, splashing into the valley, coming tight on the plow and the bruce. Swinging thirty degrees to port with her timbers groaning and her bows rising as the gulf stands her on her keel end, forcing me to stand on her wheelhouse wall. Her sampson post has ripped loose from her keelson and stem post. Tearing through her forward deck, busting the anchor chute off her stem post then skyrocketing through the air with the windless whirling, its ratchets whining as it disappears into the wall of the following breaker.

Falling into the crest to starboard and she's broaching, burying her cap rail, her bulwarks and half of her deck in the foamy spume. Plunging into a trough that has bottomed out, swinging 270^0 as she goes then rolling hard to port, slamming her beam ends into the coral heads amidships, crushing her gunnels, her galley bulkheads, and rupturing her deck. Righting herself on the swell, water pouring over her rails and gushing from her scuppers, her rigging thrashing violently and her jam cleats shattering, only to be heaved upon the reef, with relentless pounding breakers filling her to the cap rails, grinding her keel and planking into the coral heads.

Under my feet the deck feels firm, but I can hear her fragile ribs moan with their cracking. As the raging gulf and the stone hard reef snaps her keel and hogs her, I hear reports like heavy guns firing as her shrouds and stay wires are bursting, then whipping and lashing, becoming encased with St. Elmo's electric blue fire humming and sizzling. As the breakers roll her across the reef, pulling away her rigging, she breaks apart into two pieces and sinks in the lee. The sharks are eating my mutton snappers. All the other fish are hiding, knowing only vigilance before dying.

Lashing some of her busted timbers together, I'm looking death and Ol' Davy Jones in the face and making them wait. I've been here before and I'll have my way only to be here again. Riding her timbers on a swell flowing to the sow'west at break-neck speed, I can see the Australian pine trees and the Malaysian coconut palms bending to the wind among the jungle brush of Loggerhead Key. Cast upon that beach, taking my bounces smartly, rolling in a ball up the rise, over the flat through the brush and down into the lee, hunkering behind the root ball of a blown over pine tree as the wind hurled sand, spray and sea-born critters past me.

There was a windblown and bruised aloe plant tangled in the roots of the pine tree. I pulled it to me and split one of the long, thick leaves with my knife. I smeared the contents on my numerous cuts and scrapes. As I did so, I thanked all the hogs I've eaten for making my skin too thick to bleed for more than a few seconds. Standing up after the worst of the blowing is over, wandering around to find some raw cracked conch and green coconut milk for an afternoon snack. I made my way through the tangled jungle brush and the blown over trees to the east side of the island. I sat upon a white sandy beach covered in an array of dead sea creatures, coral, turtle grass, sargasso weed and human trash piled in long rows and heaps two fathoms deep. As I gnawed on the sweet, rubbery flesh of the queen conch, I gazed off to the southeast, and I could see some white bone porgies hanging in what was left of the prickly pears, their silver bodies and gold fins glistened in the blazing gulf sun. They will give me the ballast I'll need to face a black sunset.

On the horizon, beyond the porgies and prickly pears, rumbling up the straits, bucking the gulfstream and the ebbing tide, a sinister darkness has formed over the warm waters of the colliding currents. A black squall, flanked to the north and south by six gray funnel clouds bracing the leading edge of the thunderhead. Their cold, swirling vortexes veined and shot through with shattered purple lightning blasting from the core of the squall.

I need to bake them porgies before the rains come. It

shouldn't be too hard to get a fire started. There are plenty of Bic lighters sticking out of the trash heaps and most of the driftwood has been blow dried. I can use the shower to wash off the gulf born microbes. I hate microbes, especially the little round ones that are mostly teeth and asshole, that dig in deep and clog the pores and create a cerbatious cyst that can lead to years of irritating, stinking aggravation.

Perhaps the Coast Guard gents tending the lighthouse will see the smoke and invite me in to ride this one out in their rec-room. If that's the case, maybe I can win a few bucks playing nine ball on their pool table and eat some free hot dogs until I can work someone's deck for a ride back to Fish Mongers Hill.

There will be plenty of ghostly fishing boats tied to the seawalls at the packing houses, and the fish mongers will let me take what I want. I can fish her until her gear is worn out. By then I will have sprung her butts and pounded the caulking out of her. They will have to haul her out with the railway and refasten her.

That will give me some time off to catch a cab to the Green Parrot bar and find a pretty young nurse to help me cure my ills. If there are no nurses drowning their boredom, there will be some social workers, secretaries, and some rich, foxy man-killing bitches from Europe looking for a free boat ride with a hog tough man, and not caring where in the mayhem of hell it goes.

CHAPTER 1

Of Ominous Radio Calls

IT's 35 years later. Youth and humor have been worn thin by high seas and too many thieving salad girls, and there isn't anything left but the devil as I lay sleeping in my recliner. In the pleasant dream, I'm a grumpy dragon smoldering in my cave. Only to be awakened by someone cursing outside of my living room window.

Sitting up, rubbing my eyes, to see my gardener squeezing his enormous bulk past the bulging frame of my patio doorway. Coming through sideways, hunched over, his chin resting on his chest, fists balled up and his biceps flexed. Standing erect and growling, windmilling his arms in the air, rapping his knuckles on the ceiling. Then like the moldy, sour smelling old Dinosaur that he is, he stomped and fumed through the house, leaving me and the dog spinning and whirling in a putrid cloud of gas, all because she was burying her bone in my roses.

Terrified by this arrogant display of ignorance, the poor dog upchucked on the pretty rug. I got out of the Lazy Boy I've been laying around in for the last ten days in my rags and filth, stinking up the place smoking joints of Jamaican Chocolate. I moved the furniture, folded the rug, pulled it out on the patio and hung it over the railing. I got the water hose and sprayed the upchuck into the saber plants that surround my patio.

I love my saber plants. They do their job and demand nothing of me. Though I doubt they love me, because I have thrown more than one noisy, aggressive, overly drunk, pushy person into them. It didn't always shut them up, but it invariably sobered them up for whatever was coming at them next, which was usually the hurricane-proof deck chairs and the gas grill. Many times I tried to help those sort of people. To quote anonymous, "No good deed went unpunished."

Now in my prime years, I manage to derive a certain amount of quiet respect from shooting at them, but only if I just wound them the first time. I monitor Channel 79 on the house VHF. All the guides, weekend warriors and bucket fishermen do the same. Sometimes a commercial fisherman can hear something interesting, funny or gruesome.

As the Dinosaur was squeezing himself through the patio door with a bucket of soapy water and a brush, an ominous call came over the radio waves.

"Wolfredo Comanche calling Cross Bones."

I became transfixed and transported to strange places where even stranger and sometimes very dangerous events occur. Wolfredo Comanche owns a small private airline in the Bahamas that keeps him in trouble. He also owns a commercial fishing boat, "The Swashbuckler." To law enforcement, he is known as The Man in the Bermuda Triangle. In my neighborhood he is called Narly Spiker.

The radio squawked again. The Dinosaur looked at me with raised eyebrows and said, "Want me to answer that?" I gave him my worst frown. He looked away and began scrubbing the rug. I stomped into the house, shaking the floor and rattling the windows. I didn't want to answer the call, but I will have to sooner or later. He owes me big bucks. The least I can do is piss him off.

I keyed the mic attached to the radio and said, "Wolfredo Comanche, you ol' syphilitic wreck. How the hell are you and how are your space herpes? You still blowing whistles and dropping dimes?"

He keyed his mic and said, "Cut the crap. I've got a load of fish coming up the pike to Rye Lee's Hump, and I need you and your clones to help me deal with it."

I said, "Well, we don't need you. We would rather be locked in a room full of squawking, talking parrots. They would make more sense than your ball of wax wrapped in red tape."

He said, "I've got your money."

I said, "I'm looking at my L.T., but the numbers aren't changing."

He cursed and said, "Give me a second."

When the numbers changed I said, "OK, that will get you some talk. But you won't like it."

He cursed some more and then said, "What is that supposed to mean?"

I said, "You've got to hack through some of that red tape, then cut a slice in the ball of wax and tell that malignant can of worms inside that if we like what we hear, I've got to see the same numbers on my L.T. before I pull my braced grapnel out of the coral heads of the Dry Tortugas. Anything that comes up in between must be paid for on sight or it isn't going to happen."

He asked if there was anything else. I said, "Yes, you can balderdash your name over the radio all you want, but if I hear something other than Cross Bones about this end, I'll have Snarly run 'em through the chum chopper along with whoever was listening."

I suffered a barrage of curses. Then I asked him where

he was. He said, "I'm south of Boca Grand Bar, deep dropping coral patches in 400 to 600 feet."

I asked if he was catching anything, and he said, "Some gray and golden tile fish along with some mixed grouper."

I said, "What's your ETA at Rye Lee's Hump."

He said, "Five days." I asked what the wind and current were doing there.

He took a moment to make some observations and then said, "The wind is light out of the north, and there is a trickle of current to the west alongside the gulfstream."

I said, "I'll be on the water tomorrow. Don't call me on this channel anymore. You shouldn't have called me on this channel to begin with. I'm switching over to the sixes." I turned the channel select button to 18.

He keyed his mic and said, "So tell me why I shouldn't have called on 79?"

I chucked and said, "Seeing as how some of the home boys were listening, I couldn't resist hearing you step on your dick."

I suffered another paragraph of unmentionable curses, and then he said, "Who all was listening?"

I said, "The dockmasters at Oceanside, Boca Chica Naval Air Station's U.D.T., the Key West Coast Guard, U.S. Customs, the DEA, Border Patrol, Immigration, the FLA Wildlife Commission's Marine Units, the Monroe County Sheriff's Office's Marine Units, all the fishermen who work a shift for the Key West Police Department, and of course, on the other side the ones you should post a watch for – wwwanydrugs.com.

"Now, that bunch of commanding jacktars, Slim Jimmys and Johnny Come Latelys with their horde of foxy pistol packing, pocket picking Amazon road whores from hell that pussy whip the hardest of the hard cases are going to try to pull some tomfoolery. They can't promptly and properly club you on this side of the gulfstream, now that you have accidentally alerted the home boys, but if they find you out of bounds in an uneven stand-off with all those bastards and bitches cocking their hammers when it's time to blast and blaze away or haggle, the head jacktar will try to hornswoggle you first in the hope of getting the whole load cheap and saving his crew from a bloody slaughter. Then, you will choose between blasting his boat and crew to the bottom of hell with a few quick sweeps of the miniguns and risk suffering another long, tedious bout of relentless retaliation, similar to the last time when some of the jacktars that were smeared with a thick layer of their namesake escaped using their scuba gear because that extensive school of hungry bull sharks dogging your stern in your pouring chum slick didn't find the tar to be very tasty while they were eating up all the bullet-riddled Slim Jimmys and road whores. Or, you can set your first haggling price at what you can get for the load after the weight has been doubled with cut then stepped on by the mules, because that's what's going to happen to it, and that may reward you with a few brief moments in dying time to do some serious haggling."

He was too pissed off to curse, so he pretended to be important by saying, "Only the DEA was supposed to be in on this one. Why did you let me blab to everyone else?"

I said, "Did you drop some LSD that sent your mind into dead space and left it twirling around a quasar? Or, are you just brain dead with no memory?

"You need to think back to the last time I was following you all over the Caribbean on a double 'banger,' trying to piece together a big enough load to draw the viper-eating Mussarana out of his hole in the mountain of Valhalla. Well, as I recall, I was hauling ass from a nautical graveyard of ships cluttering a beach in South America, pounding and slicing through roguish waves in a brutal nor'wester, headed for the windward passage to meet the cutter

Diligence with one load in hand stacked to the poop deck and one more trick to play when the officer of the watch on the Diligence called to inform me that your Jamaican home boy crapped his pants worrying about retribution, and it was already global news about what we had done and what we were going to do.

"Well, the payback is going to be a mofo, and I hope you haven't brought any unstable people into my part of the gulf to make matters worse. So hide your personal stash and your pack of rolling papers. Get out your other paperwork and prepare yourself to answer a thousand questions, because the local home boys are going to be all over you like the flies on your fish stink that you should have heaved a bucket of seawater on while it was still wet."

He said, "Thanks a lot. At least I know what I'll be doing for the rest of today. I'll get the crew to work right away on the fish stink. I don't mind a little company, they being respectful gents and all. Maybe one of them knows how to fish and can work one of the bandits so I don't have to run back and forth."

I cursed, then said, "Why are you feeding a crew that can't fish? I don't care for the sound of that!"

He ignored my complaint and said, "Can you get a hold of Jolly Roger for me? He won't answer his radio."

I said, "Find him yourself. Catch fish and don't be aggravating the hell out of me every five minutes until we are in place to talk. I've got things to do."

He said, "Like what? Beat your clones with a rubber hose?"

I said, "No, no – their mother handles that part of the deal, and they know the drill. But, I need to get rid of you temporarily, seeing as how I can't do it permanently without killing your corrupted ass. Unfortunately, there is something that prevents me from doing it right away."

He said, "Clue me in and ease my worry."

So I said, "The cold hard reality of the matter boils down to one of your respectable backers putting me in prison for it, where I would most likely have to fight to preserve my unadulterated ass from being butt-fucked by some crazed murderer, be it a big black buck or little Charlie Manson. That ain't no life for an old Indian unless I've got something to scalp them with.

"Besides, I need to pet my dog. She's had a rough morning. When I get done with that I've got to punish my Dinosaur. I'm switching back to Channel 79. You can motor mouth all you want over there, but if you screw this up, you are going to be Pablo's weak sister to bleed and his cell block's pussy boy before they dress you up with a Colombian necktie."

I quickly changed the channel to void his curses into the dead space that occupies the surface of the gulf. As I gazed through the window at its vast emptiness, it gave me no relief as it normally does, for soon, he will be popping up on that horizon like an irritating pimple on a big fat ass that can't be reached by rhyme nor reason.

CHAPTER 2
Preparations

I turned away from the radio, doing a one-eighty in the swivel chair. The Dinosaur, with his arms crossed and his eyes squeezed into slits by the smirk on his face, was leaning against the two massive refrigerators that contain his daily intake of secretions, along with some excretions such as eggs and amber-gris that are among his global cornucopia of other anal by-products he buys that supposedly cultivate healing spores and a variety of nourishing fungi, which must be OK if you have a taste for dung-eye fungi.

I puckered my lips and issued a whirly siren whistle which told The Bone Digger that I wasn't mad at her, and it was time to play. She came wiggling through the hallway, slapping her tail on the walls, shaking her head from side to side and snorting. She sat on her butt in front of me. I cupped her ears then rubbed her head. She looked at the Dinosaur, laid her ears back and curled her lips, exposing her fangs, and issued a low, menacing growl. I stood up from the chair, reached into the top cabinet and pulled out a large leather bone. She began to leap two feet into the air as if her legs were on pogo sticks. I stuck the bone in her jaws. She turned, ran out the back door, dug a big hole in the flower bed and buried it.

I faced the Dinosaur and said, "Call the Rug Rats."

Fishing the Devil's Triangle...

His look of amused contempt faded to one of fear and loathing. His lips trembled and his jowls quivered as he asked, "What do you want me to tell them?"

"Tell them to bring all their gear and sea stores for ten days. Pop-top cans only. I don't want any rusty so-called stainless steel can openers leaving brown stains on my counter tops. Tell 'em to bring plenty of Bounty cooking paper towels. I don't want any damp, sour smelling dish rags in the galley. You can wash a sink full of dirty dishes with one cooking paper towel, rinse it out, and it's still tough enough to remove that crusty dewberry that's stuck in the crack of your hairy ass because the whole roll of toilet paper missed, which will greatly reduce your hemorrhoidal tissue.

"We will need lots of ripe and green bananas and fresh green bell peppers. I don't want their calves going out on 'em at three o'clock in the afternoon because of some super-fucking-stition."

He said, "What superstition?"

I said, "Many fishermen believe it brings bad luck if you take bananas on a fishing trip. But actually it's bad luck if you don't. If you have to stand on your feet all day pulling fish, you need the potassium from the bananas, along with your other food, and a gallon of water to keep your legs from locking up at sunset. If the fish keep biting after dark you should drink some more water and eat a raw green bell pepper that has enough potassium to shift your muscles into overdrive. Make sure they bring mangos, Key limes and avocados."

He said, "What are they for?"

I said, "I'm sure they will keep me from becoming a gout ridden, staff infected, rum scurvy dog like you. If you don't lay off that Jack, you will be sprouting shingles on your rump. They are going to hurt worse than anything you ever felt unless I'm cutting your head off with a dull hacksaw. You've got to take mind-altering drugs to get rid of them. They are going to cause you to suffer from personality trait disturbances, but since your mind is already altered, you are going to become a wild, mazed cracker-brained loony dealing with periods of paranoia and mania at intervals, and your condition will only become slightly moderate briefly, just before you go schizoid, with a positive result of the drugs reducing your infestations of assorted worms, termatoads and dramadafites.

"Tell Snarly to bring the galley table that holds the seven sawed-off, ten-gauge shotguns that cover a hundred and eighty degree spread, the key to the trap house and his special stool.

"When you get off the phone, go into the underground tunnel and take a pound of that Jamaican chocolate out of the freezer. We are going to do this truly Willie Nelson style. Shake all the seeds out of it, chop it up in the blender, then roll me four hundred joints. I don't want to be stuck in a blow behind the fort with a herd of Jonesing Bogarts and not have anything to rob them with."

The Dinosaur asked, "Why you got to rob them?"

I said, "If I don't they will Jones me. When you finish rolling, fill the galley hold, the saddle boxes, and the stern packing box full of ice. Put the splash boards in the chill barrels and fill them half full. Take out two of those seventy pound cases of ground-up bunker from the walk-in cooler and mix me up two one-hundred and fifty-pound tubs of chum dough. Use the heavy silica sand. If the chum is watery, use some steam-pressed oats to tighten it up. Make it firm all the way through. If I get out there and start fishing with it and find wet or dry areas that fuck up the fishing, I'm going to chain your blubbery ass to the mangrove roots in Crocodile Creek. Take ten cases of ground sardines and five cases of whole threadfin herring out of the cooler and put them in the freezer on the back deck.

"There's a list on the galley table for tackle. Make sure

each bin is full. Pump out the holding tank, cap off the oil and fuel, water the batteries and restock the sea stores. Cut the heads and tails off of fifty pounds of the threadfin herring and feed them to the jewfish under the boat. Cut the bodies in four equal pieces. Put them in bait tubs, cover them with plastic wrap and bury them in the ice in the stern packing box.

"Go in the bilge, clean the sea strainers, change the oil and fuel filters, check the stuffing boxes on the propeller shafts, make sure there's a one-second drip. Lift the float switches on the pumps to see if they are working. Bring to the mark the hydraulic fluid in the trap puller and steering helms. Open the lazarettes, grease the rudder shaft bearings and the quadrants. Grease the roller on the anchor chute and squirt some in the fittings on the one-armed bandits. Then do the maintenance on the generator.

"You've got eighteen hours and don't give me that overworked look. We will be gone ten days, and you won't have anything to do except take care of the dog and complain, so go on about your bad-self and get it done."

He decided to be a smart ass by saying, "Is there anything else?"

I said, "As a matter of fact, there is. I'm totally over telemarketers' constant badgering bullshit. Go buy a phone with an answering machine."

He said, "What do you want me to put on the greeting?"

I said, "I don't know. Think of something!"

He placed his massive hand over his mouth and nose, closed his eyes and began moving his head from side to side. I observed his erratic and suffocating meditation for a moment and then said, "I know just the thing! Two weeks ago, when I was out fishing, The Cactus Man from NOAA called to tell me that the Air Force had stopped bombardment of the target ship, 'Patricia,' and it is going to be charted as a marine sanctuary for the little critters. He went on to say that he had a short underwater movie of the ship that was filmed recently, and he wanted me to watch it, then identify the different critters that have claimed the ship for a habitat. I called him when I returned from fishing, and his answering machine rapped out the most clever greeting. It said: 'I'm trying to avoid someone right now, so please leave me a message, and if I don't get back to you right away, it was probably you.' Let's steal that and hook it up to the land line. I'll suffer for it later if I have to.

"And, wash that sour reek from behind your ears."

CHAPTER 3
Post-Nasal Drip

I stomped down the hall, out the back door, down the steps, over the pea rock, down the gang plank onto the floating dock and boarded the "Scally-Wags!" She is forty-eight feet long and extra beamy to hold large fish packing boxes port and starboard. She is made from Kevlar and laid up heavy in the places where she takes her beatings. Her hull is hard chimed and shallow v-ed. Her twin turbo charged Sea Tech engines roar out twenty-two hundred horse power and spin their props in semi-tunnels recessed into her hull, allowing her to maneuver in skinny water with a load on.

I went to the starboard stern quarter and reached into a shrimp basket that I keep my hand lines and spools of leader line in. I pulled out my one-hundred pound test grouper line. I prefer perlon because it doesn't tangle up like other lines. The first two hundred feet have been sanded three times with two-hundred grit wet and dry sandpaper so it won't slip when I'm setting the hook on a large grouper. I cut away the used leader from the last trip. I began pulling the line through my fingers, feeling for nicks and chaffed spots.

A fishing boat named the "Bumpy Gizmo" came up the canal and tied to the seawall across from me. She was manned by three young fishermen. They had been fishing for two days and their eight-hundred pound chill barrel seemed full. The captain watched as the mates began gutting and washing pound-size fish. This told me they were working the top of the outer bar in sixty feet of water instead of the drop-off in ninety feet where the bigger yellowtails are.

The young captain went into his cabin and began chopping something on his galley table. He bent over the table and I heard snorting sounds. He came out of the cabin tweaking his nose, then covered it with the palm of his hand and blew a white residue into the water. Then mumbled, "Fucking cut!"

I was tying a new swivel on my grouper line when the young captain asked, "How come you fish with a hand line when you could use a rod and reel? Isn't that primitive and outdated?" Then they all snickered and giggled.

I was already slightly irritated over the unknown reason why it was necessary for me to help Spiker do something he usually does himself so that people in high places concerned with the worry of the world could be happy and assured that something was being done about the growing number of cartels being added to the "Risky Shit" hit list.

The youngsters snickering and their misinformed assumptions only set my jaws a little bit tighter. I relaxed, swallowed my rage, saving it for later and began to feel better as I realized this was just the thing I needed to take my mind off Spiker's insanity. I decided to put everything aside in order to rob and humiliate these post-nasal drips and get them to help me do it!

I turned away from my tackle and faced them, displaying my broadest grin that I normally reserve for a foxy bitch sporting a high ass, then said, "Primitive you say, outdated! Well, I tell you what there, me young hot shots making a lot a snot, I'll bet all three of you one thousand dollars each, that I can take these two chicken-shit Mickey

Mouse plastic yo-yos poured in a cooling mold by a raw flesh-eating yubanggee in Ethiopia, and I'll put them against your racks full of spinning buggy whips and stand up meat rods, and I'll out fish the three of you, so put your money where your mouth is or cease with the snerty snickers."

The young captain wanted to know what "snerty" meant. I informed him that I wasn't sure if it was a verb or an adverb, but it was definitely derived from the noun snert, which is something that will lick anything anywhere. Take my dog over there, for instance, much as I love her, she's a pure snert. They didn't know whether to be offended or amused so they did neither.

The young captain said, "All joking aside, mister, I believe I'll take you up on that bet."

He looked at his first mate who said, "I would love to double my pay for a hard day's fishing."

I looked at the second mate and he said, "Sure, I'll go along, I believe you will be hard pressed to do it."

I said, "Aye, maybe so, maybe so. But when we get down to basics, it's just going to be a jerk on each end of the string, and whosoever pulls the bigger, faster shall win." I asked if they were fishing close by.

The captain said, "Yea, we're working the east end of Eastern Dryrocks outer bar."

I said, "What are conditions like?"

He said, "Winds light out of the northeast, a trickle of current to the west, the water is green and cloudy."

I said, "Sounds good. I'll meet you there at seven o'clock in the morning."

I took my sixty-pound test pulling line for snapper out of the shrimp basket, cut away the old leader, then tied 15 feet of 30-pound test "Seagar" to it. To the end of that I tied a wired gig for catching mackerel for grouper bait. A U-Haul truck backed down the driveway, stopped at the seawall and

17

the Rug Rats jumped out. Snarly, Ruckus and Hubbub, born in that order, minutes apart. They were barefoot, wearing camouflage cut-offs only. Their close cropped silver-gray hair glistened in the sunshine. Their dark tanned bodies were pock-marked and crisscrossed with many small and large white scars, some to the bone and, in Snarly's case, beyond. They looked at the post-nasal drips. The flash in their emerald green eyes and the expression on their faces was as hard as the blistering concrete of the seawall that they stood on with their heavily calloused bare feet.

They came down the gangplank, then jumped on the Scally-Wags! and walked to the port caprail. They gave the youngsters a wicked grin. The young captain said, "Are they going to fish, too!"

I said, "No, they are here to watch my back, and I pay them a few bucks to gut and pack fish." I looked at Snarly and said, "squwimps"! I walked into the galley and sat in the swivel chair in front of the console and steering helm on the starboard side of the cabin, just forward of the galley counter tops. I fired up a joint, leaned back in the chair, closed my eyes and pictured all the large green-eyed black groupers the youngsters had chummed up.

Across the canal, the captain asked, "What did he mean by squimps? Was he being facetious?"

Snarly said, "No, no. He doesn't like to talk much, and that's his way of saying he wants fried squid and shrimp for dinner. I usually do the talking for us. We were wondering why he was speaking to you. He only talks when he's mad about something. What did you do to set him off?"

He said, "I suppose I was a mite critical of his hand line."

Snarly said, "Oh, that ain't so bad. Many people have criticized his hand line, but they were mostly inept, lesser fishers and misinformed by conscientious environmentalists. There are worse things you can do to his line, like step in it, or pour a bucket of water on it. We've suffered his revenge for that. No one is allowed on the stern when he's working because they might tangle it up."

I stopped daydreaming about the groupers. They were in the box unless the water clears up, allowing the sharks to dog me. I stepped out of the galley and told Snarly to help the Dinosaur ice the boat. I looked at Ruckus and Hubbub then glanced at the U-Haul. They began unloading gear.

I asked the drips if they would please bring cash tomorrow because I will not be returning to port after fishing. They said, "No problem."

After they loaded their fish on a truck and headed to the fish house, I began removing the galley table. Ruckus and Hubbub installed the one containing seven sawed-off shotguns. They opened the top of the table to inspect the guns, which were arranged in a Chinese fan pattern and operated by push-button hydraulics.

Ruckus said, "What load do you want in them?"

I said, "Since I don't want to kill anyone in my neighborhood, put in stun bags. Leave the breaches open and engage the breach blocks, then cock the hammers. Help Snarly finish unpacking then fry up some grub, make it crispy."

"Have breakfast on the table before dawn. We'll be leaving as soon as I can see to get through the canal. This north wind has filled it full of the white man's trash and no sane Indian would try to run it in the dark. As it is, one of you will have to get on the bow with a push pole and move the big stuff out of the way."

Snarly wanted to know what was up. I said, "I'll answer that when I know myself. Right now it's time to eat and get some rest after we burn some weed. The Bone Digger is standing watch so smoke all you want. There won't be much for you to do until I'm done fishing
Tomorrow afternoon."

CHAPTER 4
Of Fishing and Catching

I awoke to the sound of the youngsters cranking their engine. I overslept. Fishermen can do that. I got out of the bunk and entered the galley. The Rug Rats were sitting at the table eating. I went to the sink and brushed my mouth with some Listerine then went to the console and cranked the engines. As they warmed up, I took a joint out of a bag of two hundred, fired it up, went forward and aft, threw the dock lines off, then pulled out behind the youngsters as they plowed through the white man's trash, clearing the way.

The surface of the canal was covered in a thick layer of dead eel grass and turtle grass that floated up after they were killed by an algae bloom that was born in a fresh - water runoff from some so-called environmental development. The decaying vegetation was littered with a multitude of plastic water bottles, chemical jugs and five-gallon buckets of various colors. Only the fish could see what was under the mess created by the white man in the everglades. When we reached the end of the canal, the "Bumpy Gizmo's" engine shut off. He eased her to the seawall in front of perfect Richard's winter haven. We were out of the trash by then. One of the mates put bumpers between the boat and sea wall while the other was stripping down to his underwear.

I pulled the throttle back to idle. As she slowed down I eased her into reverse, stopped along side of them and asked if there was anything we could do to help. The captain said, "I've got something in the prop, he will have it out in a minute or two." The mate jumped into the water with a knife and dove under the boat. A minute later three round sections of a brown, slimy, rotting, fifteen-foot long banana tree popped to the surface with the mate rising among them. The captain asked if that was all of it. The mate informed him that there were still four plastic garbage bags, one hundred feet of polyurethane trap rope and one hundred yards of one thousand-pound test long line monofilament still wound tight around the shaft and prop with some wire that required a hacksaw.

I put her in gear and waved good-bye. As I motored past Hazard Reef, Snarly placed a bacon and egg sandwich and a cup of espresso on the console. I gulped them down then turned on the fish finder. The display revealed the depth at ten feet and told me that we were moving over turtle grass growing in a mix of sand formed from crushed coral, sea shells and thin layers of gray dust carried here by the southeast winds whipping across the Sahara. This combination of current events is the habitat of the nimatoads. The screen showed small but numerous schools of lane snappers and porgies preying on various crustaceans and small fish that spend their juvenile life in the turtle grass. As we entered fifteen and twenty feet, the picture changed to hard-pitted caprock sprouting sea fans, a variety of sponges, seawhips, short corals and coral heads that were inhabited by many species of grunts, snappers, groupers and tropical fish.

Suddenly, the screen turned red from top to bottom as it revealed a school of pilchards surrounded by a school of cero mackerel. I asked Snarly to take the wheel after I put the boat in a three knot, three hundred and sixty degree turn. Then I said, "Don't watch me, keep an eye out for trap floats." I went to the stern and pulled my jig rigged snapper line out of the shrimp basket. I flipped the jig in the water and trolled it thirty feet behind the boat. I caught six three- to five-pound ceros for grouper bait. I put them in a five-gallon bucket of ice water. I walked to the console. The "Bumpy Gizmo" went by on a plane headed to the reef.

Snarly said, "Want me to pass them up?"

I said, "Don't assume to know what I'm going to do! Second guess your clones. Put her on a course to the moaning buoy at the entrance to the main ship channel and hold her present speed.

"Let them get to where they are going. After they have anchored up, put out their chum bag and gathered up all the trash fish, I'll anchor on their deep side and catch the groupers they've chummed up."

The VHF radio was tuned to Channel 18. The Dinosaur called to say that the Bone Digger has dug up the rose bushes and kicked them into the pea rock. "If I try to pull her out, she snaps at me."

I said, "Leave her alone, she's just digging up a bone she buried awhile back. She likes to gnaw on her leather bones after they are soft, slightly chewed and riddled with a herd of fat, juicy, meaty worms. She doesn't dig until she smells a lot of different worms, so quit digging them up and throwing them in the trash. They cost more than the real ones. If she's growling at you when we get back, I'm going to let the Rug Rats dig up their rusty tomahawks and skin you alive, like their great grandpa did to some hapless immigrants that skinned his buffaloes.

"On the other hand, if she's licking your hand, there might be some hope for your deteriorating carcass. While you are sitting there praying that we won't come back, get off you pimply ass and vacuum up the dog's hair and don't call me on this channel anymore unless she corners some meddling rogue agent that's not following orders and snooping around trying to find my personal stash so he can smoke it up!"

I went to the stern, took the mackerels out of the ice water, cut their tails off and threw them overboard. As I was cutting their bodies into two-inch chunks, Hubbub came down from the flying bridge and said, "There was a large lizard on top of the overhang."

I asked, "How big?"

He said, " 'Bout eighteen inches."

I said, "Is he green and round with a long tail with black stripes?"

He said, "No, he's cocoa brown, long, broad and flat with a short, stubby tail. He has a long gator snout and long legs with very large foot pads."

I said, "Is he still there?"

He said, "No, I tried to grab him and he ran down the side of the cabin then under the caprail."

I said, "Then it's hell and death to ya' you goggling, geeking bookworm that ain't learned a damn thing. You'll get more time in the field for this and if I have my way you will be wearing some fresh goat crap to draw the predators. You should have gotten the rat gun from the console and shot it, no matter what was in the way. You've gone and let it get under the caprail where there is no way to get him out. He can go wherever the hell he wants to and we'll suffer his racket."

Hubbub said, "Why are you raising so much hell over a little ol' lizard?"

I said, "That's no ordinary lizard. He's a Barking Bull gecko! Come sundown when he starts his mating call, he's going to drive you stark raving mad. When she doesn't answer, it's going to get worse. After he's been under there

24

for a few days, he's going to get hungry. They get mean when they are hungry. He'll come out and latch on to the first thing he sees and won't let go until he has twisted off a big hunk of meat, so you will have to wear him. It might be the only chance you'll get to kill him, unless he gets you by the pecker while you are leaving a leak over the caprail. It will be the end for you, no more road whoring. I'll have to stop what I'm doing and build you a monastery to live out the rest of your life as a peckerless prophet. But before all that happens, which won't be soon enough for me, you need to stand by with the rat gun in case you get a shot at him."

I scowled at Hubbub and said, "This stinking bucket of guts is your fault, you are on a sixteen-hour watch unless you figure out some way to kill that noisy bastard before sunset, or you will be cutting everyone's bait 'til the end of the trip."

I put the mackerel chunks in a bait tub and covered them with ice. I told Snarly that I was taking the wheel. I climbed the ladder to the flying bridge and increased her speed to fifteen knots. The youngsters were anchored on their spot and had a long chum slick covering the surface of the water to the west. As I approached them from the north, I took out the binoculars and looked behind their boat. There was a large school of chubs, spadefish, bar jacks and speedos chomping on their chum bag. Just behind them were some large amberjacks and yellow jacks. Beyond those was a large mass of small yellowtail snappers flanked by four large barracudas waiting for a yellowtail to act erratic after it's been hooked, then they dart in and grab it. The youngsters were only boating one out of three fish hooked. I anchored up in ninety feet of water fifty feet south of them. The fish finder was marking large yellowtail from thirty to seventy feet. They were not hugging the bottom. This told me that there were some predators under them.

I went to the chest of drawers bolted to the port galley

bulkhead that held my tackle. I removed a roll of duct tape, tore off a four inch strip and tore it down the middle. I curled a strip around the first joint of each index finger. I covered each index finger with a three inch piece of double layered bicycle inner tube. This allows me to grip the sanded line and keep the large groupers out of the coral heads without splitting my fingers to the bone.

I walked to the stern and clamped the chum table to the caprail on the transom. I took out one of the one-hundred and fifty pound tubs of chum dough from the stern packing box and placed it on the table. I filled a two gallon bucket with seawater to wash my hands in, then put it on the table along with the tub of mackerel chunks. I squeezed some large lumps of the chum dough into tight balls and dropped them in the water. The current was slow so they went almost straight down to the bottom and began to disintegrate, drawing groupers to the place where I will present my bait. I took the cover off the grouper chill barrel. I poured some five gallon buckets of seawater into the ice then worked it into a slush with a plastic shovel. All snappers and groupers must be chill killed in heavily iced seawater to preserve their color. If they're not, the fish mongers won't buy them.

I glanced at the drips. One of them was putting blocks of frozen chum into a chum bag. As he did so, he was throwing the paper boxes it came in overboard. Snarly went into a rage saying, "They are tossing their paper into the sea."

I said, "There's nothing we can do about it. The white man has made a law that says it's OK."

He said, "I know that, but they are supposed to tear it into five-inch squares."

I said, "That will only spread it wider and kill the smaller turtles too!"

I took my grouper line out of the shrimp basket. I

removed the point of the number 7-0 super strength hook from the tuck of line that held it in place and stuck it through one end of a mackerel chunk, then pulled five hands of line off the yo-yo.

About ten feet, I reached into the chum-dough tub and grabbed a lump the size of a baseball. I flattened it out in the palm of my hand with my thumb. I placed the chunk of mackerel in the pancake then wrapped it tightly around the mackerel with both hands. I gently lowered it into the sea, being careful not to step in my line and break the ball prematurely before it gets to where I want it to. I quickly pulled thirty more hands of line off the yo-yo into the sea. As the chum ball pulled the seventy feet of line toward the coral heads, I quickly rinsed away the sand and chum stuck to my hands in the bucket of water. Any excess chum slime can cause the line to slip when I'm setting the hook. When I could see the line coming tight, I quickly pulled off another fifteen hands of line from the yo-yo. The chum ball landed on the bottom just before it came tight. I pulled the slack out of the line until I could feel the weight of the chum ball. I raised it two feet off the bottom then jerked the chunk of mackerel out of the chum ball, causing it to explode into a blinding cloud of sand and chum.

A heavy fish ate the mackerel. I quickly pulled on the line as hard as I could, setting the hook and pulling the fish a few more feet off the bottom before it realized what I was about. As he dove for the coral heads, I laid the line over my right hip with my right hand then laid the line over the caprail with my left hand and pushed down hard, taking the weight of the fish on my palm and index finger. As I held it there, it took some inches of line and pulled my hand to the top of the caprail a few times as it struggled to get back into the coral heads. When it became weak I slowly pulled it to the surface and stuck a short, heavy gaff in its heart, then heaved it into its chill barrel. Its weight was about sixty pounds.

I repeated this process seventeen more times and put as many thirty- to sixty-pound black groupers in the chill barrel that filled it to the four hundred and fifty pound mark. When I broke the nineteenth chum ball I hooked a fifteen pound mutton snapper. This told me that I had caught all the local big grouper or scared the hell out of the ones left. I caught twelve more mutton snappers then hooked a small fish.

As I was pulling it up, something grabbed it, biting it in half. It was a bright orange dog snapper bitten off behind the head with a curved bite. This told me that the sharks have picked up the scent. Bottom fishing was over.

It was time to move the sharks into the drips chum slick and concentrate on catching the large yellowtail. The thirteen mutton snappers raised the catch to six-hundred pounds. I removed the head of the dog snapper from my hook and placed it on the chum table. I rolled up my grouper line and put it in the shrimp basket. I squeezed together a dozen large chum balls and threw one ten feet from the boat between me and the drips, then threw the rest a little bit further each time, hopefully putting the sharks in their chum slick. I removed two quarts of chum dough and put it on the table. I mashed it into a pancake to dry out. I asked Snarly for another bacon and egg sandwich. I looked at the fish finder. It was showing large yellowtail from thirty to ninety feet. I broke off some small chunks of the pancake and sprinkled them into the water then watched the screen. As the bits of chum gradually sunk to twenty feet, some yellowtail began rising from the school to eat them. They were ready to cooperate. I removed the double layer of inner tube from my index fingers and replaced them with a single layer.

As I chewed on the sandwich, I gazed at the drips. By now they were being dogged by sharks but still catching small fish. I sprinkled more chum and watched the screen. Again fish rose to it.

Suddenly, a large void appeared in the school on the bottom as fish scattered in all directions. I sprinkled more chum, then picked up the head of the dog snapper and put it on the circle hook on the one-armed bandit. I lowered it to the bottom then sprinkled chum. The yellowtail disappeared from the screen. A few moments later a large fish hung itself on the bandit. It gave the Kevlar leaf spring some hard jerks, but it didn't pull any line off the reel with the drag set at one hundred pounds, so I didn't engage the electric motor. I slowly hand cranked it to the surface and saw that it was a fifty-pound cubarra, snapping its one-inch fangs. I stuck it in the heart with the gaff then heaved it into the chill barrel. I removed the circle hook from its rubbery lip then hung it on the bandit. I sprinkled chum then looked at the screen. The fish were hugging the bottom.

I went to the galley counter, poured a cup of espresso and fired up a joint. After a few drags, I passed it to Snarly. I returned to the stern and sprinkled chum. I removed a bait tub of cut herring from the stern packing box and placed it on the chum table. I grabbed my snapper line out of the shrimp basket and cut away the mackerel jig. I tied a 5-0 nickel-plated J hook to the end of the thirty pound test leader.

It was ten o'clock. The wind switched from north to east. I sprinkled chum then went into the galley. I took the joint from Snarly and sucked on it for awhile as I finished my coffee. I went back to the stern and sprinkled chum. I put a chunk of herring on the hook then wrapped a small pancake of chum dough around it. I lowered it into the water and quickly counted off ten hands of line from the yo-yo. I rubbed my hands quickly in the bucket of water. When the line came tight, I jerked the herring out of the chum dough then put out one hand of line. It came tight with a large yellowtail on it. I pulled it off the top of the school, hung it over the dehooker and shook it into the ice water. I repeated this process two hundred times. The fish averaged two and a half to three and a half pounds each and filled the snapper chill barrel to the six hundred pound mark.

The wind switched to the south. I rolled up my line and put it in the shrimp basket. At this point there were twenty five other fishing boats anchored to the west and north of us. It was three o'clock. The wind kicked up to ten knots.

I went into the galley and sat at the gun table. I fired up a joint, inhaled a heavy drag, and then we passed it around as we ate fried grouper sandwiches. The south wind slowly pushed the gulfstream over the outer bar of eastern dry rocks. The current slowly turned to the east. As it did so, all of the fishing boats turned with it, then it picked up speed and began to rip to the east at about four knots. The drips were still anchored to the bar but lying in one hundred and ten feet. A school of large yellowtail rose up into their chum slick. They caught a few then the barracudas moved between them and the fish. As they hooked the large yellowtails, the barracudas began chasing them to the bottom where they were eaten by black groupers and sharks. The buggy whips and light line the drips were fishing with just weren't tough enough to pull the fish away from the big, toothy critters. They soon tired of feeding the predators then switched to their heavy stand ups.

The young captain hooked a cobia about seventy pounds. The fish swam hard and fast with the current, pulling about one hundred yards of line from the reel then it slowed, rose to the surface and began swimming against the current, directly at the center of my transom. It was obvious that the fish was going to swim between my propellers and most likely cut itself away. I reached under the transom and removed from its rack a heavy solid stainless steel trident with an extended center point and bladed struts. As the cobia approached the stern, I heaved the trident. The center point struck the cobia in the center of its boney head. The bladed struts allowed it to cut deep and hold fast, stuck tight in the bones. The fish trembled briefly. With two quick pulls on the retrieving line I had the hilt of the trident in my left hand. I grabbed the shaft in the middle with my right hand, lifted then heaved the cobia into the grouper chill barrel.

As I did so the young captain's line came in contact with one of the bladed struts and it cut it away.

He grumbled then said, "Was that my fish?"

I said, "How in the hell can it be your fish when it's on the point of my trident?"

He said, "I'm sure I saw it on my line when you stuck it with that oversized frog gig."

I said, "I suppose that could be so. I don't see fishing lines very well these days and I wondered at how it was shaking its head as I put it in the barrel, seeing as how it was already dead as a doorknob. I'll give it to you later when we settle up. I don't usually fish for turd eaters anyway."

The young captain said, "Why did you call it a turd eater?"

I said, "Because that's what it is. I have been observing cobias for fifty years. If they are not in your chum slick gobbling up your ground sardines they are swimming in the wake of some large shark, grouper or ray, waiting for it to take a crap so it can rush in and eat it all up before the sucker fish do. It will eat them too if they get too close. If the wind is blowing hard and the water is cloudy with all the scents mixed together and they can't see a target to follow, you will find them hanging in the lee of the sea buoys and range markers in the effluent zones using them as ambush points to catch small fish and an occasional floating feces.

"If I'm requested to cook one, I slice the flesh thin in the pursuit of the termatoads. Cobias have a tendency to pick up one or two when they stop for brunch at the end of the sewer pipe to help them to continue on their hapless wondering as they follow the stink from one sewer to another in anticipation of a hardy lunch."

The young captain was flabbergasted as he said, "Say it isn't so. Well I'll be damned, isn't that something. It just goes to show you that something good can come out of eating crap, for they are very tasty."

"Aye," I said, "Tasty indeed, but if you like to eat it raw or poorly cooked and underdone, you may suffer a variety of parasitic hazards."

The young captain said, "No doubt. Let me see if I can catch another one." He tied a new hook to his stand up then stuck it through a chunk of cut fish, lowered it to the bottom and hooked a large fish. As he fought it out half way to the surface, a bull shark took it away from him. The instant release of the pressure on the locked down drag caused the young captain to fall backwards on his ass while he banged the back of his head on his port caprail. He slowly stood up, groggy and cursing. As he vigorously rubbed the back of his head, he confessed that he had had enough of this shit and could he tie stern to stern to look at my groupers?

I said, "Aye."

They did a one-eighty on their anchor, put it in their boat and tied stern to stern. As they came aboard I asked the Rug Rats if they would please gut and wash the fish. Snarly reached into a fifty-five gallon plastic drum with its top cut away and drain holes cut in the bottom. He pulled out a four by eight foot gutting carpet and placed it over the stern packing box. I walked to the starboard stern quarter and sat on the caprail. At that moment the stinking breath of Mariah entered my nose. Ruckus and Hubbub removed the large mutton snappers and black groupers from the ice water and laid them on the carpet. Snarly began gutting them, his hands were a blur. Ruckus helped him from the other side of the pile. As they put the fish back in the ice water to wash away the blood and gore, Hubbub grabbed yellowtails by the tail and laid them on the carpet six at a time. The drips paid close attention to the quick and efficient way the Rug Rats handled the fish.

The young captain walked over and sat next to me. He confessed that they had only caught five hundred pounds of yellowtail and a hundred and fifty pounds of cobia. Then he apologized for being such a jerk about my hand line. As he said, "Here's your money," he handed me thirty one-hundred dollar bills. He stared intently as Ruckus and Hubbub put the fish head first into eighty-pound shrimp baskets to drain away the last of the blood. As it dripped from the scuppers a three hundred pound bull shark rose to the surface behind the stern. The leader of the pack.

The young captain said, "How much fish you got there?"

I said, "I believe there's about twelve hundred and fifty pounds of sellable fish there, but the total weight is closer to fourteen hundred when you add the buckets of guts."

"Aye," he said, "No doubt!"

I asked if he was selling to the Rusty Anchor.

He said, "Yes."

I said, "You got anything in your packing box?"

He said, "Just a shallow bed of chill ice."

I said, "Perfect, would you like some of your money back?"

He smiled and said, "Always."

I said, "I'll give you four hundred dollars and each of your mates three if you will haul these fish to the master monger so I can get on to the west. Tell him to hold the ticket until I return."

He said, "No problem."

Ruckus removed the carpet and took it to the stern. He tied a rope through a grommet in one corner of the carpet then lowered it into the ripping current. As the blood and gore washed away, a mixed bag of sharks sliced the surface with their fins in a frenzy. Hubbub came to the stern carrying the two ten-gallon buckets containing the guts. He threw them in the gulfstream. The sharks streaked in, rolled and turned in the guts, closing their eyes as they inhaled mouths full, thrashing and splashing violently, churning the water into a red boil. It was over in a few blinks of the eyes as they swam away in search of another snack.

The Rug Rats and the drips transferred the fish then capped them with four baskets of ice from my stern packing box. We talked briefly about future meeting then said our good-byes. We walked into the galley where Snarly had been preparing fried black grouper sandwiches. We sat down at the gun table. I fired up a joint, inhaled a heavy drag then passed it to Snarly, who Jonesed it. As Snarly puffed away, we took a bite out of our sandwiches.

Hubbub laid his sandwich back on its plate in the hopes of grasping the joint then he said, "What's that odor?"

Snarly said, "I don't know, I can't smell anything but this joint I'm sucking on. What does it smell like?"

Hubbub said, "Carrion, moldy jungle rot, spoiled crabs and precipitating ozone."

Snarly said, "Aye, you have a keen sense of smell, me bra snatching brudder, but your brain has failed you, for you are not but a shiftless lubber if you don't know when the foul breath of Mariah is in your nose. Aye, it's her, she's seeping in from the sow'west, she will be huffing and puffing like us soon, only she will be an ill wind that will blow us no good and I'm glad I can't say the same for this joint," as he finally passed it to Hubbub.

I said, "Snarly's right, there's no sense hauling ass into the triangle before the wind shifts to the northwest. There is some heavy turbulence forming in the sow'western gulf. The northerlys and southerlys are going to shoot it through the straits. We need to stay close until there is a window in it so we can cross Rebecka Channel."

I cranked the engines. Ruckus went to the bow with the flotation ball and resting ring, then put them on the anchor line. I put the engines in gear and slowly turned to port until I could see the anchor line then increased her speed to ten knots and did a one hundred and eighty degree turn on the line. The braced grapnel came loose without breaking its trip, floated up and hung in the resting ring. Snarly pulled it into the boat. Ruckus pulled the drain plugs from the chill barrels. The sharks came back.

CHAPTER 5
The Eastern Apex of The Devil's Triangle

I increased her speed to fifteen knots and put her on a course to Satan Shoals. As we were passing Sand Key Light the fish finder began marking small schools close to the surface in fifty feet of water. I pulled back on the throttle, hoping they were mackerel. I asked Snarly to drag a gig. He hooked one right away so I told him to catch ten for grouper bait. We dropped the anchor in one hundred and ten feet at the west end of Satan Shoals. The current was ripping to the east. The water was cobalt blue and gin clear. The sow'west wind kicked up to fifteen knots and formed a three-foot chop on the surface. I know nothing about the mysterious events that gave Satan Shoals its name, nor do I care to. Other fishermen never come here, making it a haven for mixed grouper, and that's good enough for me. The flow of the current was too fast to fish with chum dough. I took out my grouper line from the shrimp basket. I cut the leader three feet above the hook. I put a sixteen ounce lead sinker on the leader. I tied a one hundred pound test swivel to the end of the leader then tied the three-foot piece of line with the hook to the other eye of the swivel.

Snarly removed a two by three foot piece of carpet from the plastic barrel and laid it on the stern packing box. He cut away the spine bones and tails of the mackerels, leaving the fillets attached to their heads, then minced the flesh on the lower part of the fillets without cutting through the skin.

I pulled the re-sharpened mustad 7-0 super strength hook through both lips of the mackerel. I slowly lowered it, letting the current carry it to the base of Satan Shoals in ninety feet, which is the north and south passage for large fish hunting around the seamount. I gave the line some quick, long jerks, breaking away some of the minced meat at the end of the fillets. Yellowtail snappers rushed in and tore at the fillets, spreading the scent around the seamount from west to east. The pecking and tearing of the yellowtails increased then ceased abruptly as they scattered in all directions.

I bent over, pulling some slack out of the line, gripped it tightly with both finger stalls and braced myself for the leader of the pack. The grouper inhaled the mackerel head first, catching itself in the corner of its mouth, the toughest part of its head. I heaved on the line with both hands, pulling it off the bottom and forcing the point of the hook through the thick, rubbery skin. It struggled desperately to get under a coralhead and cut me away. The mate's knot at the hook and swivel held so I slowly pulled it to the surface, gaffed it then heaved it into its chill barrel. Its weight was about seventy pounds. I removed a fillet knife from its holder and cut the hook from the corner of the fish's mouth. The head of the mackerel and half of the fillets were still on the hook.

I removed the mauled mackerel from the hook and tossed it into the bucket of ice water that Snarly had put it in after he caught it. This told him it was his bait to cut in pieces and fish with when I was done with the big ones. I caught five more black groupers from thirty to fifty pounds.

I rolled up my line then put it in the shrimp basket. The Rug Rats began cutting the mauled mackerels into four-ounce chunks and baiting their hooks. I fired up a joint and passed it to Snarly. I went forward and sat at the gun table then consumed the cup of hot espresso and the fried grouper sandwich placed there by Snarly.

The Rug Rats began catching a mixed bag of fish, mutton snappers, and red, gag and yellowfin groupers in the ten to fifteen pound range, and some large mangrove snappers five to six pounds. By the time I was finished with the sandwich and fired up another joint they were out of mackerel. The chill barrel was over the five-hundred pound mark. I asked them to roll up their lines, put a cap of ice on the fish and get everything ready to tie to the trees.

I stood up from the gun table and walked to the swivel chair in front of the steering helm. I fell into it, pulling my shoulders back to release the tension on my pinched nerves. I took a long drag on the joint, sucking it deep into my lungs and holding it in as long as I could. I went numb, my skin felt thick as a brick. As I exhaled, all the pain left my body, riding on the smoke then blown away by the sow breath of Mariah.

CHAPTER 6
Trappers Cut

I took another drag on the joint to motivate my foggy mind and painless body, then another one for effect. I changed the channel on the VHF to the NOAA. I neither liked what I heard nor what I could see. I changed the channel to eighteen, keyed the mic and said, "Talk to me, Spiker."

He keyed his mic and said, "Yea, where you at?"

I said, "I'm leaving Satan Shoals and going to Trappers Cut on the northwest corner of Boca Grand Island. I've got to take my antennas down to get in there and tie to the buttonwood trees. You will need to do the same, so listen up and I'll tell you how to find the Cut."

He said, "Can I follow you?"

I said, "Where are you?"

He said, "I'm drifting in six hundred feet, west by sow'west of the sunken rock."

I said, "I'm not going to lay here side-to in this crap for an hour and beat our heads against the bulkheads waiting for you to play catch-up."

He said, "I've got a chart here. I'll find my way in there I reckon."

I said, "You're a rectum, all right. No 'Bout a' Doubt it. Trappers Cut isn't on that chart."

He said, "Why the hell not?"

I said, "Because it was made by some white men, and there will never come a day when they show you everything. There's lots of things out here you won't find on your chart that only half a century of exploring will reveal."

He said, "How do I find the Cut?"

I said, "After you enter Boca Grand Channel, stay half a mile off the beach to avoid sandbars until you are due west of the first green stake that marks the entrance to the Dog Leg Channel that leads into the lakes. Come in slow around the south side of the stake, it's close to the beach. Make a port turn to the north as you approach the stake that marks the turn into the Dog Leg and the lakes, look along the beach and you will see the cut just before you reach the northwest corner of the island. Don't tie up behind me. Tie up across from me on the north side of the cut. Enjoy your ass kicking on the way in, I'm outa' here."

I passed the half joint to Snarly and cranked the engines, giving them a few minutes to warm up. We finished the joint except the roach which I put in my stash bag for lean, shaky times. We put the anchor in the boat then I slowly increased her speed to twenty-five knots. Fifteen minutes later we arrived at the cut and tied to the shady black buttonwood trees.

Snarly began deep frying chunks of beer battered black grouper. I fired up a joint and passed it around. Ruckus and Hubbub cleaned and packed the fish then scrubbed the stern. I cleaned and sliced some bell peppers then put them on a paper plate. I peeled then cut some mangos and avocados into chunks and squeezed two large Key limes onto them in a gallon bowl. We puffed and munched. The sow'west wind kicked up to a steady thirty-five knots. We finished stuffing our faces and choking on the chocolate.

I stood up from the bench surrounding the gun tale and went to the chair at the helm. The Rug Rats shifted their positions to the end of the table and braced their backs against the port cabin bulkhead. Under their feet next to the center bench leg is a turned-off floor switch that executes the last two functions of the gun table. It is wired to a toggle switch on the control panel under the console that is duct taped in the OFF position. One heel-press on the floor switch disengages the breach blocks and closes the breaches. A second heel-press on the floor switch pulls the triggers that release the already cocked hammers.

Snarly reached into his pocket and pulled out a bag of weed with a pack of Bambu' rolling papers.

I said, "What's that?"

He said, "Some white widow from the bluegrass lands."

The pale green buds coated with white crystals sparkled. As we puffed away a flock of terns and laughing gulls landed in the buttonwood and mangrove trees. They screeched, squawked and pecked in their fight for the best roost. The constant racket became irritating. The Rug Rats began to nod in and out of reality.

I asked Snarly to get the binoculars then said, "Let's all take a walk up the path to the beach. I want to see what's coming at us besides Spiker."

When we arrived at the beach, six-foot waves were crashing onto the sand bunkers of sea oats and the long sandbar that banks the channel into the lakes. I asked Snarly to look to the sow'west for Spiker.

"Aye," he said, "I can see him. It's the Swash Buckler all right and she's a-swashing and a-buckling. She's too long in the tooth and too narrow in the beam to get any respect from these short, choppy seas. Her round bottom is pitching her bulwarks and dipping her cap rails while she's running a zig-zag course in a following sea. All the makings for a catastrophe. Her ass end just came out of the water on the down roll and I can see why she can't stay on course. Half of her rudder is gone."

I said, "If that was the case then she wouldn't have any rudder at all, because she never had more than half a rudder. I told him that thirty years ago when he built that tub of rotting timbers, but he's as hard headed as a dried out coconut. He wouldn't listen then and he won't listen now."

The wind huffed up to a steady forty knots and gusted to fifty. The horizon beyond Spiker turned charcoal gray. North of the darkness white mist was forming. Lobster traps were being heaved onto the beach and sandbar among hills of salt foam and spume.

I said, "Snarly, put the binoculars on that white thunderhead to the north. What do you make of it?"

He said, "At the moment it's spiraling down four black water spouts. I can't see beyond the wall of swirling turbulence."

I asked if they were going to miss us?

He replied, "I believe so. They should be north of the lakes and in the bay when they pass us."

I said, "What about that mess behind Spiker?"

He replied, "Well, the sky is turning a very deep cobalt blue above the horizon. The sun is turning fire engine red, so is the water. Because of the glare I can only see a mass of squalls with a whole lota' lightning. It's pretty to look at, but it ain't naturally normal nor will its effects be."

I said, "Let's get back to the boat."

When we boarded we were greeted by large yellow biting horse flies. Snarly cursed, then grabbed a swatter and began rushing about the boat smacking them and leaving the guts on the bulkheads. I asked Hubbub to bring up the Doppler on his L.T. It showed a deep red area fifty miles wide, east and west, a hundred miles long north to south.

Snarly said, "That's a lot of rain, it's going to be a toad strangler."

Spiker turned into the cut and tied to the trees across

from us. He stood on his back deck, his long arms folded around his six-foot-eight frame, his long red hair and fu manchu flopping in the gale force wind. He smiled and said, "How's everything in the neighborhood Bones?"

I displayed a grim scowl and said, "Well, all those who portray me as the devil seem to be handling the satanic curses, all 'cept one."

He said, "Oh! And who might that be! Say, where's Dynamite? She in the bunk seasick again?"

Snarly growled and said, "Leave him alone about her. We ain't seen that twisted screw faced whining blood clot, but that's because we only look for her in the obituaries."

Spiker frowned and said, "What happened?"

Snarly displayed a wicked grin then said, "He made the mistake of showing her how to chum up the groupers and hook them. Lately that's all she's been doing. She bought her own boat with the money she weaseled out of him. Now she's running around here and there to all of his numbers that she stole, hooking the groupers and leaving her gear in their mouths because she doesn't have enough ass to keep them out of the coral heads, tho' I dare say it's big enough for busting balls. We heard it through the seaweed that she's looking for some bumbaclod to squeeze her blackheads, pop her zits and scrub the crap stains out of her five-gallon Chevron port-heave-a-potty but she ain't having much luck with the bumbaclods because she's still smashing feeling and killing fun as she pets her loaded stolen gun. If you see a blue boat on the horizon you might want to do a one-eighty.

"I swear, she's so confused by her mixed emotions, quirks, traits and hereditary flotsam and jetsam that she's deluding herself into believing that she's in possession of something as noble and heartwarming as a soul. But, after she's run aground a few times and destroys her running gear, then sucks her intakes full of sand and turtle grass that burns her engine up when she tries to back up and sinks a few times because she didn't change her moldy green brass through hull fitting and her rusty so-called stainless steel hose clamps. Then she will realize that she's just like everyone else around her and the neighborhood will be pure hell again."

I told Snarly to put a lid on it. He gave me a sulky look, refusing to be silent. He changed the subject by delivering a dagger shooting glare at Spiker and said, "Why did you bring a pair of Jonahs out here?"

Spiker, being unaware of his meaning, seeing as how he is a Jonah himself appeared dumbfounded then said, "What Jonahs?"

Snarly smiled with amazement and said, "There is a skinny old man and a very large gorilla wearing fancy red jogging shorts peeking through your curtains."

Spiker said, "What makes you think they are Jonahs?"

Snarly twisted up his face into a scowl then said, "They sure as hell ain't fishermen, if they were they would be on your back deck wanting to know what's going down. No, no, only Jonahs, frightened women, children, people who can't pay their bills and drug crazed crack freaks peek through the curtains. And since gorillas can't talk, call that old man out here so we can see what he's about."

Spiker yelled, "Fairel get out here!"

Upon hearing that name, Snarly growled and said, "Are you out of your fricking mind! Don't you know who in the hell that is?"

Spiker looked perplexed then said, "No, not really. He lives on a boat next to my slip at Oceanside. He said he could fix my autopilot so I brought him along."

Fairel shuffled out the galley door then over to the cap rail. When he saw Snarly he moaned then wrapped his arms around himself and shuffled back into the galley. Snarly cut loose with a barrage of curses then declared that idiocy was prevailing and no amount of autopilots can steer a semi-rudderless boat.

"If he's been fooling around with your electronics then one night in the future you are going to find yourself with nothing working except your engine and you will be running your course with a flashlight super-glued to your compass."

Spiker said, "Why's that?"

Snarly said, "A new head boat chartering out of the Fish Mongers Hill hired him on as engineer. They were on a three-day trip with eighty fishermen aboard. The first night the light in the ladies room went out. The captain told Fairel to go below and see if the wire was loose on the panel. About ten minutes later all the lights began going out then the electronics. The captain passed out flashlights to the crew then went below and found all the wires off the panel with the nuts lying in the bilge. Fairel was setting on a cross beam with a bottle of rum in one hand and a sack of coke in the other with a straw sticking out of it, saying he could fix the problem in a minute.

"That ain't half of it!"

He entered the galley and quickly returned with a loaf of bread. He began breaking the bread into small pieces then threw it in the water between the boats. The birds increased their chatter then shrieked as they left their perches and dove for the bread. The racket intensified as they flew around us.

Snarly continued breaking and throwing bread as he said, "Jonsey bought an aluminum flying bridge for his boat and paid Fairel to mount it. After he had it in place and all the nuts finger tight, he decided to have a drink and toot then wrench the nuts down hard. Well, that never happened.

"The one drink and toot turned into many. Jonsey came back to his boat in the afternoon and found Fairel nodding in and out of consciousness from the rum and cocaine. He asked Fairel if he was finished. Fairel assured him that he was, took his money and left in pursuit of more rum and coke. Jonsey went about mounting his electronics on the flying bridge and getting the boat stocked for a morning trip then went home to get some sleep.

"The next morning the wind was out of the south at ten to fifteen knots, creating a three-foot chop inside the reef. Jonsey cranked up and headed south to Eye-Glass Bar. As the boat bounced along on her course the nuts and lock washers began to rattle off the bolts holding the flying bridge to the cabin roof. Jonsey was setting on the bridge's seat with his feet propped up on the console, smoking a joint while the auto-pilot steered the boat. Half way to the reef the bridge collapsed. Jonsey fell onto his engine cover head first and knocked himself unconscious. The boat kept going south until it ran aground on the outer-banks of Cuba.

"He woke up in a hospital where the chief of police informed him that his suicide attempt had failed and he was recovered from a concussion. 'Your boat has been confiscated and you are under arrest for illegally entering Cuban waters and possession of marijuana. Now that you are feeling better our mental health facilities are quite adequate here and Dr. Shocker will be with you shortly!'"

Spiker said, "That makes a sad day and damn the bad luck. I reckon I'll lock Fairel in the fore-peak so nothing else happens and look over my wiring."

By now the birds had a belly full of bread and began crapping in flight. Spiker didn't have an overhang on his back deck. He reached into his galley door and removed a slicker from its hook and put it on raising the hood.

Snarly threw the birds some more bread and said, "You need to get him on the first boat going east to Key West. You've already let him do the damage and most likely you won't find it until it happens. That's the way things go with Jonahs. And we will be cursing you some more in the future for it.

"What's the story on the gorilla?"

CHAPTER 7
The Dirt

Spiker yelled, "Hey Morese, step out here."

He waddled through the galley door onto the back deck. He was as wide as he was tall. His entire body was covered in long black hair except his eyes and nose. His fingernails and toenails were long and filthy. Spiker smiled then said, "Gentlemen, meet Morese Digler."

Snarly growled and said, "Dock-handles only on this one crap stain!"

Spiker gave Snarly an irritated look then said, "His handle is The Dirt."

Snarly said, "Well, it's the Dirt Digler now and he'll wear it like the bird crap on his back!"

The Dirt looked at Spiker and said, with a Cuban accent "Whoose dees mangs?"

Spiker scowled and said, "They are the devils' spawn."

The Dirt asked, "House day get so cut up?"

Spiker said, "Mostly from fooling around with wild women in the jungle and their toothy pets. They got some of those scars at picnics and barbeques messing around with the wrong woman and working for the devil. That will be him standing in back."

The Dirt waved and said, "Kapaso hombres?"

Snarly said, "We don't speak Spanish on this boat. We

only converse in English nautical terms over here. You need to remember that and them when you hear 'em!"

The Dirt tilted his head to one side and said, "Haaang?" Then he smiled, revealing a mouth full of bright yellow teeth that faded into moldy green at the gums with his incisors hanging over the corners of his bottom lip, giving him a vampirish look. He said, "I don' know nutsing 'bout no nogable termanites, but I speak Englace, jew know what I ming mang, haaang?"

Snarly said, "Hang you? Aye, that we can do from those buttonwood trees, and since we can't do it sooner, let's do it now."

The Dirt said, "Hah, jew berry funny mang." He gave Snarly a long hard look, then said, "What'sa matter for jew, how cung jew looky me like thack? Are jew stoned, are jew flucked up or what? Or mablee jew got a pralum' wiss me. Don' jew worry 'bout me, I do my jog, nutsing goes downg wissout me ang what I say."

Snarly chuckled and said, "That might be the way things are on that hulk of worm eaten timbers, but on this boat we answer to Cross Bones only. You will do the same or I will suffer the banshee of your death rattle."

Snarly looked at Spiker and said, "What in the hell is he talking about?"

Spiker said, "Nothing to be shouting over. I need to talk to the old man in private. Can I slack off my lines and tie alongside of you?"

Snarly said, "Sure, you can tie alongside and good luck with keeping us out of your red herring!"

Spiker boarded the Scally-Wags! and entered my galley. I gave him a nasty look and said, "You're like an itchy bump on a bull's ass that keeps him scratching it on a fence post until he knocks it over, then running wild and terrorizing the peaceful valley. Spit it out, harbinger. Tell me why you've got your bandits mounted with the covers off when you should have the miniguns mounted with the bandit covers on them."

He cringed and said, "They changed the contractors' rules and took away my toys."

As the Rug Rats gave each other knowing nods, I said, "Well, that certainly explains the unknown reason why you think we can help out, but I have my doubts. What does this Dirt have to do with anything?"

Spiker picked at a large scab on the outside of his arm as he said, "He thinks he can set up three of the heroin cartels for big loads and offer them to the Mussarana, which might draw that cannibal out of his hole. All he wants in return is to spend some of his time at a halfway house with a TV and pool table."

I looked at Hubbub and said, "Do some fishing in the net, bring up this bottom feeder and tell it all."

As Hubbub punched the keys on his L.T., the sow'west wind increased to a steady fifty knots. Then the squalls were upon us. The rain swirled around us, pounding on the roof. When the squalls moved into the bay heading for the lower Keys, Hubbub received a transmission from the satellite. He whistled loudly and said, "The Dirt is a very bad man. There's warrants out on him everywhere for any crime imaginable. He hasn't made it to America's Most Wanted but he is posted on Unsolved Mysteries. They don't know he's in custody of the DEA. The DEA wants to keep it that way so the cartels won't hear about his capture. He was an informer for Batista throughout the Cuban crisis. During the overthrow, he was indicted twice for murder. Both killings were ruled justifiable homicide. After Castro took over, he moved to the jungles of South America where he became well connected to the multitude of cartels and respected as a ruthless and brutal labor enforcer among the poppy fields. He was captured by the DEA in Great Inagua while he was living on his sailboat in the harbor turning tricks. That's all I can find on him."

Spiker said, "His sailboat is still in the harbor at Great Inagua. Upon his capture he agreed to cooperate with the DEA. He called one of his mules to watch his boat and keep the tricks turning while he was being briefed and pumped for all he knows. The DEA is finished with the office work. They've given him to me to set him in motion. I've got to remove his mule from his sailboat and put him back aboard to make arrangements to have a load dropped off the Turks soon. Until then I'm stuck with his ranting and raving."

I said, "Can you control him?"

He said, "Sure, he knows I'm his only way to the halfway house. He's seasick most of the time. Any rocking of the boat and he upchucks then lays on the galley floor useless. I can't let him go below because he can't make it to the back deck in time, so I have to let him stay underfoot and in the way for a short crawl to the galley door."

I said, "What makes the DEA think he can pull it off?"

He said, "As you know, the King Cobra has been putting a lot of pressure on the cartels. He's watching every move they make so nothing's moving. It's stacking up in their warehouses and going stale. Anyone they have done business with in the past that didn't rip them off can get a hundred-and-fifty million dollars worth fronted for a million bucks down payment if they have the balls to move it. The three cartels The Dirt deals with fight among themselves and don't trade information on rip offs."

I interrupted and said, "We are well aware of that fact, seeing as how it's the only reason we are still alive from your last attempt. Tell us something we don't know."

He said, "The Cobra is giving The Dirt three million dollars to set up the deals in the hope of keeping four-hundred-and-fifty million dollars worth of scag off the streets."

I frowned and said, "You are talking about the future.

What are you doing in our back yard now?"

He slapped at a horsefly then said, "Some Coast Guard gents captured five tons of raw opium coming out of the Middle East. The Black Mamba sold it to one of The Dirt's connections that he doesn't deal with very often for a low price with the option to buy the finished products for five million dollars. They will be coming through the Yucatan Straits in four days on an old worn-out shrimp boat named the "Dragger." I've got to meet the captain and mate in one thousand feet of water south of Rye Lee's Hump, place them under arrest, take the morphine off the boat, put it on an airboat that will fly it to Boca Chica Naval Air Station, where it will be put on a c-one-thirty flying fortress, then flown to the Middle East to ease the pain of the war. I've got to burn the Dragger with the scag aboard. If they arrive heavily armed with a sizable crew, I'll have to pay for the drugs and take them into Fort Jefferson for the airboat."

As the Rug Rats' jaws dropped, I smiled and said, "You've got five million bucks on board?"

He nodded his head and said, "The payoff is four million in gold bullion and a million in one-hundred-dollar bills. It's in wooden crates and paper bundles under the lower bunks in the forepeak with two mini-transponders to keep track of it in case it's moved from my boat to wherever they may take it. The Cobra is pulling rank on the Boomslang and taking him out of his meager retirement. He's now in charge of the Caribbean operations."

Spiker reached into his shirt pocket, pulled out a small slip of paper and handed it to Hubbub then said, "Punch in this code, then Slime Line. He may have some useful information later on when things are being set up."

I said, "What has he done so far?"

He said, "Not much. He's just waiting for some cooperation over a dispute about his authority. The word on the river is he's an incoming, pissed off animal because he had to stop fishing. The King Cobra has shown his sympathy by giving him a free fist for pounding on bureaucratic doors in pursuit of a stack of U.N. warrants. Risky shit is going down everywhere. He's ordering cases of cuffs and tasers. Any viper that isn't getting any results from what he is doing is being transferred to Valhalla and assigned to the Mussarana. They are dressed as junkies so they can follow the mules that come out of his hole.

"They mostly put red dots on rural maps, but the Green Mamba was a little too green. He got inside posing as a replacement for a mule that was sick. He stuck a straight pin numerous times in the veins of both arms then squeezed some of the punctures until they bruised making them appear older, hoping the guards would take him for a heavy shooter. His plan was to look the place over, pick up the mules' dope and walk out.

"He might have pulled it off if he had put some pink eyeliner on his eyelids. Every guard knows that a junky with that many tracks would have pink eyelids. He made it to the Mussarana's table, but he came out as so many turds in the sewer. I haven't heard anything else."

The wind eased up to twenty knots and there weren't any formations showing on the Doppler. The Dirt stuck his head out of Spiker's galley and asked if he could come aboard the Scally-Wags!

Snarly frowned when I said, "OK."

Then he said, "You've got to clip your claws and dig the gunk from under them. We don't want to die from monkey scratch fever over here. You need to file your fangs and scrape the carrion off of them. We don't want to die from oral fallout, either."

Ignoring Snarly's commands, The Dirt came aboard and entered the galley. There was no place for him to sit. He was too big to fit between the bench and the gun table. Snarly opened the utility closet, hooked his foot to a leg on his special stool and pulled it out onto the galley deck. He looked at me, and I shook my head.

The Dirt said, "Cang I sit on it?"

Snarly said, "No. This stool is reserved for irritating interlopers that I need to get rid of in a hurry. Besides, some very close friends of mine live on it. They possess the strength of a mighty warrior, seeing as how they came from me. I've seen them run many nosey bastards off the dock faster than I can talk them away, hopelessly scratching and digging at their asses until they reach a bottle of rubbing alcohol and a tube of Cortisone Ten."

The Dirt looked at the stool and said, "I don' see sung bodies."

Snarly smiled and said, "That's because they are microscopic and extremely toothy. They don't like being sat upon."

The Dirt asked, "What's day eats?"

Snarly said, "Every other day I take them to the Stren Scuppers and urinate on 'em. Keeps 'em happy and pissed on until I make an offering of an unsung ass to chew on."

I interrupted Snarly by saying, "Pull out those Kevlar boarding steps for him to sit on."

He said, "Aye, they are strong enough to hold his weight tho' his butt will be square rigged on the spread!"

The wind changed to a light breeze from the sow'west, and the horse flies returned. One bit The Dirt, and he hissed a stream of curses.

Snarly said, "Don't be making a lot of racket. Over here you're just a shiftless lubber who can't kill his meat. That means someone else has got to do it for you, so don't rile 'em or you will find some fowl on your plate that used to be turkey. Pick up that swatter and make yourself useful."

The sun disappeared below the horizon and Trappers Cut became shrouded in darkness. Among the black buttonwood and red mangrove trees the birds ceased their pecking squabble. The lull in the wind crated a gloomy silence that was disturbed by a ringing in my ears – a sign of unhappiness because I knew what was coming, and I wasn't looking forward to it.

The silence was shattered as the Barking Bull gecko started his mating call by inhaling a long, deep breath into his air sacks that generated a series of loud, lip-smacking sounds like a baby sucking on a dry tit.

Everyone except me and The Dirt jumped up as Snarly said, "What in the hell was that?"

The gecko blasted out a noisy, progressive sequence of deep-throated croaks that reverberated and amplified off the bulkheads. It sounded like a very large bull frog saying, "Fuck you, fuck you," over and over again. It went on for about ten minutes with some brief lulls as he refilled his air sacks. When he stopped, everyone looked at me and laughed. I gave them a "what the fuck is wrong with you" look and growled at Hubbub. They frowned and confessed that they had never heard such a thing. Five minutes later when the female didn't show, he cut loose with another round of croaks on a higher scale.

Hubbub reached into his dive bag and pulled out some ear plugs. He looked at me, and I shook my head. As he was putting them back in his bag I said, "You've got first watch. Ruckus will relieve you in eight hours. Stand by with the rat gun where the gecko went under the cap rail. He might get hungry and try to catch some horse flies."

Snarly asked if there were any female geckos on the island.

I said, "No, geckos are not indigenous to the Keys, but many species have been turned loose on the islands that have been bridged. The only creatures indigenous to this island are these biting horse flies, along with some large red-and-white striped ants that will bite the piss out of you. There are some prodigious orange centipedes and black scorpions that will do the same. There is a sizeable species of walking sticks that live on the white mangrove trees behind the sand bunkers of sea oats that the sea turtles lay their eggs in on the sow'west corner of the island. If you get too close to a female walking stick she will squirt a rank fluid on you. There's no small beasts that can get to the gecko and eat him."

As the gecko continued to croak, The Dirt stood up, walked to the back deck and began urinating over the port cap rail near the stern.

Snarly growled, "That stupid idiot!"

I said, "What's he doing?"

Snarly whined like an old woman, saying, "He's pissing into the wind and getting it all over the cap rail where I sit when I'm fishing."

Snarly reached into the cabinet below the galley sink and pulled out a two-gallon bucket and brush. He filled it with water and added some dish soap. As The Dirt opened the sliding door to enter the galley, Snarly put his hand on his chest and said, "Back up there, butter ball, you've got a mess to clean up!"

The Dirt said, "Haaang! What mess?"

Snarly handed him the bucket and said, "Listen up! I'm damn proud of my cherry asshole, and I'm extremely particular about where I park it. You've gone and pissed on its favorite spot. Do you know what's going to happen when I sit there?"

The Dirt shook his head and looked away.

Snarly hissed, "I'm going to get zits on my ass. Your zits on my ass ain't happening! Scrub the rail then rinse it off."

As Snarly watched The Dirt, he removed a ten-pound black grouper from the stern packing box. He quickly filleted it, heaved the six-and-a-half pound carcass into the cut, then carried the three-and-a-half pounds of fillets into the galley and gave them to Ruckus to fry.

The wind huffed up to twenty knots again. Snarly groaned, "I was hoping it would swing around to the northwest. Hubbub, bring up the Doppler."

The screen showed another line of squalls coming at us. By now the gecko was totally frustrated. He filled his air sacks and issued a burst of raspy croaks then a long blast of quick, repetitious rattling barks that sounded like a burp gun emptying a hundred round clip. This slowly settled into shrieking squeals similar to a Tasmanian devil chewing on a dead wombat. He ended the session with a hideous cackle.

Fairel stuck his head out of Spiker's galley door then asked, "What kind of beast was in the woods?"

Spiker said, "It's a big lizard."

Fairel whimpered and said, "Can you take me back to Oceanside, my ulcers are bleeding out of my butt because I'm going into the DTs. I need a drink bad!"

The Dirt spoke up, "Shut jour mouse jew crasee bassard. I killa jew mudder fluck!"

Spiker said, "Lighten up, you are going to be like that some day if you don't get over your seasickness."

The wind increased to thirty knots. The squalls pounded us with heavy rain again. Lightning flashed, thunder boomed and St. Elmo wrapped his electric blue fire around the short LORAN antenna. As it buzzed and sizzled, the disconnected connectors began to click and hop around on the console, tapping out an uncipherable but holy code. As we ate fish and chips, Spiker squirmed and fidgeted with woe and worry on his face.

I said, "Spit it out."

He said, "I don't want to put you in a rage, but the King Cobra doesn't want anyone killed on this go-round, which puts the contractors out of their element and taking orders from the DEA.

I said, "Is that so. Alright, but I can't make any promises if they start popping caps."

Snarly smiled and began dancing a jig on the back deck. Spiker asked why he was such a bundle of joy.

I said, "If he can't kill them, it means he can torture and tase."

Spiker said, "He's a sick bastard with a knack for subterfuge."

Snarly frowned and said, "You may be right, but that statement is going to cost you some suffering. No man can criticize me out here and motor away without paying sooner or later. You want it now?"

Spiker huffed up his chest and said, "Have at it bad boy, I'll wear you!"

I stepped between them, fired up a joint, cleared my throat, spat into the water then said, "If you two can't get along then swim or sink."

I passed the joint to Ruckus, he sucked on it then passed it to Hubbub. The squalls passed on toward the bay Keys causing another lull in the wind. The gecko filled his air sacks and rattled out a succession of clamorous burps. The birds squawked and flapped their wings in protest."

The silence returned only to be broken by sniffing sounds coming from Spiker's galley.

Spiker stood up, boarded his boat, stuck his head in the galley door and said, "Stop snorting that coke, you'll be up all night fooling around. There's half a gallon of Crown Royal in the top drawer by the sink. Drink on it until you pass out. Don't spill the rest."

Fiarel tried to break the unopened seal on the bottle but the coke had drained the last of his limited energy. Spiker broke the seal then grabbed the bag of cokc from his galley table and dumped it in the sink drain. As he turned on the faucet, Fairel whined like a wounded beast then chugged on the bottle.

When Spiker returned to the end of the gun table he said, "I can't believe that a man his age can snort so much coke. He was chopping rails that makes scar-face look like a whimp!"

The Dirt had his moment on stage by saying, "One tieing a freng of mineg snort to much coke ang he hada braing hengroid."

Snarly smiled and said, "Is that so. Are you sure about that?"

The Dirt said, "Ung hung."

Snarly said, "Aye. That you are but the trees are still close. So, tell me Digler, how long has your friend been crapping through his ears and improperly wiping his asses? He would have to do a whole lota' that to fire up a brain hemorrhoid."

The Dirt said, "No, no, no, no, no. He was bleeding frung hiss ears!"

Snarly refused to carry on the conversation by dropping his gaze to the top of the gun table. His light Cherokee red face deepened to burgundy. His jaws flexed, the muscles rippled. His eyes swelled from their sockets and the corners of his mouth turned down as he looked at The Dirt with a disgusting sneer. He stood up from the gun table and walked the length of the counter tops looking them over. Then he stooped down, staring at the rug that covered the recessed hatch to the galley ice hold. He stood and walked out the galley door and stooped down on the deck space between the saddle packing boxes, gazing intently at the surface as if he was privy to some sort of cloaked demon that only he could see.

I realized he was seeing something I couldn't because of my windblown cataracts. He stood up, walked back into the galley still displaying his grim expression and reclaimed his seat at the gun table. He leaned his back and head against the bulkhead. As he closed his eyes, all the color vanished from his face giving him the appearance of a white man. His eyelids fluttered.

Ruckus said, "He's having a stroke!"

Hubbub said, "No, he's fallen asleep and having a nightmare."

Snarly mumbled, "I never completely sleep, I'm merely observing the colors of my attitude."

Intrigued, Hubbub said, "Are you saying your attitude has colors?"

Snarly said, "Aye, all my attitudes flash different colors on my third eye. Sometimes they appear polished and translucent like a pile of sparkling multi-colored precious gems. Other times they are dull and faded."

Hubbub ventured to ask, "What are the colors of your attitude now?"

Snarly uttered in a grueling tone, "Turkey turd brown in a gray area with a mass of thin black lines crisscrossed and stacked on top of each other."

He opened his eyes, smiled at The Dirt and said, "You shed more hair than a kennel full of black labs."

Spiker interrupted and said, "I swear, the devil is my witness, he's telling the truth. The son of a bitch is weaving a throw rug on my galley deck where he lies by the door until he has to crawl to the scupper to heave up regurgitated air and green bile."

The Dirt whined, "I don' know why I loose my hairs, day cung back wheng day fall out."

Snarly grinned and said, "That shouldn't be too hard to figure out."

The Dirt was astonished and said, "So jew know why I got dees hairs?"

Snarly said, "Aye, I believe the entire catastrophic event occurred before you were born. Apparently in the first moments of the abortive conception when the sperm that helped create you penetrated the surface of your embryo on an angle. A most difficult approach to pre-creation. As it struggled in a frenzy to break through, it inadvertently triggered a single premature and misguided electron shock causing the embryo to drop the gene that inhibits your hair growth, which activated the gene that stimulates your hair growth. So in other words, you are devolving, and there isn't any way to reverse the genetics."

The Dirt twisted his face into a scowl and said, "What jew ming deballbing?"

Snarly grinned then said, "There really isn't any other way to explain it, unless I put it in more simple lay man's terms. For instance, if you screw one of your road whores and she gives birth to a son, he will appear more apish than you, and if he screws one of your road whores then she gives birth to a son, he will appear more apish than him, so and so on down the line until you're all a bunch of quirky baboonish apes picking and eating each others' fleas and ticks.

"There might be some hope for you yetis yet. I heard it through the seaweed that a scientist is attempting to employ the impossible application of mythical molecular electronics. If he can do it then he can send in one of those micro-bots to run a diagnostic on your genetics, locate the dropped gene and put it back where it was. But until he can do all of that, you must wear the hair and your offspring will continue to devolve onto a dead-end branch of the evolutionary tree. I must say it grieves me deeply knowing that there isn't any way of showing my overwhelming affection to that single misguided electron."

With that, he stood up, reached into the storage closet, pulled out a bright red portable Dirt Devil and shoved it into The Dirt's arms then said, "On this boat you must vac' it up. Don't even think about being lazy and going shiftless on me, I'll be backing the vac' with a hazer taser."

The Dirt's eyes popped out of their sockets as he said, "I know 'bout tazers, day use theng ong me in dee big house all dee tieing but I nebber heard uh no hazy tazer. Cang I see it?"

Snarly removed his taser from the bottom pocket of his coveralls. The Dirt said, "It looky like all dee udder tazers I've sing, udder dan doze three red linegs, what's day ming?"

Snarly said, "They mean I have injected the charge with three grains of uranium which gives it an extra boost that leaves the perpetrator with a bad case of the jerks and poor vision. If you don't pull the barbs out quickly, the charge makes contact with static electricity in the air that stands your hair on end while it glows electric blue and nuclear green. I haven't been able to test it further for any other outstanding side effects, but I'm hoping you will present me with such an opportunity shortly if you don't suck in your gut and suck up your hair."

The Dirt switched on the Dirt Devil and moved around the cabin, uprooting his sticky hair from the rug. Snarly went to the back deck, turned on the deck hose and sprayed the hair out the scuppers. He returned to the cabin, picked up the heavy boarding steps and carried them out the door, then placed them on the deck between the door and the port packing box. He came back in the cabin and sat in his place at the gun table.

His brothers twisted up joints as they exchanged sly smirks, snickers and grins. The Dirt finished with his hair, turned off the vac', opened the storage closet and placed it on the deck.

Snarly growled, "Pick it up, carry it to the stern and dump the hair into the water. For each hair a shark will acquire the stink of your fear, assuring me that they will follow you wherever you may roam in this cosmic bubble of shifting water and rock with a growing fire in its heart much like my own."

The Dirt waddled towards the door to return the Dirt Devil. Snarly stood up and met him at the entrance, grabbed the vac' from his hands then pointed at the boarding steps. He put the vac' in the closet then looked at The Dirt who returned his glare and shook his head.

Snarly said, "You must sit there and hose the deck hair out the scuppers when it piles up. That will intrigue more sharks. The tides flow northwest and southeast in the gulf. All the sharks in those directions are picking up your unending scent. I see you are not happy about the arrangement. It's for your own good, and you should be grateful. It's sparing you the extent of the wrath of my rage. If we are cooking or eating and some of your hairs get in our food, it may unleash the devil in me. I'm stating that fact in the presence of two captains. I can't be responsible for my own decisions.

"I might do what my mother always did to a three-hundred-pound boar hog after she shot him in the brain and slit him in the throat, bleeding him out, heaving him over the fence, and tying a rope around his back feet to lower him with her A-framed block and tackle into a fifty-five gallon drum of scalding water to loosen the hairs. After the drum of scalding water has been brung to a boil by the heat from six old, dry-rotted flaming truck tires, she removes the boar from the water with her block and tackle, then moves the rolling A-frame to one side of the drum so she can scrape the hair off of the skin with her butcher knife while he's still steaming. After she shaves away all of the hair, she slits his belly and removes each innard one at a time, washing it in a bucket of salted water to loosen the gore then heaving it into a large cooler containing a bed of frozen water bottles.

"When us kids filled the water bottles to be frozen sometimes some of them exploded if we didn't leave a one-inch void at the top for expansion.

"After all the innards were washed and cooled she would cut away the thick skin in strips and chunks then toss them into the drum of boiling water. When all the skin was cooking down she would throw in hands full of herbs, garlic and salt, then go about removing the other parts from the backbone with her hacksaw, saving the pork shoulders and the prodigious hams for last. After she wrapped them in cheese cloth and stored them in the cooler she smashed the backbone with a six-pound steel maul and fed it to her watch dogs. She would return to the drum some hours later to spoon the thick layer of fat off the cooled water into mason jars and cold store it to season the sautéed flesh, boiled beans and fried potatoes with chopped onions.

"I don't suppose that school of hungry sharks sniffing and tracking your scent would care about such careful preparations, but if we cast you adrift and leave you floundering in the surf anywhere along the Ivory Coast, a hungry tribe of mad cannibals might find such an event quite tasty, but not right away. First they will bind you with tough thorny vines and make you walk to their cooking pot. The women and children will surround you in a fire dance as the men dig a large pit and let it fill with ground water. When the deep pit has filled to the level of the ground water they will keep you bound in the vines and club you until all your bones except your head are broken, keeping you alive.

"They will lower you into the pit of water with your head above the surface where you will stay for a day, a night and another day until you have swelled up half again your size. When you are bursting at the joints oozing watery fat, they will put you out of your misery with an adequate club, pull you from the pit, remove the vines, sever your joints and put the members into the cauldron of boiling water seasoned with roots and tubers."

I told Snarly to put a lid on it. Spiker said, "Now that's an option I never considered."

The Dirt, who appeared unaffected by Snarly's brow beating, poked around in the hair on his right wrist exposing the face of his watch. He held it to his ear, shook his arm a few times, put it to his ear again then said, "It's no worky, what tieing iss sset?"

Snarly immediately became alarmed and said, "Why do you need to know what time it is?"

The Dirt shrugged his shoulders and looked away. Snarly said, "Nobody else wants to know what time it is. Right now time has no meaning until we've made up our minds about the next move and when we are leaving. So, tell me what you've got going down, what's your deadline. Spit it out before I grow impatient and tase it out of you!"

Spiker said, "Give him a break, he's just trying to guesstimate about where his friends are right now while they're bringing up the dope. He's worried about 'em."

Snarly grimaced then said, "That's a lota' road whore crap, nobody other than a pair of love birds would give a flying fuck over his emotional concerns for a couple of mules that he's about to stick it to in more than one way if he gets the chance. No, no, this scheming, shaming pig raper is up to something besides the goats and sheep, and I need to know what it is. Has he been talking on your cell phone or the VHF?"

Spiker said, "No, he won't be doing any of that until he's back on his sailboat. Snarly gave The Dirt a doubtful look then shook his head in dismay.

The Dirt said, "Dhere's nutsing going downg. I like to know what tieing it is 'ing case sungsing happing so I will have more tieing to get aheada' tieing."

Snarly breathed a sigh of frustration then said, "Well, we would all like more time, but if you really want it you must buy two watches. As for getting ahead of time, you need to be hauling ass faster than the earth is spinning, so good luck with just keeping up with the twilight zone."

Ruckus rolled a joint then passed it around, filling the cabin with smoke. No one was sleepy except me. I took a puff on the joint and felt re-energized. The gecko was silent, worn out from croaking and hungry or OD'ed from bilge fumes. The birds slept on their perches and I was glad that I didn't have to hold on to a branch with my feet to sleep.

CHAPTER 8
A Bumbaclod with a Hard Head Fighting an Irate Humungous Hammerhead

Spiker, unable to sit still for more than thirty minutes without going stir-crazy, boarded his boat, taking The Dirt with him, who laid on the galley deck next to the door. The half empty bottle of booze was on the table. Fairel was below passed out and unaware that he was sleeping on a small fortune. Spiker turned on his blinding deck lights filling the Cut and all the trees on both sides with a reasonable facsimile of daylight. The birds began to screech and squawk a groggy protest, flapping their wings and pecking their neighbors.

As we sat around the galley choking on the chocolate, we gazed down the Cut at Boca Grand Channel. The wind continued to blow mounds of spume, seaweed and white man's trash into the Cut while the waves heaved more lobster traps onto the sandbar that shielded the entrance.

Fishing the Devil's Triangle...

Swimming among the flotsam and jetsam with its tail fin and dorsal fin exposed was a fourteen-foot hammerhead shark approaching us on a zigzag course, snorkeling in and out of the oily scent from the grouper carcass Snarly threw in the Cut before dinner. The girth of the shark was enormous, obviously a pregnant female with a dozen or more two-foot long pups in each ovary. The most difficult creature to deal with among any species.

Spiker hopped around on his deck like a spoiled brat, then said, "I'm going to catch it."

I gave him a horrified look and said, "Why would you want to catch it, it's close to bunk time, and we need some rest. All you are going to catch is unholy hell."

He said, "I ain't making any money tied to these trees. I can get two hundred for the jaws and three hundred for the fins and tail. I can use the meat to rebait the fifty lobster traps I dropped on the edge of Nelson's Channel south of the Cay Sal Bank before I crossed the stream."

I said, "Good luck with that. It sounds like a lot of work to me, I don't want any part of it, I'll get stoneder while I watch." I gave Ruckus a break on his stash by taking a joint of mine and firing it up.

Spiker went about taking his yellow-eye snapper rig off his one armed bandit and then put a sixteen 'O' super strength hook on the heavy snap-swivel-eye-spliced to the eighth-inch aircraft cable pulling line. As Spiker reached into his chill barrel and pulled out a small fresh barracuda, the shark swam past the port side of his stern on top of the water, lost the scent, turned around, found the rising oily scent then dove under his stern took the carcass in her mouth and shook her head from side to side as she chomped it down. She began swimming in a circle, searching for more snacks, stirring up the silt on the bottom and clouding the water. Spiker put the point of the sixteen 'O' hook through one eye of the 'cuda then out the other. He lowered it to the bottom. She ate the 'cuda, pulled the cable tight, hooked herself and hauled ass down the Cut, headed for Boca Grand Channel, smoking the drag on the bandit.

Spiker locked down the drag which slowed her down and put her in a hundred- and-eighty degree turn. He slowly hand cranked her back towards his stern as she jerked her head from side to side and thrashed on the surface, pulling back with everything she had, splashing spume and spray high into the air.

Fifty feet from the boat she became aware of the cable, the bandit and Spiker standing behind it. She ceased her tug of war with the cable, turboed herself on top of the water then streaked towards the stern, shaking her head trying to dislodge the hook, forcing Spiker to quickly crank up the slack. As she streaked past the bandit the cable came tight, forcing her into a ballistic turn that launched her out of the water and slammed her head into the bandit, causing Spiker to fall back on his ass as she took a hard blow to her midsection falling on the caprail then back into the water.

Still enraged, she tried to streak away again forcing her into another ballistic turn that slammed her head into the side of the boat. Dazed, she raised herself half out of the water and repeatedly pounded her hammers on the gunnels until she was exhausted. She relaxed and settled back into the water. Unable to do anything else, she twisted and turned on the cable until she became motionless and suspended perpendicular in the water.

Spiker cranked hard on the bandit raising her hammers out of the water. He entered his galley and returned with an old World War II M-1. He held it at arm's length with his right hand, turned his face to one side and shot her in the head. The M-1 once belonged to his father, who fired it sixteen hours a day on a three-year tour during the battles for the Phillipines. The weapon wounded so many Japs at long range and killed so many Japs at close range that the breach was worn out. If you held the weapon to your shoulder to fire it, the semi-useless breach speckled your face with specks of burning powder. He confessed that it was the only weapon the DEA would let him have with The Dirt on board. He went on to confess that it pissed him off because he couldn't possibly defend himself while he was carrying The Dirt's dirt around for three months.

He removed a long gaff from the rack of nautical tools hanging on the back of his galley bulkheads. He hooked it around the shark's tail and pulled it to the surface then looped a rope around it. He lifted the tail to the top of the caprail and grabbed it with both of his massive hands. Then with a Herculean effort he lifted the shark up and rested her gargantuan belly on the caprail. He paused for a moment, catching his breath, then pulled on the rope repeatedly, trying to pull her the rest of the way into the boat, but she wouldn't move because her expansive pectoral fins hung over the caprail and were wedged against the gunwale.

Spiker sat down on the caprail next to the five-hundred-pound female beast that wouldn't budge, hyperventilating on the edge of cardiac arrest.

Snarly, who had been eagerly waiting for the opportunity to give Spiker his promised suffering, realized that just such a moment had arrived so he offered to help. He knew the screw-in lock bolt that prevented the bandit from swinging was loose, a dangerous situation when fighting large aggressive fish, but that was Spiker's way. He boarded Spiker's boat, picked the shark up by the tail and told Spiker to put his hands under her fins and lift up, "Then I'll pull her aboard."

Spiker studied Snarly's face for a moment, decided he was sincere then said, "Well I suppose I could use some help, this toothy overweight bitch is still fighting me with dead weight. He stood up, put his arms around the shark's belly, put his hands under the fins and lifted. Snarly heaved on her tail and she came aboard. The short cable on the bandit caught the weight of the shark as it fell onto the deck. The bandit swung a hundred degrees with a brutal force. The end of the Kevlar leaf-spring that held the line block whacked Spiker on the side of his head, leaving a three-inch horizontal gash above his left ear that rendered him unconscious. He fell against Snarly, and they both crashed into the chill barrel. Snarly shoved him off, then he fell onto his engine box where he laid inert with blood squirting out of the hole in his head.

Hubbub was there in a flash applying a compress and scolding Snarly. He probed the wound. The long gash was shallow and appeared superficial. The small hole made by first contact contained an open vein that required a few stitches. As the wound swelled he swabbed it with rubbing alcohol. He gave it a few moments to dry as he opened a tube of triply antibiotic cream, then applied a thick layer overall. He asked Ruckus to bring a roll of duct tape, sneered at Snarly then commanded him to hold up Spiker's head and hold a compress on the wound. He put a strip of tape around Spiker's head and then Snarly rested it on a pillow.

Hubbub said, "That's all I can do until he comes out of the coma." He sneered at Snarly again and said, "Could you try to be sympathetic and helpful when he comes around. I know it truly isn't in you, but we need to move on and get this long ordeal over with."

Snarly nodded his head and said, "How long until he's awake?"

Hubbub said, "Any minute or never, I'm no brain surgeon, so I can only guess at anything in between."

By now everyone except Fairel stood around Spiker's engine cover staring down at him. His body began to jerk with spasms as his internal system completed its realignment. Ten minutes later after his brain received proper blood flow through the swollen vein, it began to function.

He came out of the coma slowly, shifting around on the engine cover and moaning. He opened his eyes and rolled them from one side to the other then started at us with a wild, crazed expression on his face. He said, "What did you bastards do to me?"

Snarly pretended to be offended by saying, "We didn't do anything to you crap stain, you're the one who left the lock bolt unscrewed on the bandit. Don't try to blame it on us, ass wipe!"

Hubbub looked at his brother, shook his head then returned to his analysis of Spiker's condition. He took him by the right arm then raised him to a sitting position and looked intently into his eyes. Seeing that things were all clear, he smiled and said, "You'll be OK."

Spiker, who is always unsure about the outcome of anything, showed his doubts by touching the left side of his head. He felt the tape and bandage which compelled him to press harder. When he felt the searing pain he screamed like a woman giving birth without an injection of saddle block, then fell back, resting his head on the pillow and cursing Snarly for the rake he was, mumbling something about being set up.

As Ruckus and Hubbub helped him up to support him below to his bunk, he gave Snarly a murderous glare. He shook off the brothers, then removed a twelve-inch scimitar from the tool rack and cut away the fins and tail from the shark. His hands became a blur as he skillfully removed the jaws from the flesh, then hacked, sliced and tore the body, guts and the two dozen pups into chunks for trap bait.

Hubbub, certain that his patient was in prime shape pulled the rat gun from his belt and handed it to Ruckus. In consolation, he took his stash out of his pocket, sat at the gun table and rolled a joint to smoke with his rational brother. As he did so Ruckus, preparing for his watch, went to the galley stove and cooked up a pot of homemade bucci. He placed one-ounce bucci cups in a long row then asked his brother how many he wanted. He requested a double. Ruckus poured three of the heavily sweetened and condensed espresso for himself. They shared the bucci and joint with each other before Ruckus had to sit on the portable and uncomfortable chopping block to stand watch for the gecko. The birds that had scattered to all points of the compass when Spiker shot the shark were returning to their roosts.

Snarly went to the counter and poured himself a triple bucci then said, "The last time I had a triple bucci, I was having breakfast with a political science teacher at the Fisherman's Café on the waterfront where the drunk road whores crap in the street. When I ordered my bucci the teach' said she would have one, too, so I told her to try a single first to see if she could handle it.

"Being a ball busting bitch from hell she said, 'If you will recall last night, I believe I'm as tough as you are.' When the bucci came before the breakfast I grabbed mine and chugged the triple in one gulp. She did the same. Five minutes later when the food came she stared at it, turned milky white, stood up from the table and hustled into the ladies room to heave up the load of semen she had for her first breakfast, hustled out of the café and ran down the street toward Sloppy Joe's to work off the buzzer up her ass. She never spoke to me again."

He passed the joint that he had been Bogarting to Ruckus who said, "When I anchored in Morgan's Harbor at Port Royal, the people didn't pass joints. Everyone rolled and smoked their own as they went about their daily routine with it between their lips, which caused the end to become soaked with spittle. So it was considered a health hazard bordering on barbarism to pass the joint. I learned that the first day of my arrival when a Jamaican named Booky came out in his banana boat to see if he could get me anything after I put down my mooring. He had three-quarters of an unlit joint in his mouth. I was out of weed so I asked if I could have a toke on his joint. His eyes bulged in their sockets as he looked at me as if I were insane. Then he passed it with some reluctance. It was then that I noticed half of it was slobbered on. I tore the wet part off and dropped it on the rug then smoked the rest while I promised to replace it as soon as he scored me a stash.

I said, "Spitball, the Brutal Boxer from down under does the same thing, hoping you will be disgusted and pass the joint back so he can double suck. The only way I could break him of the habit was to tear the end off and throw it on his floor and complain that I was never much for sucking on spit."

The Rug Rats continued to sip enough bucci to propel them into a two-day "stay awake" as if they were king crab fisherman on the Bering Sea, that they could only come out of by blowing a joint. Spiker finished packing his bloody meat, washed the boxes and deck then entered his galley where he was bombarded with a barrage of questions from The Dirt. He continued on and went below to see if Fairel was still breathing and then laid in his bunk with a pounding headache.

The sow-breath of Mariah periodically slammed us with swirling squalls. I went to the counter and poured myself a single bucci then reached under the console, removed my two log books and placed them on the gun table. I sipped the bucci as I opened the first log book that only contained three LORAN-C locations that held large schools of fish I recently discovered.

I opened the second book then printed the last three numbers of the four-line and the one-line by omitting the decimal that signified the tenths and memorizing the hundredth number of the four-line for each location. I created an uncipherable code that only I could understand. Even if a young, incoming and computerized "high liner" were to come across them and figured out they were LORAN-C positions, he would have a very difficult time finding them unless he could pay the price for the memorized hundredth number in my brain. His only other option would be to run all over hell's creation to all the hundredth numbers of the four lines then continue west to bring up the last three numbers. Even if he reached that point with all the hundredth numbers, he still wouldn't know if he should run north or south on the one-line in the hopes of marking fish without the hundredth number on the one-line. I never need that because most of my locations are in fifteen fathoms, and if not, the depth would be one-tenth of that printed.

Spiker, unable to sleep because of the headache, smelled the rich aroma of the bucci, got up, came over and poured himself one. He glared at Snarly. Then he looked at all the numbers in the second book as I was ripping up the page from the first book that the complete LORAN-C positions were printed on. As I threw it in the trash, he said, "What's all those numbers for?"

Knowing that his favorite way of finding fish is to run up close to someone and write down their location, I said, "They appear somewhat ambiguous and unimportant, but they're actually part of a numeral equation for the design of a combustion chamber that can contain a series of minimal nuclear detonations and be navigated with electromagnetic vent controlled radial exhausts."

He laughed and said, "What's it for?"

I said, "I'm going to put it in a spaceship so I can get the hell out of here someday. I'm sure its velocity will blast me through the sound barrier and the spheres then shoot me into dead space far an' fast in any direction with the capability to turn on a dime instantaneously. I'll probably install a video void chart to map what's on the other side and electro-nuke the hull to avoid or devoid alien clingers on the way there. So what's it to ya?"

Afraid to laugh, he mumbled, "Nothing, nothing. I just need to bum a few joints. Fairel got pissed off because I washed his coke down the drain into the Cut, so the fish hanging under the boat could cop a buzz, so he flushed my stash of Humbolt County Original Gangster into the holding tank hooked up to the shitter. I'd love to strangle the sorry bastard but it might put things on hold, and I can't afford that. The old lady is screaming about retirement money for a cabin in the mountains. The health inspector downgraded her rating at the fish market from an 'A' to a 'B' because the flopper door on the ice machine has a crack in it. She's too embarrassed to show her face at work so the help is running another business out the back door. Her son had half a key of coke mailed to her house and the sniffer dogs found it. Now she's pissing our money away on lawyers to keep him out of prison. After she bailed him out he smoked too much crack and wrecked his Mustang. The airbag reshaped his face so she's wasting money on a lawsuit against Ford. Tragedy seems to pursue her whenever I go away for a few months in spite of her best efforts."

He stood up and poured a round of buccis. We all sipped.

I said, "I'm going into the lakes tomorrow and troll kingfish spoons for gag groupers. You can follow me around in there if you like and see what you can catch. The gag groupers are spawning in the turtle grass now. There's thousands in there, I just want twenty or thirty. There will be a lot of great barracudas dogging us, but you can grind them for chum. They make good deep drop bait, too."

Spiker said, "I was thinking about heading west

tomorrow, why can't you?"

I said, "I don't want to go into the Triangle until this wind goes around out of the northwest. There's no telling what might come at us from that disturbance off of Mexico, it's still swirling a mass of squalls this way every two or three hours. You've got four days to get there and it's just a five-hour run. Chill out until better weather."

The Dirt came out of Spiker's galley and threw some paper plates into the Cut. Snarly saw him do it and said, "The Dirt is a regular Trasher Smithy!"

He yelled, "Hey! Fish that stuff out of the water with a net and put it in a garbage bag. If you do that again I'm going to scalp you, lazy bastard!"

Spiker said, "Who's Trasher Smithy?"

Snarly grumbled then said, "He's a professor who lives in the mountains of North Carolina. He teaches environmental development in the valley, but when he's at home on the mountain he throws his trash to the wind and puts his deteriorating chemical containers in a rusted out shed next to a stream flowing down hill. He didn't like the doors in his house so he bought new ones and piled the old ones in his driveway. Then he set them on fire. Instead of sweeping up the ashes and the hardware, he drove through them repeatedly, going up and down the mountain, not practicing what he was preaching, which created a baffling situation where he couldn't figure out why he was having so many flat tires. He's an oxymoron moron, which is a common occurrence out here that literally creates nightmares backed up with conscious daymares causing me to go from conscious to subconscious, never getting anywhere near unconscious, having a dreamless sleep in a skunk weed void. After a number of years with you temporarily interrupting fishing and carrying out your government backed paybacks, I'm positive two flew over the cuckoo's nest!"

Spiker gave me a dubious and doubtful look then said, "Are you serious about that spaceship?" The clones snickered.

I said, "Absolutely, it's a well baked piece of cake if you've got the right woman at the oven. Merely figuring out the correct combination of the lightest and toughest metals for the chamber will put you halfway there. You must construct it in the middle of any large desert and dig a long, deep trench on a fourteen-degree angle for a launch pad. At this point mankind will have reached the last stage of no stages. After the glorification of such an event has been suffered with hangovers, he must endure mind-boggling and repetitive calculations that only change slightly in their progression to the end results handed over be a number of nuclear physicists in order to determine whether one, two or three electromagnetic vents should be open in the radial exhausts upon the initial detonation in the progressive series to be initiated upon slowing down so you can continue to haul ass."

Spiker placed a hand on my log books. When I didn't protest he opened the thinner first book with half the pages torn out. Finding no numbers to ogle over, he looked baffled then opened the other one containing the coded LORAN-C positions. He studied the numbers for a moment then said, "You get all of that out of these numbers?"

I said, "Yes, it's quite simple if you can see numbers as something other than amounts you can send home to your wife."

He said, "That's alota' crap, these are just your fishing holes tho' I can't make them out. Light a joint so I can come down from this bucci and get some sleep."

I was glad that he was tired of my bullshit and convinced he couldn't get at my fishing holes. As he sucked on the joint a call from his wife came over the radio waves on his sideband. We could hear her muffled questions coming from his galley door.

Spiker said, "I don't know what to tell her, ain't shit happened yet except some financial loss."

Snarly, always being the messenger of doom said, "Don't tell her anything, it won't matter anyway. She's looking through a long tunnel and sees a big pile of gold at the end. She can't see all the obstacles and difficulties the tunnel passes through to deposit it there. She can only watch it grow as she bleeds off a little bit here and there to keep things on an even keel so she doesn't have to worry about her son being tied to his bunk with the bed sheets and butt-fucked while he's in jail."

Spiker took his last toke on the joint, stood up and exhaled with a scowl on his face then said, "One of these days I'm going to bop you in the chops, sending you into never, Neverland. Then I'll ream that inverted set of lips between your ass that persists with talking all that crap. You've got more'n a stopped up toilet!"

He boarded his boat, turned off his deck lights then stepped into his galley and tripped over The Dirt who had rolled in the way. He cursed him viciously then stuck his head out the door and asked me how I was going to spoon the groupers tomorrow.

I said, "It's only twelve to fifteen feet in there at mean low tide which will be in one hour. Seven hours from now it will be high tide and I can cover more bottom trolling. I just lower the bandit lead down about two or three feet with the wired spoon on a thirty-foot leader. I Super Glue a barrel rattle on the underside of the spoon. It compels the grouper to shoot off the bottom and slam it full throttle."

He said, "I've got some rattles in my freshwater tackle, I'll see you at ten o'clock." He entered his galley, turned on a light and answered the radio that had been periodically squawking, "Are you there?"

I slid my galley door closed and sat at the steering helm.

Snarly grumbled, "Why did you invite him along tomorrow?"

I said, "What's it to ya?"

He said, "I really don't want to play nursemaid to the hippy Navy."

I said, "Well, you won't! If you had been listening when I told him how I was going to spoon the groupers, you would have realized that I plan to use him as much as I can before he catches on. While he's trolling two feet below the surface catching barracudas as fast as he can go, I'll be trolling two feet above the bottom catching groupers. He doesn't care what he's catching as long as something is biting his spoon. He has a use for anything that swims. I don't and he will keep the 'cudas off me. That's a big help in a long day on your feet for a few fish, but we won't be taking any ass kicking."

Snarly asked if he could work the port bandit.

I said, "Whoever isn't standing watch can take turns manning the helm and working the bandit."

Snarly's face sagged into gloom an' doom until Ruckus offered to stand half his watch for the same in return.

I said, "Whatever, but somebody better be scanning the horizon. I don't know how many jacktars are looking for Spiker. Somebody has got to give up some of their stash and give mine a break. Let's eat a fish sandwich then get some shut-eye. We'll be spinning spoons soon."

I drank a pint of water to wake me in six hours. Ruckus poured a bucci. We ate fish, smoked then went below and I fell into a dreamless sleep.

Ruckus poured another bucci, picked up the rat gun and returned to his hard seat on the chopping block, his long hard day almost over.

CHAPTER 9
Treasure Hunting
An' Trolling

I awoke to hear rain pounding on the forward deck above me. Mixed in the roar was the squeaky whining of Fairel and the choking rasp of The Dirt barfing. It reminded me of the early mornings I shared with my wife in the first stage of her pregnancy with the Rug Rats. Such events preceded a series of personality trait disturbances with a depressive reaction that fortunately could become catalytic. I could only hope for the same concerning The Dirt and Fairel.

I left a whiz in the head then stepped up into the galley and cleaned my mouth, preparing it for the filth it will have to converse with Spiker. Ruckus poured me a bucci, then one for himself. As he reached for it I said, "Blow a joint and get some sleep. I'm not fishing in the rain."

We smoked then he passed the rat gun to Snarly who took his seat on the chopping block. Hubbub cooked some bacon and eggs then put them on the table. He carried a plate to Snarly and put it on the port packing box next to the chopping block. Snarly laid the rat gun on the box and began eating. Spiker, forever ready to plunge into oblivion without bothering to look at what was coming at him, cranked his engine. I stepped outside and motioned for him to shut it off then come over for breakfast. Squalls howled around us as we ate and smoked. The wind increased and stayed out of the sow'west.

Suddenly the rat gun went off. Everyone jumped out of their skin as rat shot ricocheted off the caprail. Snarly cursed then said, "That bug eater is fast. A two-inch cockroach was crawling on the rail then the gecko was there with the roach in his mouth. I picked up the gun and fired, but I was half a second too late. He won't come out again until he's hungry."

Spiker confessed that he needed someone to replace Fairel because he wasn't able to stand watch or navigate a course. He asked if I had spoken to Jolly Roger recently.

I said, "He's fishing. He doesn't talk to anyone until he's finished or forced to go into the fort because of the weather. You might see him when we are fishing the Tortugas Banks, he's been running with Captain Lead and fishing the area. If you are counting on him to help out, he might be interested. He would be welcome by me and the Rug Rats, but don't tell him one thing then do another like you do me. If you pull that crap on him, he will scalp you. Give him his money up front in case he gets a chance to spend it."

Squalls continued to spin off the churning mass to the sow'west. Spiker began to fidget then pace the deck, pissed off because I wouldn't call Jolly. Snarly, also pissed off because he had to sit on a hard seat for eight hours, staring down the Cut at Boca Grand Channel or looking under the caprail for an easy shot at the gecko. Unable to sit still he asked if he could take a hike in the rain.

I said, "For what purpose?"

He said, "I would like to muck around in the pirates' watering hole."

I said, "Aye, bring the metal detector, we can all go."

Spiker said, "I've got to stay here and keep an eye on those two while I wait for a call from the old lady about the next catastrophe."

Showing the fortitude of a king crab fisherman, Ruckus came from below with his gear, still slightly buzzed by the all-night bucci. He put on his slicker top and waders then went to the counter to pour some buccis. We did the same and wandered up Trappers Path to the beach. The stinking breath of Mariah was piling up mounds of salt spume, eel grass, turtle grass, Sargasso weed, pin shells, conchs, sea pigeons, sea cucumbers and horseshoe crabs among the lobster traps on the beach, creating a putrid, swirling mass that intensified her reek.

We turned south following the sand until we came to a wall of red mangrove trees and roots. We walked along the edge of the mangroves in a northerly direction, through the sea oats, over the sand bunkers, past the white mangroves and other brush into the sand and mud that surround the water hole. The wind and rain swirled around us. Snarly moved the detector from side to side around the water hole. After an hour of searching and finding a five-gallon bucket of pop tops and beer cans with other useless trash, he found two quarters of recent mint that were mostly corroded away except a paper thin shell of what appeared to be nickel silver still displaying old george and the eagle but too thin to spend.

Snarly became terrified by the discovery which compelled him to blurt out another one of his prophecies of doom as he said, "Thus goes the economy as we devolve into mangrove mutants. Aye, you must toughen your guts me bra-bra brudders so you can eat the creatures raw while on the move in stealth mode. If you can't hack it and stop to cook your stone-killed critter on a campfire, you will give away your position to some crazed terrorist which will only shorten the number of days you have left to eat raw, cracked conch soaked in Key Lime juice to kill the scurvy before the heavy shit falls!"

He continued to sweep the detector from side to side as we completed our walk around the water hole and headed south toward the beach. The detector beeped loud and long for about ten feet to the south then stopped.

Snarly said, "It's not very wide, it's a shaft or piece of pipe. He moved the detector back to the north end then swept it east and west. The beeps continued to the sow'west and southeast on each side of the north end of the shaft.

Hubbub said, "What do you make of it?"

Snarly said, "It's an old wooden ship's anchor. Judging from the size of the anchor, the ship was well over one hundred feet and perhaps a hundred and fifty tons. Since there isn't any tilt bars under the mooring ring I would say it was the captain's second best. A wise ol' captain, he had his crew bury it deep here to ride out the northeast winds from a passing hurricane. He would have been standing at her helm with his crew standing behind her bowsprit at her sampson post, ready to cast off her mooring line when the wind switched from the northeast to the sow-west. When the wind was due-west he would give the order to take up a foot of slack and heave off her mooring line, then put her main boom to port with a reefed sail on a course to the sow'west to gain some leeway to clear the sandbars offshore of the southwest corner of the island. Upon making his leeway he would have come about lashing the main boom to starboard to reach his mooring ground at the northeast corner of the Marquesas Islands on his initial and only tack. He may have met his end there. The sow'west wind can be the most treacherous and he didn't return for his second-best anchor. Or perhaps he was a pirate and would only give a hoot an' a poot for his best borrowed anchor, seeing as how there was more riding the waves on his horizon."

He continued to scan the beach as we made our way back to the boat. He found no booty, only white man's trash with some recent pennies and dimes that were in such a corroded condition they were only fit for scrap.

When we boarded the boat there were horseflies everywhere. Snarly slapped at them with a fish rag, chasing them away from the door so we could enter and close it quickly. Ruckus went below to get some sleep. I spared Snarly the hard seat on the chopping block and the horseflies but insisted that he must keep an eye on the Cut and Boca Grand Channel until Hubbub relieved him.

Spiker boarded our boat going ape shit about heading west to find Jolly and an unfortunate captain that might take Fairel off his hands before it was necessary to call the Coast Guard to airlift him to an institution.

I said, "I wish you would leave Jolly out of this, he's a good fisherman and that's what you should let him do."

He said, "Call him and find out where he is. He will talk to you."

I said, "I'm not going to drag him into this. If your forked tongue can convince him to come along, then it's on your head that you might lose. You must remember that he is a friend of ours and we are on his side. If he doesn't want to risk it, don't go digging through his past trying to find something to force him into it. He was framed by some white men for most of the slander on his rap sheet and the rest were just well deserved paybacks that we can't hold against him."

I asked Hubbub to bring up the overall picture of the Gulf. I looked at it then said, "There's a two hour window before the next mass of squalls get here. If you leave now they will hit you halfway there. They look nasty, ship weather only. The ebbing tide will be three hours on the fall, peaking to its rip to the southeast colliding into the sow'west wind creating an extremely turbulent cross sea with massive waves crashing into each other. If it doesn't roll you over in the toss about the least you will suffer is bruised, dislocated shoulders and a bunch of lumpy knots on your head from being slammed into your bulkheads when she dips then pitches her caprails shipping water faster than the pumps can keep up with it. It's not a good time to cross Rebecka Channel, but if you want to venture blindly into it I can't stop you."

Snarly said, "Let him go about his bad self, it might put an end to his vendettas and we can go fishing."

I looked at Spiker and said, "You need to throw off your tie lines and move to the other side of the Cut so I can go trolling until the squalls hit."

Spiker moved out of our way. We motored out of the Cut then turned north for a few hundred yards up the channel and turned east into the main lake. The sow'west wind was honking and whistling at twenty-five knots and gusting to thirty. Protected by a string of islands with miles of sandbars between them the lake's surface was only rippled with a one-foot chop.

I gave the helm to Hubbub with her speed at three knots and told him, "Hold a course to Archer Key cut then make tight turns to the north as we troll back and forth until it shallows up at Turtle Channel. Then make your turns to the south until it shallows up north of the islands. If Spiker crosses your bow just keep going and cut his gear away on the shaft choppers."

I went aft, lifted the dog on the starboard bandit and lowered the kingfish spoon two feet above the turtle grass. Snarly did the same to the port bandit. I told him and Hubbub to keep an eye on the east and west entrances and Turtle Channel to the north.

We trolled back and forth for two hours. The grouper strikes came minutes apart. We caught thirty six gag groupers that filled the chill barrel to the four-hundred-pound mark along with six large 'cudas for Spiker. The squalls were approaching the sow'west corner of Boca Grand Channel. I motored back to Trappers Cut. Spiker followed. After he tied alongside he confessed that he had killed twenty seven great barracudas and nine gag groupers. Snarly threw the six 'cudas we caught onto Spiker's deck.

Spiker gave Snarly a suspicious look then said, "You don't want those?"

Snarly said, "No, we've got plenty of bait and I don't want them stinking up the chill barrel."

Spiker was certain it was some sort of trick. He grabbed the 'cudas by the tails and laid them on his packing box. He opened all their mouths and gazed intently down their throats. Finding nothing, he began squeezing their bellies, feeling for anything that shouldn't be there. Five of the 'cudas were lean and had been hungry, which compelled them to eat the spoon. One had a hard lump in its belly.

Spiker stuck the point of a gutting knife in the rectum of the 'cuda. With one swipe of the blade he slit the belly to the throat, and with a short slice to the stomach he removed a fresh fourteen-inch gag grouper from the viscera.

He looked in its mouth then said, "I'll have it for dinner."

Seeing that Snarly was sincere with his offering, he thanked him for the 'cudas which was a waste of time.

The incoming squalls roared past us, leaving a light breeze from the sow'west, but the screen showed more turbulence breaking away from the center of the main storm and moving toward the straits.

Snarly and Ruckus cleaned and packed the fish. Hubbub stood by with the rat gun. I told him, "Put it under the console and fry up some fresh grouper, make it crispy. The gecko isn't hungry and he won't come out unless he hears a road whore croaking. He's full of cockroaches and palmetto bugs he caught while we were mucking around in the watering hole, which foretells another evening of his frustrated racket."

As we smoked and choked on joints we ate fish

sandwiches with lettuce, tomato and tartar sauce. Spiker cursed the stinking breath of Mariah, Fairel and The Dirt, who were eating crackers and sardines then washing them down with Crown Royal. The Doppler showed the storm slowly moving to the north with the incoming squalls dissipating.

Spiker smiled then said, "Let's crank 'em up and head west."

Fairel moaned as The Dirt gagged. Snarly, knowing that no one was going anywhere until the wind switched due west – and ever ready to mess with Spiker's Jonah mind – said, "Aye, great idea, I'm tired of floundering under these trees with a bunch of birds fighting and crapping all over the boat, getting my ass chewed in my sleep by these horseflies and smelling that rank hill of decaying sea life constantly piling up on the sandbar."

He stood up and grabbed Spiker by the hand, shaking it, then said, "I'll see you in the mooring basin at Fort Jefferson. May your crossing of Rebecka Channel be blessed with a dozen rift squalls."

Spiker pulled his hand away, looked at it to see if Snarly left anything on it, then wiped it on his t-shirt, scowled and said, "What in the hell is a rift squall?"

Snarly said, "When the sow'west wind goes calm and doesn't switch to the west then increases as it goes to the northwest and honks, it creates a lull, turning Rebecka Channel into a flowing doldrum. The surface reflects the sun's heat causing it to rise. Small swirling cores of turbulence form that can develop a vortex. If you cross her shipping lanes when Rebecka is spawning water spouts, she will give birth to a rift squall. It will be born on, then attach itself to and feed off the intense heat from your engine exhaust which is more than twice as hot as the surrounding and already volatile air. Since there is no wind to break it up and blow it way, it follows you wherever you go as it intensifies until you become shrouded in a gray, misty gloom that blocks out your bright blue horizon and leaves you navigating blind with a sat nav because your wife won't let you buy a radar.

"All of these facts add up to a hazardous situation that can go from rapture to rupture without notice when you crash into another poacher running blind and defying Murphy's Law like you, or a ship that sees you on his radar but really doesn't care that you are there and won't alter his course for a small blip that he can't see with his naked eye because he has a schedule to keep. It happens all the time. Just ask Lloyd's of London. They can prove it."

Spiker grinned, shook his head, looked at me and said, "What about it?"

I said, "You can go whenever you want, but I'm staying 'til dawn and watching the weather."

He said, "Why?"

I said, "There's no light breeze from the west. The wind isn't trading. Everything is still hanging to the sow'west in a heating lull. I'm not going to buck an ill wind that is deceiving. We haven't had the worst of it yet."

Spiker whined, "What in the hell does that mean?"

I said, "The longer it hangs in the sow'west the nastier it's going to be when it does trade around. If this lull lasts another two or three days it's going to trade with temporary hurricane force winds. I've seen it before and I'll see it again. We will have a light breeze from the west that will come with the sunrise, another cunning trick from Mother Nature to lure us into the Triangle, but she will leave a window of light wind for about eight hours. That's long enough to get to the fort and get settled in the mooring basin before it swings to the northwest honking or goes back to the sow'west."

Spiker gave me a Jonah look then said, "How do you know what it's going to be like in the morning?"

I said, "Mother Nature can be a lovey dove or a heartless killer like anything else female. After more than half a century of dealing with her, she becomes predictable in her ways if you bother to observe and remember."

I fired up a joint then passed it around. We ate fish and fruit until the sun went down. Enjoying the lull, the birds went to their roosts elsewhere. The Doppler showed the storm moving back toward the sow'west. With the darkness came the gecko's mating call. In comparison to the night before, his demand for affection was somewhat subdued as if he knew there weren't any bitches about.

Snarly went below and pounded on the forward bulkheads. The gecko ceased his racket for a moment then croaked louder. He came up the steps into the galley then went into a huddle with his clones. Hubbub went to the console and removed the rat gun from its holster, then went aft and laid on his back on the port side of the deck between the packing box and the cabin bulkhead. He aimed the gun up at the underside of the hollow caprail at the spot where the gecko went in and the only place he could come out because the starboard side of the hollow caprail was blocked by an air vent that funneled fresh air onto the engines.

Ruckus opened all the cabinets under the galley counter, moved everything onto the rug then laid on his back inside the cabinets and posed his arms to jab an' stab.

Snarly went below, entered the head on the starboard side and began pounding on the bulkheads. Moving forward, he came out at the level of the caprail, moving forward then to port and aft pounding as hard as he could.

The gecko tried to pass Ruckus, running upside down inside the hollow. He jabbed the point of a knife into the bottom of the Kevlar caprail in front of the gecko, who crashed into the back of the blade. As Ruckus stabbed with the other knife, the gecko jumped on the inside of the hull and stared him in the face causing him to miss his mark again. The gecko extended its wet tongue and raked it across his long, serrated teeth as he licked his eyeballs. As Ruckus raised both knives to stab, he jumped back into the hollow of the caprail behind the storage closet then streaked past Hubbub who saw only a blur as he fired and missed. He sat up quickly, jammed the gun and his fist into the hollow of the caprail behind the packing box then fired the nine remaining rounds of rat shot down the length of the caprail where it ricocheted off the inside of the transom and then fell into a harmless pile on the deck and rolled out of the port scupper.

Hubbub went to the console and reloaded the long-barreled revolving target pistol. He took a Maglite out of the storage closet, stepped out the door then stuck the gun under the starboard caprail behind the packing box and discharged five rounds down to the transom. He walked to the starboard side of the transom and discharged three rounds under its caprail to the port side. He shined the Maglite under the transom caprail, the port and starboard caprails, then the spaces behind the packing boxes and found nothing.

Snarly cursed then said "How in the hell did he survive that?"

Hubbub said, "Damned if I know!"

Ruckus said, "He's fast, most likely he jumped on the deck behind the packing box after you shot at him the first time. While you were blasting under the caprail he ran down the deck then jumped up under the transom. That's where he was when you reloaded and blasted under the starboard caprail. While you were walking to the transom to blast under there, he was hauling ass up the port side back into the forepeak behind the bulkheads where he will stay until he's hungry, but I think I have his ass, tho' I won't be surprised if I don't.

"When he gets hungry he takes up station behind the storage closet where he first entered the caprail. That's where he was when he came out and grabbed that cockroach while Snarly took a shot at him and missed like everyone else. I'm hoping by tomorrow evening he will be over his fear of the gun play and hungry enough to attempt an ambush on a cockroach. If he's under the caprail in the storage closet when I stick the gun under the rail between the cabin bulkhead and the packing box then blast two rounds at him, he should fall dead into the storage closet. Best laid plans."

He looked at Spiker and said, "I've got to stand watch soon for your jacktars. Please move your boat to the other side of the Cut so I can fish for mangrove snappers later tonight instead of going bug-eyed staring at shadows."

Spiker went about throwing off his tie lines. Ruckus went to the stove and began preparing a large pot of bucci. The sow'west wind renewed itself then slowly increased to twenty knots, gusting to thirty. Snarly and Hubbub went to the stern then removed a seventy-pound case of ground Spanish sardines and a bait tub of cut herring from the packing box.

As Snarly threw chum into the center of the Cut, Hubbub rigged three eighty-pound pulling lines with ten feet of sixty-pound leader and a six 'O' hook for night fishing.

Snarly stopped chumming and they came forward to sip buccis and roll joints. We sat around the table munching on snacks and choking on the weed. I turned on a weather cube because my VHF antenna was down. The NOAA forecasted the possible development of a tropical depression in the tropical wave covering the sow'west gulf. The narrator went on to inform us that a long line of squalls with heavy rain and gale force winds was approaching from the sow'west and would reach the lower Keys in six hours, which would hit us an hour sooner.

Snarly said, "How depressing. Sad day. Fishing will be over shortly after midnight."

I said, "It's eight o'clock. We can fish 'til twelve. That will give you an hour to gut and pack before it hits us."

We all took our joints to the stern and fished in the Cut as Snarly chummed, then sipped his bucci between puffs and worked his line. Catching mangrove snappers was slowed by some jewfish that kept grabbing the snappers after we hooked 'em, forcing us to grip the line tight and bend the hook to release them because they were protected. Spiker hooked one on his bandit, fought it to the surface and reached for a long gaff to hook it with.

Snarly said, "Don't hurt that fish."

Spiker said, "Why not?"

Snarly said, "You're already fishing illegally over here. You haven't caught any flack from an ack-ack because the Florida Wildlife Commission knows you are doing something for the government. But, if they hear that you are killing protected species, they will put your sorry ass under the jail."

Spiker grabbed a knife then bent over his rail to cut the leader close to the hook.

Snarly said, "Don't let him go, yet."

Spiker cursed then said, "I can't keep him and I can't let him go! What the hell is wrong with you?"

Snarly said, "Nothing, there isn't any law yet that says you can't have him in the water with your hook still in his mouth. That's OK, you can look at him all you want and take pictures, so let's leave him there. We can use him in that spot."

Spiker laughed then asked, "How can you use him?"

Snarly said, "I'll show you after you catch the other one on your other bandit and let him hang by your boat with his mate."

Spiker quickly hooked the other hungry two-hundred pound jewfish and had it treading water next to the boat in a few minutes.

Snarly said, "Well done, now we can catch fish without them eating everything we hook and running the other fish back into Boca Grand Channel. It takes forever to chum them back."

The snapper bite was still slow, but we were boating a two- or three-pound fish every minute or so. By midnight the chill barrel was filled to the four-hundred-pound mark.

Spiker released the jewfish.

The Rug Rats cleaned and packed the fish in a misty light rain. The leading edge of the squalls was over us. Birds that were fleeing from it began to roost in the trees. Five huge manatees, protecting a small baby from a twelve-foot saltwater crocodile that was also protected, swam into the Cut then hung out between the boats with the baby manatee surrounded by the huge ones. Its small body was covered with green algae growing on its skin. The parent manatee let it grow because it stank, making the baby less desirable to the crocodile. The baby constantly raised its head above the water then moaned and shrieked like a frightened child when it could see the crocodile. The wailing was ear-piercing and wretched, striking us all with its fear.

Snarly said, "Should I shoot at the crocodile and scare it away?"

There was no time for a reply. The squalls whistled through the trees and slammed us with a force that rocked the boats vigorously then shrouded the landscape with violent, swirling torrents of thrashing, stinging rain. I stood on the back deck between the saddle boxes and waited for a water spout to come twirling through the Cut, sucking everything out of it. The leading edge passed over and it didn't happen, which isn't always the case so we were good to go for now.

As the force of the wind settled down to twenty knots the constant bawling of the baby manatee returned, raising its voice to high-pitched screams then lowering it to whimpering snivels. Unable to help it, we suffered remorse as a herd of cockroaches, palmetto bugs and snapping beetles with nuclear green eyes that glowed crawled from the tree limbs onto the tie lines and boarded the boat then scattered about here an' there and under the caprail. More food for the gecko.

I threw my hands up into the air then we entered the galley and closed the door to keep the critters out. We sat at the table and smoked some chocolate to come down from all the buccis then went below to get some sleep.

Ruckus stood his watch with his stainless steel twenty-two magnum auto. A bad ass gun. A standard twenty-two magnum round couldn't kick the breach back, but the magnum auto round blasted a ball of fire out of the breach the size of a honeydew melon with the tone and recoil of a three-fifty-seven magnum. It could easily kill a ballsy crocodile that decided to crawl on land and board the boat.

As the wind eased up the manatees swam into Boca Grand Channel. The croc followed them, staying close to its prey.

CHAPTER 10
Into the Devil's Triangle with Two Shiftless Lubbers And a Frustrated Gecko

I awoke to the rich aroma of fresh brewed bucci that makes me crap. As I sat down at the galley table, Snarly placed a sandwich in front of me made with toasted Cuban bread, bacon, eggs and cheese. The dawn to the east was all the colors of a ripe peach. I fired up a joint, took three long drags then passed it to Snarly who finished it with the help of his brothers as they discussed the meanings of the blood red sun rising. The sow'west wind ceased to a brief lull then slowly shifted out of the west.

Spiker came out of his galley and gave me a befuddled look then shook his head. As I finished eating I looked at the Doppler and saw nothing foreboding. I cranked the engines then gave them a few minutes to warm up. Spiker did the same then untied his lines and backed out of the Cut into

Boca Grand Channel. We headed sow'west across the channel. Ruckus raised the VHF antenna.

Spiker keyed his mic and said, "Where the hell you going, the short route is the north side!"

I said, "You can run the north side and save an hour if you don't crash into one of the wrecks that are scattered everywhere, but it's mostly a nursery for the small critters. The big fish are swimming on the south side. I need to get some of them in the boat before the wind trades to the northwest and blows twenty-five to thirty for a week. I'm going to grouper dig the deep side of the first, second and third set of humps. When I get to the end of the reef on the edge of no-man's-land, I'm going to fish for large yellowtail before I cross Rebecka. You can tag along if you want, but don't count on catching much without chum dough. You should be able to catch plenty of trash fish to grind into shark chum when we cross the stream to your neighborhood next week.

"I know you like to travel with a large school. They are very efficient at removing incriminating evidence and helpful security against an underwater jacktar sent by a commander, but one of these days a commanding jacktar is going to come at you in force. He will be swimming behind a herd of his Slim Jimmys and Johnny Come Latelys with their wetsuits smeared in a thick layer of tar. He will let the sharks maul them until all their jaws are stuck together with cold bloody tar then he will make his move, and most likely you won't be ready for him."

He said, "Thanks for the heartwarming information. I reckon I'll install an underwater camera mounted on a rotating harpoon gun."

I said, "I reckon you're a rectum and good luck with that. Personally, I never felt comfortable working the back deck on a rough day surrounded by a school of hungry sharks. All it takes is one slip on some unwashed fish slime then it's over the caprail, into the water and out their assholes!"

He said, "Life can be a bitch but only if you are lucky."

I said, "You need to bugger off and go into a monkey-see-monkey-do mode so I can plot a course and get this baby on top. Her engines are hot and she wants to move. Just keep your course to the sow'west until you run off the reef. You will see us to the west."

I increased her speed to twenty knots. Her bows rose out of the water. I pushed the throttles forward until she was cruising at thirty knots. Her stern rose to the surface. She leveled off then planed out, skipping over the surface at forty knots, ejecting twin fifty-foot rooster tails of water from under her stern. She bore the weight of tons of ice and fuel without coming apart.

I pulled back the throttles when we reached the south side of the first set of humps. The Gulf Stream was south of the reef. It's ripping current to the east created a slower current to the west on the reef. I slowly cruised to the west at idle speed on a zigzag course in forty feet of water. A few minutes later I passed over a large school of small yellowtail. I turned around then anchored on the east side of the school.

We fished the bottom with half a herring double-hooked and wrapped in a pancake of chum dough. In fifteen minutes we caught six thirty-inch red groupers and two black groupers in the twenty-pound range as we lost a dozen hooks to sharks and 'cudas. I never use wire while fishing for groupers with a hand line because I don't want to fight the sharks which wastes time and scares the fish away. It's cheaper to let them have the hooks.

There is another series of events that can occur when setting the hook in a large fish after it has taken the bait. If you jerk on the line at the moment you feel the fish you may hook it in the skin of its upper lip which may pull out, or you might just jerk the bait from its lips. I usually wait a few seconds and let the fish pull a few feet of line through my fingers then set the hook, because if it's a five-hundred pound bull shark it will have swallowed the bait biting through the monofilament leader. If you jerk too soon you might hook the shark in the corner of its mouth where it can't bite it away, which will compel it to haul ass down the reef, ripping line off the yo-yo through your fingers. The easiest way to separate yourself from the beast of burden at this point is to grip the line hard by pressing it between your thumbs and index finger stalls. Then wrap one arm around your ass and brace the other one in an upright position with the upper part of the arm and elbow resting against your rib cage as you continue to press down hard with your thumbs on the index finger stalls and pull with everything you've got until the knot breaks or you turn the fish.

In either case you must not allow the line to slip when the fish is pulling hard. If the line slips with such pressure on it, it will cause coils of line to rise into the air from the yo-yo high enough to fall on your shoulders and wrap around your neck. When this occurs you must press harder with your thumb on the index finger stall of the arm in the upright position while you let go of the line from the arm wrapped around your ass and quickly remove the coils of line from around your neck. If you fail to do so and the line continues to slip through your fingers the coils will tighten around your neck. You will feel a terrible burning sensation just before you are decapitated.

I've seen it happen twice to young men I hired on as mates to learn the ropes. Only the quick slash of a knife blade from me saved them from certain death, but it didn't spare them the suffering of the deep bloody line cuts displayed on the circumference of their necks.

We made another attempt to catch grouper. Small yellowtails picked at our baits until it was gone. I pulled the anchor and moved to the west, found another school of small fish and repeated the routine until we reached the west end of the third set of humps. The grouper chill barrel was filled to the six-hundred-pound mark. Snarly covered the fish with ice then put the LED on the barrel. He removed the LED and de-hooker from the snapper barrel then put the splash boards in. Without the splash boards the fish would de-scale and turn white in rough weather. He removed the LED from the stern packing box and began chopping ice to put in the snapper barrel. I told him to wait and put the ice in when we are west of the tail end buoy and fishing the edge of no-man's-land.

We took a break, smoked some joints and ate fish sandwiches. Ruckus made a large pot of bucci. We took our buccis aft and sat on the caprail then looked to the northeast for Spiker. We couldn't see him, perhaps he was somewhere fishing. I looked to the southeast and saw him off the deep edge in a hundred fathoms. He was underway in our direction. We sipped our buccis and munched on delicate multilayered guava pastries made by a Cuban baker that complimented the buccis.

Spiker slowly pulled up to within ten feet of my stern and shifted into reverse, stopping the boat. He shifted to neutral then came forward to his bow and stood behind his sampson post with his hands on his hips.

Moments passed then he said, "Well, can you throw me a line?"

Snarly growled then said, "No!"

Spiker asked, "Why not?"

Snarly said, "The white man's law declares that if I heave you a line then I must be responsible for you, your crew and your Jonah ways. That whimsical road whore crap ain't happening. The law also states that if you heave me a line, I don't have to put up with you more than I want to which isn't very long. Wake up your motley crew to heave a line or throw it yourself."

Spiker reached into the rope locker bolted to his forward deck and pulled out a tie line with a loop spliced on the end. He tossed it to Snarly who put the loop over the stern's port sampson post.

I asked Spiker if he caught any fish in the deep.

He said, "Not much, about twenty small snowy groupers. The whole mess don't weigh more 'n a hundred pounds."

I said, "We're going to no-man's-land to fish the edge. You might catch some red grouper on your bandits there. If they won't bite your heavy tackle they will bite a lighter hand line."

He said, "I don't have one. I like fishing the deep. I never know what I'm going to hook."

Snarly said, "I heard it through the seaweed that you lose a lot of tackle, catch a lot of hell and have a lot of accidents caused by mystery fish just for that reason. Man up to a hand line."

He asked if he could borrow one of mine. I said, "No, I'm not giving you fifty dollars worth of hundred-pound perlon to fuck up. Have you got any hundred-pound mono'?"

He said, "Yes, I have a spool."

I said, "I'll give you a yo-yo and some innertube for your index fingers but you must sand the mono' with two-hundred grit wet and dry sandpaper four times."

He said, "Why in the hell should I do that?"

I said, "Mono' is slippery as an eel. When you try to set the hook the line will slip through your stalls and won't drive the point past the barb. All the fish has to do is open his mouth, shake his head then spit the hook out."

He said, "I fished with a hand line some in my youth, I didn't sand it and it worked just fine."

I said, "Have it your way. I was going to mention a few

more helpful tips but you're not listening because you don't give a shit, therefore neither do I."

Snarly, knowing that fishing for groupers with an unsanded hundred-pound test mono' line could be an extremely dangerous and dismembering experience, was eager to encourage Spiker to do so. He went to the tackle chest of drawers bolted to the port galley bulkhead and took out an empty yo-yo, swivels and egg sinkers, gave them to Spiker and said, "Use three feet of unsanded leader in front of the egg sinker with as much bait as you can get on a seven 'O' hook, hold hard and pull fast. I'll be watching to give pointers."

Spiker said, "You didn't give me any innertube for my fingers."

Snarly said, "Use some duct tape, we're low on bike tube. Put plenty of line on the yo-yo. If you hook something big that wants to haul ass, you will need some back-up line to turn it."

I cranked the engines. Spiker boarded his boat. Snarly cast off his line. I put the anchor in the boat and headed west to the edge of no-man's-land. As we passed the tail end buoy, Spiker called and asked if I knew who it was that was anchored out in the mud sow'west of us. "There's no hard bottom on the chart out there!"

I said, "That's the Admiral's replacement along with The Bone Crusher trying to catch Squirrely."

He said, "Who's Squirrely?"

I said, "He's a very large black grouper that doesn't act normal. When they are pulling large yellowtail he rushes up from the bottom and grabs them. If you toss a yellowtail in the water with a heavy line and large hook, he looks it over and won't eat it. He has been hooked many times with tackle he could break and learned from the battles. He's the only black grouper I've seen that uses his eyes and brain before his nostrils and lips, so he's probably female. Thus goes evolution. If she keeps using her brain in such a manner she might grow to the size of a whale and become a legendary mystery fish, hooked many times but never seen."

Spiker said, "Why does he call his mate, "The Bone Crusher"?

I said, "Between trips he meets a new girl and doesn't want to go fishing until the money is gone, but he wants to keep his job so he does something to lay himself up for a few weeks. The last time I saw him he was wearing a cast on his arm from water skiing on the beach instead of the water."

Spiker said, "I'm going to motor over there and write down the numbers he's anchored on."

I said, "The one thing I can't stand the most is some sorry dumb ass who can't find his own school of fish to work, and may Squirrely pull you under when she grows up. Stay away from the Admiral. He won't put up with that crap without making you suffer for it. He's been tied to his dock for the last three months repairing his boat. He went fishing by himself his last trip out because The Bone Crusher was laid up disabled but able to hump. He was anchored south of the fort, below in his galley hold, icing down a chill barrel of groupers.

"A sixty-foot blow boat left the fort on a course due south. The captain engaged his auto-pilot then went below to hump his wife. His boat was doing twenty knots when it slammed into the Admiral's starboard side amidships. The impact destroyed her gunnels, gunwale, caprail, galley roof and bulkheads then relocated her poop deck and all the fish in her ice hold. The Admiral was tossed about but not seriously hurt, tho' his boat was busted all to hell.

"I'm almost to the end of the reef, I need to get off this radio and find some fish on the south side. I'll see you later when you catch up."

The fish finder showed a large school of large yellowtail

in one-hundred-and- ten feet. They were swimming against the ebbing tide flowing to the southeast forty feet off the bottom, which told me there were a lot of groupers under them. We anchored uptide of the fish and began dropping small but numerous chunks of chum dough in the water. Small groups of fish slowly rose from the main school to eat the chum dough.

We baited our hooks with cut herring wrapped in chum dough. We counted out twenty hands of line, then quickly rinsed our hands. When the lines came tight we jerked the herring out of the chum dough creating a cloud of chum, then slowly paid out hands of line allowing the bait to move with the tide and chum until a fish ate it. We filled the snapper barrel to the five-hundred-pound mark after three hours of fishing. I asked Snarly to put a cap of ice on the fish.

We took a break and sipped buccis while Ruckus cooked fish and chips. Spiker was fishing in ninety feet, north of us. He worked his bandits and caught numerous small groupers that didn't make the eighteen-inch limit. The big grouper refused to bite the heavy tackle but some mutton snappers were hungry. He boated seven then a five-hundred-pound bull shark ate the next one, hooking itself on the bandit. Spiker quickly locked down the drag and the shark broke the hundred-and-fifty-pound leader. A few minutes later the shark came back and ate the bait on his other bandit, cutting away the hook. Bottom fishing was over. The bull shark wouldn't leave because it had the scent of the bleeding packing boxes that dripped blood and slime from the drain holes onto the deck then out the scuppers.

Spiker, having acquired the bulk of his education from a number of prisons around the entire Caribbean, was unaware of this fact. Refusing to give up, he put some duct tape on his index fingers then reached into a five-gallon bucket and lifted out the hook and lead attached to the hand line on the yo-yo. He baited the hook then heaved it and the lead into the water.

He stared at the bucket as the lead pulled line from the yo-yo. When it reached the bottom he stood up, took the line in both hands then pushed the bucket behind him with his foot.

We fired up a joint and watched. No fish took the bait. The groupers were hiding under the coral heads and the snappers moved off into the deep away from the massive pregnant bull shark.

As Spiker sat on his caprail next to his four-hundred-gallon shark chum tank that was bolted to the deck in the center of his transom, we made bets as to whether he would be hasty and lip hook the shark or give it a few feet of line to swallow the bait and bite the hook off the leader.

We didn't have to wait long. The shark picked up the herring with its teeth. Spiker was premature with his hook setting jerk and hooked the shark in its lip before it could inhale the herring. It hauled ass off into the deep, ripping the slippery unsanded line through his finger stalls. The short backing of line that Spiker put on the yo-yo came to its end. The yo-yo shot out of the bucket and whacked Spiker on the back of his left elbow rendering his left arm useless, then shot through both his hands and into the water.

Spiker rested his left elbow in the palm of his right hand, bent over at the waist and sat on his caprail cursing between moans. As he rocked backwards and forwards with the pain, he noticed that his palm was filling with blood. He looked at the back of his elbow to see a large gash shaped like a new moon. He grabbed a stinking fish rag, tore it into strips and wrapped it around the wound. Hubbub asked if he needed any stitches. His reply wasn't fit to be repeated.

He stood up and paced the deck moving his wounded arm up and down. As he did so he noticed the yo-yo on top of the calm surface fifty feet from his stern moving towards him. It stopped about twenty feet from the stern then dipped, jerked and bobbed about on the surface.

The shark was back and it was wrapping the line around

the coral heads to bend the hook.

Snarly said, "Hook it with a gaff."

He said, "I don't want it."

We passed around another joint and praised Spiker for manning up to a hand line. Spiker entered his galley where The Dirt was gagging between snores. Fairel was just waking up to a bad case of the D. Tees. He came up into the galley as Spiker was cracking the seal on a bottle of Crown Royal. He hung his arm over the sink and poured half a pint of booze on the bandage.

Fairel squeaked and whined, "You only needed a small amount, I could'a drank most of that."

Spiker took a long pull on the bottle then handed it to the whiner to shut him up. He returned to his stern and sat on his transom. As he stared at the yo-yo his boat began to move away from it. The light breeze from the west ceased to a brief lull while he was fighting the shark. It now began trading back to the sow'west and increasing to ten knots. Our boats started to swing 90 to 180 degrees as the wind pushed us one way until the current became the master and pulled us the other way against the wind.

As our boats passed each other on the swing, I told Spiker that I was headed for Dry Tortugas. "I'll see you after you play catch-up. I'm putting her in the corner."

I cranked the engines, gave them a few minutes to warm up, fired up a joint, passed it around then did a 180 on the braced grapnel and pulled it into the resting ring. Snarly pulled it into the boat. I put her on a course to the northwest for the eastern entrance to Garden Key. The wind was at 15 knots and gusting to 20. I slowly pushed the throttles forward until she rose from the water and skipped along.

We finished the joint and sipped buccis as we pounded through the three- to five-foot chop.

CHAPTER 11
Fort Jefferson

I slowly pulled back on the throttles when we were east of Bird Key. I made a port turn to the west and entered the deep channel between Iowa Rock and Texas Rock at idle speed. We continued to the end of the short but bountiful reefs then I made another port turn to the south into the mooring basin, past the rubble pile and the seaplanes landing, then eased her starboard side up against the pilings of the visitors dock. I told Snarly to tie her up with a short line amidships.

The fort was locked up. All the rangers except one were behind the walls moving everything that wasn't bolted down to the second floor in case of flooding from the approaching storm. The "Hangman," senior park ranger and captain of the supply ship, was standing dock watch. He has been served a daily ration of hell for decades in one form or another from every direction while dealing with a fleet of commercial or recreational boats and their captains. He knew what he was about. He knew all of the fishermen and their ways as well as what was coming. If he wasn't there the beach would be littered with whiskey stills and white men cooking up their white lightning that turned good fishermen into Stone Age pirates and compels young braves to hone their tomahawks and go on the warpath. Many of the existing survivors from these two historic and often brutal cultures still retain some of the traits of their ancestors that prevent them from completely understanding the youth of America and their evolution that has hurled us into the Stoned Age without a bloody revolution.

The Hangman boarded our boat, nodded to the Rug Rats, gave me a stern look then said, "You don't fish weather like this, so what's the word on the river, has the Feral Crab crawled out of the Potomac?"

I said, "Aye, it is so. The Cobra is using some free bait with an irresistible stink that is drawing them out of all of the rivers everywhere. Pirates and smugglers are turning mercenary for the bucks, free grub and the not-so-moldy ammo."

He asked, "Where's Spiker?"

I said, "He's just over the horizon to the southeast wallowing in the trough, dipping his cap rails, shipping water and wearing out his pumps. He's two hours away and crippled. He's no longer a well armed loose cannon. All the contractors have been disarmed and taking orders from the DEA. The only thing he has to pop a cap with is his father's worn out breach. The DEA figures since his father took a hill with it in World War Two, he can do the same."

I informed him of Spiker's cargo and explained its purpose then filled him in on the condition of his crew and his endeavor to recruit Jolly Roger. "The current mode on the river is shifting from attack to tact which he doesn't have so he needs all the help he can buy."

The Hangman said, "He sure picked a hell of a time to play his tricks, but I'll do what I can."

I said, "Now that the DEA has broken off some of the major spikes from his carapace and made him nursemaid to a kingpin, he's doing stupid crap like hiring the first scavenger that comes along and believing everything he says. He's grabbing at straws. He's in this too deep without his mini-guns and I don't think we can save him."

The Hangman smiled then said, "Most likely the weather will save you the trouble. He only shows up when it's at its worst. Why's that?"

I said, "He won't do anything when it's nice out here, too many eyes looking for his round bottomed scow. I would like to put my bows on the beach at the northeast corner next to the rubble pile and bury my storm anchor in the sand. This wind could trade around any minute and honk eighty knots. I need to talk with Captain Lead. He can tell me when watching the birds. Jolly Roger needs to be warned. I would like both of them to flank me."

He nodded his head and said, "That will be alright, just don't block the seaplane landing."

I said, "After we're prepared for the blow, the clones will be frying up mutton snapper sandwiches. If you are motoring around the basin later with your flashers on writing tickets, stop by the stern if you're hungry and write me one. We need to look as guilty as we can to fit in with the crowd you've got in the basin now that thinks they are going to ride this one out without a hitch. It's going to take at least five hitches backed up with four half-hitches, to keep the line from pulling down so tight you can't untie it."

I cranked the engines. Snarly untied the short line then walked to the stern and pushed it away from the pilings. I backed her away from the dock, made a 180 degree turn, motored north then ran her hard chimed bows up on the beach just south of the rubble pile. Her stern was supported by eight feet of water.

Snarly went ashore with a shovel and the storm anchor. He dug his hole a hundred feet from her bows, dropped the anchor then jammed the flukes into the packed sand with his bare feet and dug a narrow trench for the chain to lay in for a direct pull on the shaft that would not slip in a hard blow. He filled the hole and packed the sand down with his feet. He walked down her port side and climbed aboard amidships between the galley bulkhead and the saddle packing box. He walked through the galley forward and out the port galley door, climbed onto her bows, took the anchor line in both hands, heaved it tight then wrapped five hitches around the sampson post and four half-hitches around the post cleat pins. He entered the galley.

Ruckus was removing a bubbling pot of bucci from the stove. He poured some into small cups. Snarly picked one up, blew on it then chugged it down. He walked to the stern where Hubbub was gutting fish. He pulled a fifteen-pound mutton snapper out of the pile by the tail and removed the light pink flesh from the head and backbone. While he was preparing fish with spicy breading for the frying pan, Ruckus carried a cup of bucci to Hubbub then helped him wash and pack the fish. When they finished we sat at the galley table to eat. When we finished eating we piled the paper plates and cups in the center of the paper table cloth. Snarly stood up, folded the four corners of the table cloth over the pile, mashed it flat then rolled it up into a small tightly packed cylinder and put it in the garbage can in the utensil closet.

As he sat down, he said, "That's cheaper than paying a dishwasher and you don't have to listen to their gabbing or the noise from the infernal machine."

They stared at me with anticipation, hoping that I would fire up a joint without a long brow-beating about the damage they were doing to my stash.

I looked away to the south. They did the same. The Hangman was standing on the high mound that was braced with massive concrete bunkers. They once supported the steel frame of the coaling piers. All that's left is a twisted mass of rusty mangled and jagged girders jutting up from the bottom that are the devil's teeth in a nor'easter if you don't play out enough scope. There's no hope without plenty of scope. Most learn it the hard way. Some never do.

The Hangman was gazing through his binoculars, scanning the fishing boats anchored on the east side of the barrier reef that surrounds the basin, which can also be the devil's teeth upon the arrival of the approaching sow'wester.

I removed a bag of joints from my pocket and laid four on the table. As I was putting the bag back in my pocket, Snarly reached for one. I quickly covered them with my hand and said, "Take a look around the basin. How many boats have their curtains closed?"

Snarly said "Looks like about half of them."

I said, "Some of them are blowing weed and passing the joint. Some are chopping coke on their galley table, others may be passing a crack or heroin pipe. In any case the type of drug they are using will determine the extent of the damage they will receive when Mariah renders the devil's due. If they are laid up on their bunks in a crack coma or an opium dream they may well meet their end. Same goes for a bunch of passed out drunks. If they are just smoking weed they might forget a trifle that can be quickly corrected in a hard blow. I don't want to close my curtains. I need to see what's coming at me besides Spiker. There will be no blatant passing of a joint. The Hangman is watching us too, and we don't need to piss him off. We will smoke our own joint and hold it like a cigarette. The wind is blowing to carry the smoke northeast."

We carried our buccis to the stern then sat on the cap rail at our fishing spots. There was a fifty-foot and beamy snapper and grouper boat moored in the center of the basin. She was named, "Squaw Trap." Young Captain Black Heart, the fish killer for the tribe, was standing on her bows eyeing his mooring gear, looking for the slightest slip as the wind increased. He had his heavy mud anchors pulled in tight fore and aft of the hurricane chain that he was floating over in case things become cyclonic.

He was sporting a broad bladed tomahawk with a throwing handle tucked under the rawhide belt that held up his short buckskins. He was naked to the waist with his face, arms and chest proudly displaying his mass of learning scars that compel young squaws to look upon him with awe as they squabble and coo like so many pigeons to be plucked. Just for that reason he had been escorted by the young warrior council to stand before the ancient chiefs too many times to speak his plea that might justify his actions as he continues to offer all the young squaws twice the amount of their allotted share of fish if they would remove their buckskins so he could teach them the art of sex.

When it became apparent that his forked tongued shenanigans were creating the plague of obesity among the squaws in more ways than one, he was escorted by the ancient chiefs and the warrior council to sit with the medicine men that would determine his fate. Much wood was heaved on the council fire and much gunpowder thrown upon it to ward off his devil as they made sacrifices of fish to the flying raptors, their gods on high. It was all for nothing as the raptors soared away and Black Heart winked at the squaws. The ancient chiefs shook their heads in dismay as the young warriors and medicine men stood up then began stomping their feet while hacking at the air with their tomahawks because the raptors refused the fish and left his fate to them.

Many yelled, "Hang him like the white men!" Some ranted and raved about castration while others spoke of banishment to his boat and the sea. After much argument among themselves, the medicine men determined that his heart was made from a chunk of ancient coal, shining like a black diamond that couldn't be scorched by heat nor faded by light and would only pump black blood like his brother the squid. They were resolute with their conviction as they proclaimed that there was no cure for the forked tongued devil without the medicine of his father, the ancient warrior who was once the fish killer for the tribe but had been renamed "Heavy Metals."

For the crime of wanton, cunning deception, Black Heart was banished to the sea until impotent and must continue to live his oath as a warrior and fish for the tribe.

The fish killer gave no argument against his fate. He stood, faced the medicine men and said, "I give praise to your mercy for I love the sea. I will anchor out in the shallows to rest or sleep. When it's time to fish I will bring my boat to the dock to be stocked. I must continue to take a crew of two drunk and crazy white men that will learn nothing of my ways but can clean and pack fish when I sober them up. I will pay for their firewater so they can get drunk again and learn nothing more as they provide amusement for me while I'm at my labor.

"There are ten thousand islands in the Bay of Florida. If I need to stretch my sea legs I will walk and hunt on them, and may all who visit fear the name 'Black Heart' that they have given me. Many of you wanted to send me on my way wrapped and rolled in too much tar and too many feathers when all I wished to do was provide for you and the raptors and to love the squaws that will strengthen the tribe with many new brave warriors. There will be no time to forget until Heavy Metals has made his medicine."

He turned and walked the path that was lined with two rows of those who would bear witness to the sea. He was touched by many squaws until he reached the land's end. He turned and faced the agile and tenacious squaw that has been renamed "Zip-Gun" by her learning followers. She is the one who tinkers with the white man's trash as she makes hunting fire sticks from little pipes, springs, inntertubes and small rimfire cartridges. She kills her own meat so she can refuse offerings from all the other warriors. Only Black

Heart can hold her ravishing beauty.

He put his lips to her ear and whispered, "You must trade some fire sticks for a canoe. At the mating call of the lizard, I will be the star that flickers on the horizon."

With that he boarded his boat, cranked his engine, threw off the tie lines, left his hunting ground and anchored in the shallows as he is now. Satisfied that his anchors would hold, he turned and looked through his shatter-proof windows at his mutinous crew, the only kind he would feed. Two drunk land sharks, stumbling about, boasting of their wicked deeds done on the hill as they passed the firewater. Soon they would be too drunk to talk and could only crawl to the place they find sleep.

He looked into the water of the basin. A six-hundred pound goliath grouper and her five-hundred pound mate were staring up at him, hoping he would hook a fish so they could steal it, a game they play everywhere in the south Atlantic and Gulf. Certain that his crew wouldn't do any damage until he woke them to gut fish and suffer ridicule with their after-pain, he dove into the water between the groupers that turned and followed him to take any fish he might spear. With the not-so-tame groupers at his heels, he climbed on to my stern.

In all the years I fished before they became protected decades ago, such an event never occurred. Now the big groupers are everywhere. All the submerged ships, reefs, deep holes, gullies, channels, seawalls and drain pipes under the highways are occupied by goliath groupers. They have become a plague to the small group of fishermen that are allowed to fish for snapper and grouper as well as the fishery itself. The same thing is happening with the sharks, saltwater crocodiles and the massive schools of great barracuda that dog the huge schools of yellowtail and mangrove snappers in the Gulf. You can give the fishery over to the predators, but in the future that may be all that you have. The fishermen can only wait and see as the goliath groupers continue to eat a large amount of snapper and smaller mixed grouper hooked, but not boated for your table. This is prevalent among all seafood palatable in the Gulf, the barrier reefs and outer-bars of the Florida Keys because goliath groupers eat everything that swims, hops or crawls.

Regardless of what the environmentalists tell you, I've seen it myself and I'll argue the point until I'm dead! It's time to bureaucratically legalize a one-fish bag limit in a slot somewhere between the breeders and the pups so a poor man can feed his children without going broke at the supermarket and losing his pride at the foodbank. In the decades of its protection the goliath grouper has increased its range to the South Pacific. What is the significance of that? Once more only time will tell if it's going to be an instant replay. In any case people are eating them in places where they're not protected. Why are we breeding goliath groupers for the rest of the world while we can only salivate? You can only expend an unselfish crusade so far, and force fishermen to eat second-best forever.

As Black Heart and the Rug Rats stared at the prodigious groupers that they wanted to kill and eat with gluttony and garlic potatoes, a sport fishing boat that had been trolling the miles of reefs to the north and west of the fort came into the basin and anchored across from us inside the west end of Bird Key. There was a small school of very large tarpon that weighed between one-hundred-and-fifty to over two hundred pounds swimming in a circle between us at the entrance to the channel. It is their ambush point to catch fish or crabs that enter the basin as they keep an eye on the big groupers that eat them. The sport fishermen were allowed to play hook and release in the basin. Commercial fishermen couldn't fish anywhere in the park. They could only use it to anchor in the lee that blocks or reduces the rough waves in foul weather. The park offers 360 degrees of lee shore for a fisherman to choose from depending on the direction of the wind.

One of the sport fishermen baited a medium stand up rod and reel with a live blue runner then cast it into the school of tarpon. A one-hundred-and-fifty pound fish ate the bait. The fisherman set the hook and the tarpon streaked away stripping line off the reel, then jumped out of the water. The goliath groupers felt and heard the tarpon splash back into the water. They turned and charged after the tarpon, but it was already being pursued by a bigger grouper that was measured at nine feet and eight inches with a guesstimated weight of eight hundred pounds or more. The tarpon swam hard and fast toward the coaling pier to cut the line on the jagged girders. It saw the grouper coming then turned on a course of least resistance from the line toward the fisherman then leaped out of the water and threw itself into a flip as the grouper lunged for it. When it fell back into the water the grouper lunged for it again, forcing the tarpon into a series of leaps and flips that continued all the way back to the fisherman where it made its last leap out of the water then fell back and laid on its side, totally spent, between our boats in the center of the channel.

The massive grouper clamped its powerful jaws to the middle of the tarpon's body. It squeezed and rolled the tarpon in its jaws. A cascade of silver scales fell away as they were removed by the long spiked teeth hidden in the thick rubbery gums of the grouper. As it continued to squeeze and roll the fish in its jaws, all the flesh in the middle was forced into the other parts of the body. The gullet and stomach ballooned out of the fish's mouth along with the contents. Blood and guts erupted from the rectum until there was just a cylinder of skin containing the spine left in the middle. The grouper released the skin and spine then took the head and forward part of the tarpon's body into its mouth and gullet. With a few quick, vicious shakes of its head it snapped the spine and tore the skin then it swallowed the seventy-five pound chunk of meat and bone with one gulp. The other groupers charged the other half of the tarpon and head-butted each other for it with the six-hundred pounder winning the battle.

The fisherman's line was in the grouper's mouth. He pulled and tugged with the rod and reel but was unable to move the fish as it settled on the bottom and shook its head, chafing through the line.

Black Heart said, "The fishermen who caught the big one and measured it discovered a large piece of rusty metal stuck in its gullet. They pulled it on board through their marlin chute and removed the metal. As they were pushing it back into the water the grouper paid them for their kindness by hooking its tail under the bottom of the marlin chute door. Then with a Herculean heave of its body and a flip of its tail with a force that ripped the marlin chute door from its hinges and hurled it thirty feet into the air and fifty feet from the boat."

Snarly asked Black Heart if he felt any fear that the groupers might do the same to him that they do to the tarpon while he swims about the basin.

Black Heart said, "They are just dumb beasts meant for the slaughter, to be deep fried on a campfire in a teepee. I suffer no fear from them nor do they fear me, but they do not trust me."

"Why have they lost their trust in you?" Snarly asked.

Black Heart said, "They no longer care for the scent and the flavor of their own blood. To understand that you must take a long, hard look at the large, white scars on their lips. Then you will see that they have tasted the edge of my tomahawk many times for trying to bully me and take away my favorite food after I did the work of hacking some big stone crabs out of their holes and snapping off their claws."

He looked at me and said, "While you are not working, may I lay down in your sacred fishing spot and get some sleep?"

I said, "Be my guest, the foot mat is soft and padded, but first tell me what you have caught."

He said, "Yesterday was my first day out from the packing house. I made the long run to Real Milk Reef on the north side. I could see Captain Lead and Jolly Roger to the west. I spent the afternoon pulling eight-hundred pounds of large yellowtail. The fish turned small after sunset which is often the case, so I fished the bottom until sunrise and filled the other chill barrel with mixed groupers, mutton snappers and large white bone porgies.

"Tomorrow if this wind shifts to the northwest, I'll grouper dig the humps on the south side. If it doesn't trade around, I'll stay here until it does. Tonight I must wake my crew to gut and pack fish."

With nothing else to say he sat on the foot mat, curled his body into a fetal position and fell asleep in a few seconds. His lungs continued to oxidate his carbonatious atoms producing carbon dioxide with a force to be held in infamy. As he inhaled the suction was similar to a hippopotamus with a deviated septum. The exhale roared out like an old chain saw misfiring and hard to start.

We went into the galley and closed the door.

CHAPTER 12
A Pow-Wow

We could still hear Black Heart through the plexiglass doors as he continued to wake the dead in his raucous sleep. Between exhales he uttered one or two words while he dreamed, explaining how he was stomping through his hunting grounds scaring away all but the most fierce and vicious of the wild beasts as he growled with the cougars that would not flee.

I gave the Rug Rats a once-over as I located the proper scar in its proper place then focused on Hubbub. I said, "Fishing fun is over. You will always stand the first watch until the lizard is dead. Take the binoculars and the rat gun to the flying bridge. Identify and report all boats entering the basin while you keep an eye out for the bug eater."

Hubbub walked to the console, removed the binoculars and the rat gun, and then headed towards the starboard galley door. On his way there he cocked the rat gun, opened the door and stuck the gun under the cap rail, fired two shots and then opened the storage closet to see if he had killed the lizard if it was there to ambush a cockroach. There was no dead lizard among the utensils. He opened all the doors under the galley sink and counter top. No lizard. He went below into the bunk room then opened the storage closet. No lizard. He came up from below, walked out the galley door then climbed the ladder to the flying bridge and began scanning the horizon from the northwest to the southeast.

After a minute of observation, he yelled louder than Black Heart's snoring that Spiker was thirty minutes out. "There's two boats anchored at the K buoy. That's Lead and Jolly. There's a boat headed for them coming from the west. Looks like the Admiral going to the hill. There's a fleet of shrimp boats coming in from the north anchoring in the lee of Pulaski Reef and East Key. There's some other snapper boats to the north and east in Rebecka Channel. They are too far away to identify, but they are showing their bows, headed for the lee."

I raised the tone of my voice above Black Heart's snoring and said, "We can see all that from here. Now that you know where everyone is, keep your eyes on the water east and west of Spiker and tell me if you can see any fast boats coming to run a blockcade."

Hubbub yelled, "Negative!"

I zeroed in on Ruckus and said, "Go below and bring up eight quarts of blush. Put them in a cooler full of ice."

I concentrated on Snarly, knowing that he wasn't going to like what I was about to ask. I said, "Spiker can't put his round bottom on the beach without a 90 degree tilt. The only place left for him to anchor is the southeast part of the basin. It won't be rough behind the barrier, but the wind is going to whistle and put him in a swing. He will be coming over after he's hooked up, and he's going to bring The Dirt. He may need a hand getting The Dirt out of his skiff if he can get him in it."

Such a request caused Snarly to wrench his face into a very shitty attitude as he said, "I'll get right on it as soon as crap has been blown uphill and doesn't stink anymore, but that's not going to happen until some sinister war minister and his assistant murderer turn the keys on nuclear fission, so you may have to wait awhile."

I said, "Well, at least pull the boarding steps out of the storage closet and put them on the back deck by the door."

As Spiker came into the basin and passed my stern, I noticed that he had changed his rock anchor to a plow. I went to the radio and called him on Channel 18. I said, "If you put that plow down in the basin while the wind is increasing, the mud bottom will suck it down so far you will never get it back. It will also eat your fifteen feet of three-eights chain."

He said, "I've been pulling that anchor for thirty years and I've never set it without a trip."

"Well," I said, "It's smart to always use a trip. But, in this case it won't help you. There's an unknown number of plow anchors at the bottom of that fifteen feet of mud, along with their chains rusting away on top of the caprock that supports the mud. One of them is mine. It had a trip, too. Even if you can break the trip it won't budge. You can pull on it until you rip your sampson post out and destroy your anchor chute. But, you will unmoor with a knife."

Hubbub hailed us from the flying bridge saying that the Admiral stopped to talk with Lead and Jolly, then headed on to the east. "Lead and Jolly have pulled their anchors and headed this way. Spiker called and asked if he could bring The Dirt over."

I said, "Sure, just keep a leash on him."

Hubbub uttered some profanity that we couldn't quite make out over Black Heart's snoring. Ruckus gave me a sulky look. Snarly growled and cursed.

I said, "Whiners."

Upon their arrival, The Dirt managed to climb aboard himself. He went forward and sat on the boarding steps by the door. He twisted his face into a scowl as he stared at Black Heart snoring. Spiker did the same as he said, "Have you talked to Jolly, yet?"

I said, "No, I don't intend to. He knows what he's about

and he's on his way here."

The wind gusted to gale force. The late afternoon sky turned cobalt blue while the sun's surface deepened to fire engine red as the leading edge of the next black squall advanced to the horizon from the sow'west.

Spiker began to fidget and glare with impatience, then said, "Can I call Jolly?"

I said, "It's a waste of time. He won't answer, and what you have to say shouldn't be heard on a channel everyone is listening to. I'll call Lead. Do you know Lead?"

"Aye," Spiker said, "I've fished with that crazy half-breed and we've shared a few bottles in between trips. You don't want to rile him when he's guzzling his Jack and ginger. He'll have your hair flying in the wind from his flag pole. He's a pretty good fisherman tho'."

I said, "He's a lot better than good. I've got all I can do to keep up with him, and you are a jealous bastard."

I went to the console, changed the channel to 79, then keyed the mic and said, "Sea Bones calling Captain Lead."

He keyed his mic and said, "What has a half-feathered half-breed like me done to rate a call from the chief of a thousand scares, but only four hundred stitches?"

I said, "I'm gathering a pow-wow on the beach north of the seaplane landing. There's room for you and Jolly to flank me and step aboard."

After grounding their boats and burying their anchors, they boarded the Scally-Wags!

Spiker briefed Jolly on what was going down, then made him the offer of second captain plus one third of the leftover proceeds from the donated funds to complete the stings, which Jolly was crazy enough to accept.

As we sat around the galley table, I asked Lead what he thought about the weather.

He said, "When the sun shines red and the blue of the sky darkens, I think of the first day I saw such an event. It was in 1963 during the Cuban crisis when there was four or five hippies sleeping in every doorway on Duval Street because the city and county jails were full with the meanest of the bunch!

"The wind got hung up out of the sow'west for seven days. The first three days were fishable, but the wind increased each day after that and shifted to the west as it always does before it shifts to the northwest and honks. Well, it never shifted out of the northwest, but kept shifting back to the sow'west and honking harder. When it shifted out of the northwest on the seventh day, the reek of Mariah honked eighty-five knots for thirty minutes and tore the hell out of everything that wasn't nailed down. We may suffer such a blow any day now. This sow-wester will be just like all the others I've seen the last fifty years, short in duration, but brutal. Over the years I've noticed that they occur about every three years as if the extra day in the leap year might play a part."

I said, "I've paid attention to something similar, but there's no similarity in the timing if you relate the extra day to the year the sow'wester occurred. It may happen on the fourth or fifth year after the last one, but an extra day is a minor anomaly that could create another minor, unstable and erratic anomaly. But, I'm no meteorologist. What do the raptors say?"

He said, "One will show me something at sunset, but it will not speak of action, reaction, cause and effect or our uncertain hindsight. The osprey's tongue is not forked to utter deceit, it can only show me when. If it glides out of the trade winds and roosts in its nest on top of the fort's lighthouse, it will foretell another day of squally rains and wind gusts up to fifty knots from the sow'west. But, if it comes to roost and only perches on the rim of its nest then turns its head 360 degrees scanning the horizon, it may fly to the northeast foretelling the sunrise."

"Indeed," I said, "The raptors can't lie. How's the fishing?"

He said, "Rebar has been dragging north of the K buoy. We traded him a case of beer for his thirty baskets of bycatch. There was a lot of big red rock shrimp and mantis shrimp with an abundance of sand perch, maharas and sardines. We culled out the bait fish and shrimp then split the baskets of crabs and crushed them for chum. We went to the "Little Bank" and put down some balls of chum dough with ground rock shrimp in it. The hogfish lined up in a V-formation. I used the rock and mantis shrimp for bait on a fish finder rig and pulled eight-hundred pounds of hogfish before I played out. Jolly caught about the same. We left the "Little Bank" and went to the K buoy when the wind kicked up. The shrimpers have been dumping their bycatch there, and they have gathered up a large school of yellowtail plus a large school of mangrove snappers. The fish are filling an area six city blocks square and sixty- to ninety-feet deep. There's a bunch of black grouper under them, and mutton snappers pick up the bite when the sharks start taking the groupers from me. There's a huge school of great barracudas surrounding the west end of the fish, eating a lot more than we can catch.

"The Admiral stopped by on his way east. He's been doing some research with a bunch of environmentalists on the goliath grouper that have taken over the red snapper fish haven northwest of the park. There are some new kids fishing in the neighborhood. They were following us around, trying to get some numbers to work. The lazy bastards should find their own fish. This blow will teach them a few things if they have enough sense to come in out of it."

The Dirt said, "Why don' jew call dee law on theng?"

Lead smiled at The Dirt then said, "What law? There ain't no law out here. The Coast Guard stops by once in awhile to hold safety inspections, then hauls ass back to the east. The park rangers are restricted to the park boundaries. If there is any law beyond the boundaries it would be Murphy's Law."

The Dirt asked, "Whoose dees Murphy's pigs?"

Lead said, "Murphy's Law isn't governed by pigs or any other animals except yourself and you are judged by your knowledge, your experience, agility, speed, dexterity and your endurance. It helps to be thick-skinned and ambidextrous with big hands and feet. You also need to have a keen sense for timing which will do you absolutely no good unless you can see what's going to happen before it happens and get the hell out of the way. All fine qualities that I dare say you lack my hairy friend, and it seems to me by the way you sag all around that you've got all you can do just to keep your ass above your feet, but it isn't your fault."

Snarly interrupted with a growl as he said, "No! It's anus fault."

In spite of the surrounding chuckles, such a statement went completely over The Dirt's head as he gave Lead a sulky look, then smiled at Snarly and said, "Whoose fault iss sit?"

Snarly said, "Why, it's Spiker's fault."

He pulled his knife from its sheath and offered it to The Dirt as he said, "Take this and stab him four or five times, it will make us both feel better."

The Dirt refused the knife as Snarly continued to say, "He's the one who took you out of your element and put you here like a fish out of water with your guts twisted into knots, seasick beyond hope. He's the one who has to get you where you are going. Don't put all your trust in him. Sometimes he can't see what's going to happen, therefore he has more accidents than a shipload of blind monkeys. It will be Jolly that gets you to your port of call, so do what he says and don't cross him or he will wear your hair on his belt. It's so long he could scalp you every day most anywhere."

Lead fired up a joint then said, "Narly, why are they calling you Spiker?"

Spiker took the joint from his fingers then slowly took his time inhaling a half dozen tokes then letting the smoke out.

Snarly said, "The Hangman is watching, don't be passing joints."

Spiker said, "Up yours. I'm smoking your share for bad mouthing me."

Snarly growled, "Burn yourself out." Then he said, "One night not so long ago Narly came to the house to go fishing with us the next day. After we turned in, six draggers showed up and began racing the one-mile stretch between the government boundary and Crocodile Creek. After about an hour of the racket Narly became fed up and called the police. They told him that they couldn't do anything about it because the perpetrators were dragging on government property, but they would post an officer at the entrance to the county road to speak with them.

"Narly said he would do what he could to hurry them along and slow them down when they reached the county road. He took a ten-gauge, double-barreled shotgun from the rack then a handful of goose shot from the ammunition drawer and put them in his pocket. He went to the back yard where the Dinosaur was standing watch and asked him to bring some three-eights washers and some inch and a half roofing nails from the tool shed. He put those in his other pocket then walked around to the front yard. Five of the draggers pulled over a mile down the road by Crocodile Creek to cool their engines. The other one pulled over about fifty yards beyond the boundary next to the mangrove and Black Buttonwood Jungle.

"They couldn't see Narly from where they were parked.

He crossed the road in front of the house and the boundary then entered the jungle. He came out of the jungle onto the edge of the government road across from them. They saw him load the shotgun. They couldn't believe their eyes and hesitated a few seconds, which gave Narly enough time to close the breach and blast both barrels over the roof of their car. The prodigious boom and the rattling ricochet of the goose load as it shot into the buttonwood trees sent them down the road burning rubber to tell the others what happened. The draggers and their shotgun riders milled around the creek for fifteen minutes, racing their engines and doing wheelies.

"While they were smoking up the creek with burned rubber, Narly put the nails through the washers and stood them on both sides of the road in long, staggering rows in all four worn wheel ruts, then vanished back into the jungle.

"The draggers left the creek three cars per lane with the peddle to the metal and passed the house doing ninety. Two miles later they reached the county road with flat tires. We've been calling him Spiker since then."

I put an end to Snarly's moment on stage by saying, "Listen up. We are going to be stuck here for a few days, and I would like to enjoy myself. There will be no mumbling and grumbling, no moaning and groaning, no bitching and complaining. We are going to have some nautical cheer. Normally I don't mix drinking with fishing, seeing as how it creates a lot of dead dorfs, but we will open some bottles of blush and smoke your own weed. Since you will be drinking my wine, I will require a nautical toast in payment from any man who will pop a cork and pour a round. It need not rhyme, but it would put you in my graces."

I went to the cooler, removed a bottle of blush, carried it to the table and popped the cork. I emptied the contents into the six plastic anti-tilt mugs then placed one in front of each fisherman. Spiker and The Dirt were passing a bottle of Crown Royal.

I sat down, raised my mug then said –

"Here's to the brave and bold crab fishermen of the
Bering Sea —
It's rare to see them hooked up an' laying to on a hard
swing,
Wallowing in the lee –
If those sea wolves live to be old –
For their stories to be told –
Their blubbery buns will show their pedigree."

I drained my mug then slammed it down. They did the
same. I fired up a joint which caused a monkey see, monkey
do chain reaction.

Hubbub came down from the flying bridge, drained his
mug, popped a cork and filled the mugs again. He sat down,
raised his mug then said –

"Here's to the five hundred or so weekend warriors that
every year
get on their dinner boats and go out to sea –
When they should have stayed at home to mow the lawn
and trim the trees –
As they fell into their sorrow most of them died in a
minute –
For a fish for a lass, their true calling just wasn't in it –
They may have found some way to hack it –
If only they had put on their life jacket –
Or saved one hand for the boat and the other for pee –
For many were found floating with their fly open in
their cold, wet serenity – "

We drained our mugs then slammed them down.
Hubbub pinched a smoldering joint from the ash tray then

returned to the flying bridge.

Snarly popped another cork, filled our mugs, raised his and said –

"Here's to the dribble swiggers who sat at my table and claimed to know all there was to know about fishing as they dined on my tasty fair –
But, if they had to get it the way that I did, it would have stood them on their hair –
Aye, they can fork it down like it was an endless treat–
But, most of the shiftless lubbers still can't kill their meat – "

We drained our mugs then slammed them down and sucked on our joints.

Ruckus stood and went to the cooler. He popped a cork, filled our mugs then said –

"Here's to the hearty harpooners of the North Atlantic-
And bedamned to the bureaucrats that let their fishery go the way of the Titanic –
Now when the wind is light out of the east and it's time to tack the sail –
All they can do is watch their harpoons rust, guzzle their booze and raise hell –"

We guzzled our mugs and slammed them down. As we puffed and choked, I raised my empty mug at Spiker. He said, "I don't know any toasts, but I hope we will all meet here again after our run to the south by sow'west."

We all looked at The Dirt sitting outside the door. He threw his arms in the air then shook his head.

We turned our gaze to Lead. He said, "Hell, I'll give it a go." He filled the mugs, took a swig then said –

"Here's to all the ancient pirate captains who didn't like to fish,
but had their decks swarming with a horde of toothless ol' swashbuckling scallywags that all went on down in a
blasting, blazing burn her to the water line hullaballoo!
It's probably a fact that they became shark crap for sure and if that was the case –
then let's not be forgetting that they were stinkyseconds for the sucker fish, too."

We guzzled our mugs and slammed them down, then Snarly said, "Aye, and top that you slimy pond scum!"

Everyone focused on Jolly, his half-breed face burned red with contempt as he stood and pulled a bottle from the cooler. He popped the cork then poured a round. He glared at me then said, "I ain't much on rhymes which will spare me the tedious humiliation of your graces."

He gazed upon each of the others in turn, his contempt becoming grimmer as the adrenalin of a warrior raced through his veins. He said, "My egg was corrupted by the sperm of a white man. Only the blood of my mother kept me from scalping him after I dotted his eyes for making me half of one and the other, never to be whole."

He raised his mug and said –

"So here's to the thousands of white men who are killed every day,
either accidentally or on purpose by the very horrors of their own creation –
Aye, it's sad justice, but I thank the fish hawks for making it so
or I would be surrounded by a bunch of old farts farting and
turning my atmosphere into a stinking gastronomical delight for their anal born pathogens –

That being the main reason for going to sea an' all, seeing as how

I married a gassy frog-eyed princess."

We drained our mugs and slammed them down. The sky turned black as the squall slammed into us. Hubbub came down from the flying bridge. Snarly growled, "Thanks for the warning," as he pulled a tarp from the storage closet then took it to the stern and laid it over Black Heart who was saying between snores, "Lay her hard over to the south and close the windows you bleeding lubber!"

Snarly came back into the galley, grabbed a paper plate from the counter then took all the roaches from the ash tray, removed the weed from the paper, mixed the different herbs and rolled a massive joint. He fired it up. As he sucked and blew, filling the galley with smoke, The Dirt pointed at Black Heart and said, "Cang I wake hing up, he make me crasee?"

Snarly gave him a bone chilling look then said, "Leave him alone, he's been busting his ass non-stop for two days getting his boat ready and catching enough fish to pay his expenses for his long trip while putting up with two drunk gutters. He needs his rest. You shouldn't disturb a fisherman when he's bone tired. For no reason, he might fuck you up."

The Dirt stood on the deck and said, "Eyeing going to wake hing up."

Snarly roared, "Go ahead then and may the blame be on your head and whoever stitches it up!"

The Dirt was in a state of mind similar to John Wesley Hardy when it came to loud snoring. He walked to the stern, stood in front of Black Heart then poked him in the ribs with his right big toe. Black Heart woke up, lifted the edge of the tarp and stared at two very large, filthy, hairy feet and legs. Since he didn't know The Dirt, he assumed that a big gorilla had broken out of his cage on a ship headed to a zoo in the states and climbed aboard then killed everyone except him. He came out from under the tarp in a crouch, wrapped his arms around The Dirt's legs just below his expansive ass, lifted him off his feet then slammed him on the deck. Just before his back hit the deck the back of The Dirt's neck raked across the hex-head bolt that holds the handle to the hand crank shaft on the one-armed bandit which opened up a long, deep gash. Then his head slammed into the cap rail, knocking him out.

Black Heart stared down at him as blood began to pool in the rain water around his head. Then he realized the gorilla had a human face. He bent over, put his massive hands under The Dirt's filthy armpits, lifted him to his feet, then leaned him against the one-armed bandit and the support beam for the roof.

Black Heart grabbed him by the shoulders and shook him vigorously as he said, "What's the emergency, where are the dive bombers and the terrorists with their AK-47s? What kind of forked tongued devil would poke a warrior in his dreaming sleep? Such a thing is unheard of among my people for fear of death." He removed his hands from The Dirt's shoulders. They were bloody. He looked at The Dirt's back. It was covered in blood pouring out of his neck then pouring out the scupper at his feet.

Hubbub came down from the bridge, grabbed the first aid kit and went to the stern with Spiker who cursed Black Heart then asked, "Have you killed him?"

He shrugged his shoulders and said, "No, he's alive. I was going to, but I could see that he's a rare mutation suffering from many unhealthy and painful disorders, so it's best to let him live."

As Hubbub and Spiker helped The Dirt get to the boarding steps to sit down, Black Heart asked Spiker if he had the money he owed him.

Spiker said, "No, I'm still fighting the government for it."

Black Heart looked at The Dirt then asked, "Does he have it?"

Spiker said, "He doesn't work for the government."

Black Heart said, "I see you still speak with a forked tongue." He walked to the stern then jumped in the water and swam to his boat. The goliath groupers followed.

Hubbub held a compress with one hand on The Dirt's wound as he shaved the hair from around it with a Gillette Good News razor. After the blood slowed down to a trickle, he packed the wound with antibiotic cream then stitched it up and washed the blood from The Dirt's back with the deck hose.

The squall roared into the bay, the sunlight returned and the wind eased up to thirty knots. Hubbub returned to the flying bridge. Spiker walked to the stern and sat on the cap rail then motioned for me to join him, where he confessed that he needed someone else to stand a watch for eight hours at the wheel because The Dirt wasn't up to it.

I said, "Good luck with that. Me, the Rug Rats and Jolly don't care about dying. There's a lot of other men out here with that attitude but they are not crazy for your grade of risky adventure."

Spiker whined, "You know most of these men, surely there must be someone."

"Only you," I said. "They will be coming in before sunset. You look them over, the Rug Rats will tell you what you need to know about most of them. Leave me out of it."

Hubbub reported two boats coming in from Rebecka Channel. "It's ol' Dog Balls in the lead, the other boat is Twitchy and Tweaky!"

Spiker grinned then said, "Why is he called Dog Balls?"

Jolly said, "He was born with a large groove on the back of his head. He's mostly bald with a few scraggly hairs. His scalp is always sunburned and peeling, so when he walks away from you, the back of his head looks like a set of mangy Dog Balls. He's also an accident waiting to happen. He spends much of his time over the side and under the stern cutting trap rope from around his shaft and prop. Last week he was taking some bait from his boat to the freezer on the dock when a hot babe in a bikini came wiggling by. Instead of stopping at the freezer, he walked off the end of the dock. The next day she wiggled by again while he was grinding herring for chum dough and he got his thumb caught in the grinder.

"Before they became protected and renamed goliath groupers, he caught a three-hundred pound jewfish sow'west of Loggerhead at the homestead. The weather turned bad the next day, honked out of the northwest thirty knots. He wanted to catch another jewfish. We told him not to go. He went fishing anyway. As he was hauling ass in the lee of Loggerhead at full throttle heading for the sow'west point, he engaged his auto-pilot, walked to the back deck to take a leak over the cap rail, slipped on some jewfish slime he didn't clean up and fell overboard.

"The boat kept its course to the sow'west, cleared the point, shot up the first breaker, crested it, then slammed into the base of the second one at full throttle. The impact shattered the cabin windows. His fish box jumped its stop blocks, crashed through the stern and dumped his fish in the channel. The boat recovered, rode the wall of water to the crest then slid into the trough to port, did a one hundred and eighty degree turn and hauled ass back past him headed northeast where it ran aground on East Key, then sucked his intakes full of sand and turtle grass. The engine over-heated. The exhaust risers became so hot they set the fiberglass exhaust pipes on fire before the engine seized up. A cloud of black smoke rose out of the boat. Carried on the wind into Rebecka Channel, it created a long black band rushing across the horizon. As boats left the park to put out the fire and rescue Dog Balls, the ebbing tide was carrying him southeast into the gulfstream with the northwest wind pushing him faster. Everyone searched for him around East Key then the park without finding him. In spite of the increasing wind gusting to gale force, the boldest of the fishermen put it on their stern and headed southeast. While the tide and wind swept Dog Balls toward the stream, he drifted into some lobster traps. He untied the floats then stuffed them in his pants and shirt. There was some thick green slimy algae growing on the floats. It was the food source and the habitat of some very large and toothy sea lice. They chewed him everywhere.

"After working a grid to the southeast the fishermen found his chill barrel and packing box. They worked another grid to the east in the stream. When they found him the next morning he was swelled up like a sumo wrestler and covered with big red spots."

Spiker said, "Aye, you've got to clean up the slime, it's killed many fools. It got preacher Tom after he accidentally backed his car over his wife and killed her. He couldn't get anyone to go fishing with him for thirty percent of the catch. I went and caught a three hundred and sixty pound grouper and pulled in eighteen hundred pounds of snapper while he untangled his line. He only gave me twenty percent of the fish money and had the nerve to ask me if I wanted to go again. I said, "No," so he walked up the dock past the fish house door and stepped on a gob of slime that came off the big grouper I caught. He fell backwards, busted his head open on the seawall then rolled into the water between the seawall and a boat that was unloading fish. He drowned before they fished him out with a grapnel."

Lead said, "Aye, it's bad stuff. We've all slipped and busted our asses in it when we were lucky and we will be again because we're not Jonahs."

Spiker was eyeballing Twitchy and Twicky through his pocket telescope. He laughed then said, "That woman over there just slapped the hell out of one of those guys. Now she's pounding on the other one. What's that all about?"

Jolly said, "Her name is Perturbulence. They call her that because she's always pissed off with violence. If I had her job I would be, too. Twitchy and Twicky smoke so much crack they shake. They can't bait their hooks without sticking the point in their fingers. They can't cut bait or gut and pack fish without cutting themselves or getting their hands stabbed with poison fins. She has to bait their hooks. They can pull the fish in, hang them on the dehooker then shake them off, but she has to do everything else so they made her captain. She is what she is."

Snarly said, "Are you sure about that?"

Jolly took the bait and said, "Sure about what?"

Snarly simpered then said, "That she is what she is."

Jolly looked more confused as he said, "What's there to be sure about after she's been documented?"

Snarly asked, "For instance, does she get up in the morning like all other white squaws then paint her face with tubes and brushes of color like a warrior going on the war path?"

Jolly said, "I don't think so!"

Snarly simpered again and said, "Well then, that means she ain't what she ain't, only putty and paint can make her what she ain't!"

Hubbub shouted, "Boat coming in, it's the Bad Dogs, guns too!"

Snarly gazed at Spiker and said, "That's Trigger Happy, the Ax Man and the Bus Man. They catch crabs, lobsters and fish. They work around the clock and get results, but you don't want to have any truck with them."

Spiker asked, "Why not?"

Snarly gave him a callous frown then said, "They are

tough men with their own ways and they are paying off debts to the state because of that. Don't make them any offers, they won't talk to you. Don't pull any strings and try to force them into it because of what they owe. They will only leave you on the bottom half way there."

Spiker asked, "What did they do?"

Snarly said, "Trigger Happy was leasing a marine railway from the Gold Brick. The Ax Man was leasing the Gold Brick's packing house and fuel dock. The Gila wanted it all. He made the Gold Brick an offer that was substantially higher than what they were paying. The Gold Brick broke the leases by proving improper maintenance and gave the whole works to the Gila. Trigger Happy shot the Gold Brick in both shoulders and both knees. The Ax Man chopped up everything in the packing house and then the fuel dock including the pumps. While they were hiding from the law, the Bus Man came in from a week's fishing and tied up to the seawall at the packing house which was closed.

"He got in his truck to go home and it wouldn't start. Instead of calling a cab, he walked a block up the street to the bus stop. There was a little old lady sitting on the bench. He sat on the other end. An old wine-o stumbled up carrying a big loud boombox and sat between them. The little old lady asked the boomboxer if he could turn it down some. He said, 'No, I'm an American, I can do whatever I want.'

"The Bus Man said, 'That racket is hurting my ears. Turn it down!'

"The wine-o said, 'I don't have to turn it down until ten o'clock tonight. That's the law!'

"The bus arrived and the little old lady got on it. As the bus pulled away, the Bus Man stood up, grabbed the wine-o and heaved him under the back wheels of the bus as he said, 'I'm an American. I can do whatever I want.'

"Both of the wine-o's legs were busted up. The little old

lady saw him do it. She screamed bloody murder and dropped a dime on him. They put him in a cell with Trigger Happy and the Ax Man."

Hubbub shouted, "Boat coming in! There's someone at the wheel who's dressed in a monk's robe with the hood over his head and he's flying a quarantine. There is a big bloated grouper with its stomach slit open and its guts hanging out laying on his packing box."

Jolly said, "That's ol' Dead Dick. He's just passing through to gather up a fresh swarm of blow flies."

Spiker asked, "What in the hell does he need fresh flies for and what's wrong with the ones he's got?"

Jolly said, "He drank so much booze and screwed so many filthy road whores that he's turned into a festering ball of staph oozing syphilis in places. The two things that help him the most are a lot of heroin and a fresh hatch of blow fly maggots to eat his rot."

Hubbub shouted, "Boat coming in! It's Captain Starky on the 'Reformer'."

Snarly looked at Spiker and said, "He won't bother with you no matter what you offer. If he can't fish in a blow he spends his time changing the shape of things."

Hubbub shouted, "Boat coming in! It's the "Merry Chaos," Captain Bumpy's boat. I don't know the youngster at the wheel."

Jolly said, "Captain Bumpy died from too much coke and too many Camel cigarettes. The kids running the boat are the ones who have been following me and Lead around with their noses up our asses."

The captain of the Merry Chaos turned his bows into the wind between two Cuban fishing boats and put his engine in reverse to stop the boat as his mate went forward then dropped the anchor. He played out forty feet of scope which was too short for a thirty knot blow. As the boat drifted with the wind pulling the line tight, the anchor broke out of the mud and began dragging. The mate played out another ten feet of line. The anchor grabbed and held.

Lead smiled and said, "He thinks he's safe now and maybe he is until the full force of the wind occurs when it starts to shift to the west. His line is way too short for that and he's already within forty feet of the barrier reef. It's going to be chaos for 'em but there won't be anything merry about it."

A large flock of brown pelicans landed on the beach between the fort and our boats to get out of the wind. I felt safe about what was coming. The fort's high walls were made from sixteen million bricks that blocked most of the wind and flying debris. I looked to the east. A crew member on one of the Cuban fishing boats was throwing paper plates and food scraps overboard. Snappers rose to the surface to eat the scraps. He threw out a hand line and pulled a mangrove snapper from the water.

His actions didn't go unnoticed by the Hangman standing on the mound. He walked down the mound, climbed aboard his boat, cranked his engine, turned on his flashing lights and siren, threw off his tie lines, motored past the fishing boat and scooped up the paper plates that were being carried by the tide into the channel. He motored back to the fishing boat, tied up to it, shut off his siren, dumped the trash on their deck, laid down his net, pulled out his ticket book and wrote the captain a two hundred and fifty dollar ticket for littering in the park.

As the captain screamed at his mate about the money that was coming out of his pay, the Hangman picked up his net, held it out to them, then insisted that they put the snapper they caught into it. They complied, then he dumped it back into the water and watched it recover then swim away. He took out his ticket book again and wrote the captain another fine of three hundred and fifty dollars for fishing in the park from a commercial boat with a hand line.

As the evening sun touched the horizon it was blacked out by the next band of approaching squalls. The osprey dove out of the trade winds then landed in its nest. As it settled in, Hubbub shouted, "Boat coming in, it's Can't Talk and Never Listens!"

Spiker asked, "What's their story?"

Snarly smirked as he said, "They stay soaked in beer, but they will Bogart a joint if they run out. Never Listens is the captain so he drinks more and works less because of mishaps. Can't Talk catches most of their fish. He has to write short notes on where to go because he smoked so many cool non-filters that he lost his voice box and Never Listens doesn't know where anything is except the beer. He won't be any help and Can't Talk isn't a fool. Don't waste your time on 'em."

The twilight faded into darkness and the gecko started its mating call. Lead and Jolly busted out laughing. Lead asked, "How long have you been listening to a bull gecko, they are seldom seen this far north?"

Snarly growled, "Hubbub let that noisy bastard on board at the dock!"

Hubbub came down from the flying bridge and blasted two rounds of rat shot under the cap rail, looked behind the packing box, looked inside the storage closet and under the galley sink then looked at Snarly and said, "I'm the only one who saw him, but I didn't participate in his presence and I'm looking forward to the day you see something you wish you hadn't."

In spite of the gun shots, the gecko soon started its call again. Hubbub walked to the console where I was sitting and put the rat gun in its place then said, "There's no lights on the horizon beyond the shrimp boats nor any ominous evading shadows moving about. A bunch of snapper boats anchored among the shrimp boats to trade what they have for bycatch or shrimp. Old blind Muck Luck is coming in with his two boys, Squid Lips and Panic." He sat down at the table and pressed his back against the bulkhead then sighed with back pain relief.

I stared at Ruckus. He stood up and went to the stove then put on a pot of bucci.

Spiker asked, "What do they do with a little boat like that out here?"

Jolly said, "Muck Luck is mostly blind. The lens on his glasses are a half-inch thick and he still has to use a magnifying glass to read his electronics. Panic keeps an eye on him most of the time, but he can't always see what's going to happen any better than Muck Luck who runs aground on sandbars often. Last month he was looking for that wrecked ship at Half Moon Shoals and he ran aground on the quicksands. His bows got stuck in the muck so tight his small engine wouldn't back her off. So, he did what he's always done when he can't get her off. He stepped over the side on what he assumed was firm bottom to walk to the bows and shove her off. He disappeared under the muck with his hands sticking out.

"While Panic was skipping, hopping, whining and moaning around on the back deck, Squid Lips bent himself over the rail, grabbed Muck Luck by the hands then pulled him back on board where he laid on his belly flipping and flopping while he puked up sand, mud and rotting turtle grass."

Spiker asked, "Why does he call his son Squid Lips?"

Jolly said, "They fish with squid because it's cheap and Squid Lips likes raw squid. His lips and chin are usually black with ink which makes it easy for Muck Luck to tell them apart."

Ruckus poured bucci into small cups. He sipped on one as he reached for the rat gun.

I said, "Leave it be, the gecko won't come out after all that flack your brother blasted at it. Take your mag-auto with you to the bridge."

As Ruckus passed the table headed for the door, I noticed Lead smiling at me, then he said, "It seems that Spiker's bullshit has got you slightly off your mark."

I said, "What do you mean by that?"

He said, "When you put your anchor ashore you didn't put a vermin guard on the line. Now you've got a very large and pregnant wharf rat sitting on your anchor chute scratching her flea bitten butt and licking her infected paws, wanting to spread her plague."

I looked forward and saw that it was no joke. I reached under the console, grabbed the rat gun, cocked the hammer, slid the side window open and took aim at the rat.

Lead said, "I wouldn't do that if I were you."

I asked, "Why not?"

He said, "You may be killing a godsend."

I asked, "How so?"

"She's coming for the gecko," he said.

I hesitated and the rat jumped on the cap rail, ran down the starboard side, jumped on the deck then jumped into the cap rail over the bulkhead into the storage closet. It jumped back into the cap rail and over all the bulkheads until it reached the bunk room. The forepeak had an anchor rope locker built onto the stem. At the top of the locker there is an inch and a half hole for the six-hundred feet of anchor line to be pulled up to the sampson post. At the bottom of the locker there is a four-inch drain hole that allows water splashed on deck through the rope hole to flow into the bilge. The rat entered the hole to hide.

The smell of fuel fumes and burned gun powder didn't bother the gecko, but the scent of the rat deflated his air sacks with a loud sputtering hiss.

Snarly whined, "You guys fucked up. That rat isn't going to catch that gecko because it can't run upside down inside the cap rail and it's going to cause worse havoc than a lot of racket."

I said, "You may be right, but that wasn't the plan. I was thinking it might scare that noisy prick off the boat and kill it somewhere between us and the rubble pile before it gets in a crevice and starts barking again."

"Fine!" Snarly roared. "I'm going below and wash my filthy ass." He entered the bunk room, removed some shore clothes from the closet, laid them on his bunk, took out his taser, knife, quarter ounce of skunk and a large pack of bam-boo rolling papers, laid them on the bunk then removed his coveralls and stepped into the shower. The rat was focused on the scent of the gecko until it got a whiff of the skunk weed. It threw all fear aside, rushed out of the hole, jumped on his bunk then grabbed the bag of weed and the pack of papers because they smelled good, too.

It raced back into the hole as Snarly was stepping out from his short shower. While he dried off, shaved his face brushed his teeth and dressed, the rat ate the bag of weed, got stoned to the max then started in on the rolling papers, didn't care for the taste, so she pulled them all out of the pack and made a nest out of them on top of the pile of rope, laid down in it and gave birth to a half dozen pink, hairless pups the size of full grown mice.

As Snarly tied his shoes he noticed that his weed was gone. He came up from the bunk room in a rage screaming, "Which one of you pinched my stash!"

He looked at each of us in turn and received stoned cold stares with our eyes popped out of their sockets. He screamed again, "Cough it up ass wipe or there's going to be hell to pay with a hot poker and the cattle prod."

Everyone scowled then looked at the water. He focused on me, knowing that I wouldn't lie to him about the whereabouts of his attitude adjustment.

I said, "No one has gone below except you. You must have put it where you can't find it. I've done it myself when

I was stoned and brain dead."

He said, "Not likely, I wasn't that stoned. I apologize for the outburst even tho' you can understand why. There's two other critters on this boat, but gecko's ain't herbivorous and anything that can run upside down is already stoned so you gents better keep our stash in your pockets or you'll be smoking rat turds to get high."

He went to the storage closet and pulled out an old rusty rat trap. While we talked of ways to catch rats, the gecko was in a high state of fear because it was smelling a bunch of different rats so it made its exit to an ambush point in the rubble pile to catch cockroaches. The mother rat passed out into a skunk weed void as the babies suckled.

The Dirt wanted to go back to Spiker's boat to lay down. As he was getting in the skiff Spiker glanced at his boat then yelled, "She's going down by the head!" He cranked the outboard then raced to his boat. She was still swinging with the wind, but the splash rails around her bows were underwater with the stern riding to high and dry. In a few minutes water began pumping out a through hull fitting on her starboard side.

Spiker didn't call for help so we sat around the back deck watching his boat plow back and forth with the wind on a hundred and twenty degree swing.

Snarly took a piece of cheese from the cooler and molded it around the trigger mechanism of the rat trap then set it. He placed it on the galley deck behind my chair at the console so no one would step on it. He said, "She will be wearing it around her broken neck shortly after we pass out."

Ruckus came down from the flying bridge as the next band of black squalls slammed into the fort. The wind and rain rushed over and around us filling the galley with a fine mist that smelled of ozone as it swirled in through the open door.

Ruckus grinned then said, "I saw the gecko!"

Snarly growled, "Why didn't you shoot it?"

Ruckus twisted his face into Snarly's expression then said, "I couldn't without blasting holes in Lead's boat." He high jumped on it, ran up his port side and across his bows then leaped into the rubble pile moving totally ballistic.

Snarly roared, "Was the rat on his ass?"

Ruckus smirked from ear to ear then said, "Get serious. Do you really think she could catch it after eating a quarter ounce of weed! That's enough THC to knock an elephant to his knees." The squalls roared on to the northeast and Ruckus returned to his watch.

Spiker called to ask if I had a spare auto pump switch. I said, "Only if you come and get it." He arrived with The Dirt.

Snarly reached into the storage closet, found the switch then said, "Why did you take in so much water?"

He said, "When we were tied to the trees in Trappers Cut I sent Fairel into the bilge to fill up the water in the batteries and check for leaks. The stupid idiot didn't know that the packing gland on the shaft is supposed to drip so he tightened up the nuts and shut the water flow off. Sometime while we were crossing Rebecka the packing got so hot and swelled up so tight that the gland seized to the shaft and twisted the boot so hard that both hose clamps holding the boot to the shaft log broke which left the gland and the boot spinning with the shaft. Water was gushing out of the boot but it was still on the shaft log. The inside of the boot was chewed all to hell from spinning on the shaft log, so I had to repair it with layers of duct tape to stop it from leaking.

"My twelve-volt converter and starter were under water. The auto switch on the forward pump went out while other things were going to hell. The Dirt held the manual switch down and pumped the boat out while I stopped the water."

Fairel climbed into the top bunk and whined, "I've got

to pull the starter and never-seize it then install this switch. Thanks for the help. If you go fishing tomorrow I'd like to come along."

I laughed and said, "Only lunatics or desperate fools will venture out tomorrow. You need to motor around the park and find someone to stand The Dirt's watch."

He climbed down into his skiff then said, "See you at dawn."

Captains Lead and Jolly said good night then stepped aboard their boats and went below. Ruckus came down, poured a cup of bucci then returned to the bridge. Snarly set his alarm for four o'clock in the morning to relieve Ruckus, then we turned in.

Sometime before four o'clock the mother rat woke up suffering from extreme dehydration caused by the massive dose of THC. She came out of the hole then scurried across the deck boards up the steps into the galley. She smelled the cheese on the trap and ate it off the trigger without setting it off because the mechanism was too rusty to function properly without adequate pressure. She jumped onto the galley counter top and chewed holes in the plastic containers that held coffee, sugar, tea, flour and cornmeal searching for water.

She jumped back onto the deck then smelled water in the storage cabinets under the expansive port console that harbors charts, a pile of nautical instruments plus most of the electronics needed to fish the shallows down to the abysmal planes. The storage closets held extra tackle to restock the tackle box and cardboard boxes with four gallons of drinking water in each. There is a two-foot section of exposed cap rail between the cabinet frame and the step up to the port galley door for ventilation. She jumped into the cap rail over the cabinet frame onto the boxes of water, then jumped onto the deck and chewed through a bottom box. She drank her fill then back tracked to the hole in the anchor locker.

The wind howled around Ruckus. He never heard a scratch or a squeak. Snarly's alarm went off waking everyone up. He stepped out of his bunk then entered the galley and found himself standing barefoot in water staring at the destruction of the plastic jugs along with the leftovers from a hearty sugar and corn meal rat snack.

He looked down at the trap then screamed, "Holy mackerel!" which woke me and Hubbub up again.

As I was coming up from below, Ruckus came down from the bridge. I said, "I don't see any holy mackerels. You put them on ice already?"

Ruckus said, "I've heard "holy mackerel" screamed many times on that old TV show "Amos and Andy," but I've never heard the reason for or the meaning of the saying unless it was mackerels the fishermen caught when Jesus insisted that he should throw his net from the other side of his boat."

No one voiced their opinion. Snarly took a spatula from a drawer then poked the trap trigger. It tripped with a loud snap. He placed a paper towel on the counter top then went to the tackle box and grabbed a small piece of wet and dry sandpaper. He picked up the trap, placed it on the towel then sanded it to a hair trigger condition.

He molded another piece of cheese to the trigger then grumbled, "I've got the tricky bitch now! When the sun rises it will dry the cheese rock hard and stuck tight. She can't chew it off without busting her brains in." He set the trap, poured some bucci in a cup then climbed to the bridge to stand his watch.

I looked at Hubbub then said, "Take the water jugs out of the wet boxes and trash the cardboard. Wipe up the water and stuff some pillows in the cap rail over the bulkheads so she can't get back in there. Then tell Snarly we are at war with the rat and when it's dead he can stand first watch."

Snarly came down then asked, "What's the plan?"

Hubbub said, "Check all closets and cabinets and make sure she's not in them. Then stuff pillows or life jackets into the cap rail above each bulkhead. We should have her cornered when we get to the last one because there's no way to get into the bilge from the galley or bunk room."

Snarly growled, "Let's get at it."

While the clones slammed doors and shoved things helter-skelter, forcing the rat into the last compartment, Lead and Jolly came aboard and sipped buccis. After searching everywhere the clones stood before the anchor rope locker.

Snarly snickered, "She's in there. The sampson post passes through the rope locker and is bolted to its slot in the kelson. In the top part of the locker the sampson post is braced to port, starboard and the bow stem with three six-by-eight inch wood beams. The rat climbed the anchor rope onto the beam bolted to the stem then curled into a ball behind the sampson post."

Snarly said, "I'm closing the bunk room door. You gents staying or leaving?"

Hubbub clutched a claw hammer. Ruckus waved a ball peen. They didn't move. He closed the bunk room door, raised the rat gun, stood back from the locker door then reached out and opened it. They saw the babies in the nest of rolling papers then Snarly stuck his head inside, looked behind the pile of rope and up at the brace beams but couldn't see her.

He said, "I can't see her but she's got to be up on the beams."

Ruckus said, "Climb in there, grab a beam then pull yourself up and see!"

Snarly whined, "I ain't going into close quarters with a pissed off mega rat."

He took the claw hammer from Hubbub then reached

up and pounded on the sampson post below the beams. No reaction. He went up to the galley, grabbed a plastic cup and bowl, came back, jammed the cup in the drain hole then picked up the babies and put them in the bowl. He closed the locker then went to the stern and fed the rats to the goliath groupers. He came back into the galley, squirted some dish soap in the bowl, washed it and put it in the drainer then sat at the table

I asked, "Where is the mother and how did she give you the slip?"

"She's on top of the braces for the sampson post. I can't see her, but I believe she's there. Ain't nowhere else to go."

I gave him a disgusted frown then said, "It would be nice to know if she is or isn't in there."

He whined, "I ain't going in that locker. It's too tight in there and I don't need a tetanus shot. Can I spray something in there to run her out?"

"Are you crazy," I said. We've got to sleep down there."

Lead snickered a snerty snigger. I turned my face to his then said, "I hope you can run on water because your ass is skating on thin ice, god-sender!"

Snarly threw his arms over his head then said, "What in the hell do you want me to do?"

I said, "We can't leave her there in an aggravated state with a belly full of water and cornmeal, crapping and pissing all over the anchor rope while she chews it into shorty pieces only fit for a dock line. Rats eat when they can. Put the trap in the locker and be done with her."

He picked up the trap and took it below saying, "The cheese isn't hard yet!"

I said, "It won't matter if you've fixed the trap."

A boat passed the stern coming into the basin. Jolly said, "It's the Red Eyed Pike and Ikasorus who operate the Neanderthal boat repair service offshore."

Spiker heard them arrive and anchor up. He came over

with The Dirt, tied up then came to the table. He gazed around at everyone then said, "What's the story on that boat that just anchored?"

Jolly said, "There's two hard core trackers over there. They wear them everywhere. When a vein collapses they move on to another one. Red Eyed Pike shoots up so often his eyes bleed. Ikasorus doesn't do it as much so he does most of the repairs and he will find something else broke if he's low on cash and fix.

"Last year the Pike bought a hydroplane then took Ikasorus and their helper, Cromag, on a ride around Key West. They were hauling ass at ninety knots on the south side in shallow water just after the twilight zone and crashed into the long dick dock, killing Cromag. The impact broke so many bones in Ika and the Pike's bodies they remain deformed. No help unless you have a useful position for pelagic semi-parapalegic misfits."

The wind and rain let up to a lull telling me the next squall was sucking them up to slam us with a hummer bummer. The dawn revealed a sky filled with light mist capturing pink, orange and red rays from the sun. The snapper boats that were anchored among the shrimp boats were pulling their grapnels and moving closer to the fort for the reduced wind.

Snarly mumbled, "It's getting sloppy out there between the reefs and they are punking out."

Hubbub raised his eyebrows at Snarly then asked, "Have you ever asked a shrink why you are so negative?"

Snarly laughed then said, "As a matter of fact I have. She said I was too smart and that ignorant people have to ask questions while they can't keep up with their vocation which causes me to suffer personally. But it's not professionally anal-logged as a trait disturbance with a despondent reaction, and my condition is reasonably moderate considering what I do with my time."

Suddenly the rat trap went off with a loud "snap!" followed with a series of scraps and knocks on the walls of the locker. Snarly ran below and opened the door. The rat tumbled out with the trap locked tight to her snout. She rolled and hopped across the floor boards trying to remove the trap with her paws then laid still and suffocated. The smash bar hit her below the eyes and crushed her jaws and teeth into the wooden board of the trap.

Snarly picked up the rat by the tail, carried it to the stern for the groupers then washed the trap and his hands with the deck hose. He put the trap in the storage closet, ignored the rat gun then went to the bridge with a cup of bucci to sip.

A few moments later he yelled, "Boat coming in, it's After Burn and Over Load working a fish house boat."

Spiker asked, "What did they load an' burn?"

Jolly said, "Over Load soaked his kingfish net too long and it filled up. He should have cut it in half and put a buoy on part of it then picked it up later with an empty boat, but it was calm so he pulled the whole load aboard which left him with a foot of free board. He could have made it to the dock if the wind hadn't kicked up out of the sow'west and created a cross sea bucking the tide colliding with the gulfstream and washing him under. After Burn was tied to the pilings in his slip near the end of the long pier at the fish house while a nor'wester howled.

"He walked up the street to one of the many bars then drank a fifth of Jack and snorted an eight ball of coke. He wobbled and tweaked back to his boat then decided to make some coffee. He filled the pot, turned on the gas then picked up the match box on the counter. It was empty. Instead of turning the burner off he rummaged through drawers looking for matches taking far too long. After finding matches he went to the stove. By then he should have smelled the gas and shut the stove off, but he was so drunk he couldn't remember ever turning it on and his nasal passageways were clogged with coke so that's all he could smell. He reached out and turned the gas up higher thinking he was turning it on then struck a match. The explosion blasted most of his hair and the front of his clothes away then heaved him in the water onto his back as he turned into a floating blister.

"The cabin was engulfed with flames. There wasn't a fireboat in the harbor. By the time the fire department pulled a long hose to the end of the pier it was on fire along with the boats on each side of him."

As squally wind and rain swirled over us, Lead asked Hubbub how his girlfriend Maybella was getting on. He said, "I don't care and I don't know much for certain anymore except two things."

Ruckus said, "Spit 'em out."

He said, "One, I'm going to die sooner than I should because I like Spiker and what he does. Two, if you leave your recycle can too close to the street some crap-stained rectum with hemorrhoids will put his garbage in it. When I began dating Maybella I promised to give her one of everything to jump start the relationship, and I did my best to pull it off. But, she became too fond of the knick-knacks, whatnots, thingamajigs and whatchamacallits.

"I found myself while I was traversing a narrow lane to a musty antique sofa in the storage shed and her walking behind me with a large crab net to catch anything I might knock over. After she started harping about me wearing out the fabric on the sofa, I caught a few zees on some moldy plastic cushions in the palm frond pavilion then started running with Snarly after wild women in the jungle. They don't want much."

The Dirt asked, "Whats day want?"

Hubbub laughed then said, "If you can find your way around their snares, sharp staked pitfalls and their toothy pets, they like a long hard run in the hot steamy canopy then a cool dip in a spring fed lagoon."

Not satisfied until he heard more, The Dirt asked, "Ang theng?"

Hubbub said, "The rest is ancient history if you can take away their sharp sticks that have been rubbed on poison dart frogs then soaked in aggregate viper venom."

Lead gazed at Ruckus then asked, "Is Nitro still blowing the white caps from your waves?"

He said, "No! She blew me off and I can't blame her for cutting out with a scoundrel. I could have handled things differently. We were anchored in the turtle grass about fifty feet from the edge of a channel on the south side of Port Royal that flows into Morgans Harbour and Kingston Bay. Fishermen passed by day and night. One day a fisherman that was off fishing in the Bahamas for a spell returned. As he came up the channel he saw Nitro sunning her boobs on the bows. He went ape and howled like a crazy man which he was. I should have pulled the anchor and moved up the coast, but I didn't want to make long runs in and out of Morgans Harbour to buy supplies.

"The next day here comes the crazy man down the channel towing a forty foot wooden barge twenty feet wide. He anchored it on the edge of the channel next to us which put his starboard side thirty feet from our port side. I asked Nitro to stay off the bow with her boobs out. After he anchored the barge he went back to town and returned with a load of lumber, plywood, tar paper and a bunch of five-gallon buckets containing tar, pitch, paint and paint thinner. When he wasn't sawing then nailing and bug-eyeing Nitro, he was motoring around Kingston Bay buying old worn out derelict boats then tying them up alongside the barge to impress Nitro. The draft on two of the boats was too deep to put on the starboard side so he put them on the port side in the channel which pissed off some of the fishermen who go in and out on a daily basis. With eight boats tied to the barge and no room for more, he went about putting up studs for wall frames between ogles at Nitro sunning with her top on. In the twilight zone he would leave to fish offshore all night or hang out on the barge walking around in his underwear drinking beer and hanging his prick out leaving a wizz over the side.

"Days passed with squalls and rain as tempers flared because one side of the channel was blocked while the derelict boats collected rain water that bred huge swarms of mosquitoes. The bugs were so thick they ate me up when I smoked cigars on the back deck because Nitro wouldn't let me smoke inside. By the time I was covered with red spots and drinking quinine water hoping I wouldn't get malaria, a collision of coincidences occurred creating three miracles during the twilight zone, which allowed me to do what I did without setting Morgans Harbour on fire and going to jail. A fisherman was coming up the channel on his side while a fisherman came out of Morgans Habour into the channel on his side. They were going to meet at the derelict boats.

"Miracle number one! The fisherman coming up from the south had to stop his boat so the other boat could pass. In the few moments he waited his boat filled up with mosquitoes. He went into a rage and swore that he was coming back after he put his fish on ice to set the pile of trash on fire if he didn't move the derelict boats out of the channel.

"Miracle number two! The scoundrel gave him the finger then went fishing. As I sat waiting for the fisherman to come back and set his fire a rare event happened. The light wind shifted from south to out of the north.

"I've always put my life in the hands of Poseidon, the Keeper of the Benthic Realms, so I considered such a phenomenon to be his doing. It was the third Miracle because the tide was flowing south and it would carry the flaming derelicts away from Morgans Harbour with the wind's help, but someone had to act soon before the wind and tide changed.

I waited for hours to no avail as the wind held out of the north. After Nitro went to sleep I put two one-gallon cans of fuel on the dingy then paddled over to the two boats tied stern to stern on each side of the bow anchor line and poured the fuel on both decks. I struck two matches and threw one in each boat then paddled back to Nitro. The fire spread quickly to the barge and the other boats. As flaming derelicts broke away from the barge the bow anchor line burned through. The barge swung around then came tight on the stern anchor with a jolt causing the rest of the derelicts to break away from their burning tie lines. As they drifted down the channel to the south the stern anchor line burned through setting the barge adrift. Flames roared thirty feet in the air then the five-gallon buckets of paint, thinner, tar and pitch began exploding one after the other with blasts that scattered the remains of the cabin helter-skelter.

"The racket woke Nitro up. She came to the stern and watched the flaming fleet drift offshore then burn to their water lines and sink. She looked at me then shook her head and said, "Take me to the hotel in Morgans Harbour." She didn't rat me out, but she felt sorry for the scoundrel and went fishing with him to the Bahamas. I put the Viking on a course to the Ivory Coast to hook up with Snarly and Hubbub.

"She called me a year later after she realized the scoundrel was a hell of a lot crazier than I am and said she would like to see me. I caught a flight to Kingston and knocked on her door. She greeted me with a massive hybrid dog that weighed at least a hundred and eighty pounds. As he strained against his leash, growling and snapping at me, she asked, "Did you bring your boat?" When I said, "No," she seemed disappointed but asked if I would like to come in. I said, "No, your dog wants to have me for lunch and I can't kill him to do the same, so where's the fun in that?" I left the question hanging and got back into the cab I hailed at the airport.

"When I got back to the Viking, Snarly was on the phone with the Dinosaur and here we are, too far from the jungle hoeing a rutty row."

The rising sun heated up the already warm water in the series of colliding currents that flow in and around the southeastern gulf. Black squalls spinning water spouts formed over the Tortugas Banks west of Loggerhead Key.

Snarly came down and said, "It's black as night to the north and south. It's hauling ass, too!"

The bright colors on the horizon to the east faded away behind black rain as the squalls slammed into the fort then swirled about us. While the rain pounded and strummed on the cabin roof, the wind whistled and hummed past the antennas.

Spiker noticed that everyone except Jolly was staring at him intently. Jolly was looking at each of us with a sly grin on his face knowing something was coming, but he didn't perceive what.

Lead puffed on his joint, coughed up a gob of phlegm, opened the side window and spit it on Jolly's cap rail. He closed the window then said to Spiker, "If you can get away with hornswoggling Jolly it must be OK for me to defile his boat."

Snarly took over and said, "We told you how to treat Jolly because he trusts you. Instead of being fair, you've made him the same offer that you always cram down our throats up until now, and it's taken decades to get paid. He won't be crossing the stream with you until his wife's bank account is in order."

Spiker shook his head then said, "I'm going broke as

hell. After I clear customs at Run Aground Point then tie up in my slip behind the barn, the Bush Master, the Boomslang and the Golden Viper, who's in charge of the money are coming by with the scuttlebutt on our next way point. We can settle up then."

The squalls passed on to the northeast exposing the sun and revealing the osprey soaring in and out of the trade winds. Snarly climbed to his watch. The wind fell off to twenty knots. Most of the fishing boats less than fifty feet didn't like the weather report from the NOAA. They pulled their anchors, put their sterns to the wind and set a course to Fish Mongers Hill.

Snarly yelled, "Boat coming in from Rebecka, it's Big Bang the I-Beam Bender with his new boat. He slammed into a day marker without a warning light after the twilight zone. The crash bent the top of the steel girder into a ninety-degree angle and ripped out some prodigious holes in his starboard garboard."

Jolly choked on his toke then said, "Gay Fay did something similar. She was leaving Stock Rock Channel on a charter steering from the bridge. She took a hit on her crack pipe then pushed a direction button on the autopilot thinking that she had pushed the ON button next to it. She stood up and climbed down the ladder to grab a beer. While she did so, the boat fell off its course to starboard and crashed into the green day marker. The impact mashed up the fiberglass and busted a long crack in her chime just aft of the bow. The packing box full of ice and food for a three day trip jumped its blocks and slammed into the lady who chartered the boat while she was sitting on the stern cap rail, breaking her legs."

Lead said, "The High Liner left here after a long blow with a load of fish. He reached the end of the channel then made his starboard turn to the east. He stuck a cigar in his mouth and tried to light it. The wind was out of the east so he ducked down behind the console on the bridge and took too much time lighting the cigar. The east wind pushed his boat on a collision course with Iowa Rock day marker. The collision ripped off the starboard bow railing and opened her chimes."

Hubbub said, "Chokey did the same thing in northwest channel. Accidents happen if you try to do two things at the same time. I had a girlfriend who could do three things at the same time until she crashed and burned with a cup of coffee in one hand and a cell phone in the other while driving with her knees."

He looked at Ruckus then asked, "Do you know anyone who does crazy crap like that?"

He said, "I've seen and heard of other mishaps, but they are still alive and I wouldn't want it said that I was bad mouthing their cigars when a joint the same size would have solved all their problems and cured the ongoing conditions produced by their vexations. There is one among us that I could speak of."

He gazed at Spiker who turned red in the face then said, "I ain't never crashed into no I-beams."

Ruckus said, "Perhaps not, but you've crashed. Think back to that day when we were hauling ass around a big school of large black mullet setting eighteen-hundred yards of trammel net in the inter-coastal on the west side. You went into the last turn too fast while closing the net. The boat hit the shallows then leaped ten feet into the air sideways and dropped on the bank. I didn't need the bruises. You didn't like the amount of fish we caught even tho' the boat was half full of mullet, so we picked the net and reset it after the twilight zone around a school of worthless mudcats.

"When we were hauling ass back to the dock you hit a support cable holding up a light pole and flipped the boat upside down leaving me fighting my way out of a net full of stabbing catfish. I was squeezing pus balls for two weeks."

I frowned at Hubbub and said, "You need to clean the rat gun before it blows up in your face."

As Hubbub cleaned the western style long barrel single action target pistol, Lead looked at me then said, "Don't you worry about that gun jumping out of its hole when you are running in rough weather then falling on the hammer and shooting you in the head?"

I said, "We keep it locked on half cock so that can't happen and we never ease the hammer down on a live round then put it away."

Lead said, "When the Hunter and I were fishing the "Smelta" with the Magician there was a .41 mag' single action pistol on board for shooting sharks that get lip hooked on the bandit and can't bite through the leader. We kept the pistol in a chest of drawers bolted to the bulkhead like you have. One night when it was slick calm we were anchored over the submarine in a hundred and forty feet of water south of Cosgrove Light. The Hunter and I were pulling large yellowtail as fast as we could go while the Magician slept because he had to get up at dawn to gut, wash and pack a thousand pounds of snapper while we slept. The Hunter caught a blue runner, hooked it on his bandit then sent it to the bottom.

"A huge bull shark lip hooked itself. He fought it to the surface. As it rammed and slammed its body against the hull, the noise woke up the Magician. He came to the stern with the .41. He cocked the hammer and shot the shark in the head. He cocked the hammer to shoot it again, but the shark was already dead. Instead of turning the cylinder to the dead round then easing the hammer down, he eased it down on the live round, but not half cocked. He walked to the cabin and laid the gun on top of the chest instead of putting it in the drawer then went back to sleep. My bedroll was laid out on top of the engine box next to the chest of drawers because there were only two bunks forward.

"The Hunter and I continued to pull yellowtails and shake them off on the dehooker into slushy ice water to preserve the skin colors of the fish, keep the eyes clear and firm the flesh for their presentation in a fish market showcase. A freighter passed to the west and south of us. It rolled a wake at us big enough to tilt the Smelta forty-five degrees. The gun slid off the chest, landed on the hammer and blasted the round through the side and top of the engine box on an angle then made its exit out of the center of my pillow.

"After we recovered from the unexpected blast we decided that the Magician was tired of packing fish and blew his brains out. Instead he came up from below and wanted to know what we were shooting at in the cabin, then saw the gun on the deck, the holes in the engine box and my pillow with feathers scattered about. It was a sobering experience with Murphy's Law for the three of us that I won't forget."

Ruckus asked, "What happened to the Hunter? We haven't seen him around for years."

Lead said, "He made another trip with us to the "Little Bank". It was blowing twenty to twenty five out of the northwest. By the time we had thirty-six hundred pounds on board it was honking twenty five to thirty knots. Every time a wave rolled by the stern was slamming down so hard into the trough that the quadrant came apart and the rudder fell out. Water shot up through the rudder log and flung the hatch cover to the lazarette overboard. I quickly pulled off my t-shirt, twisted it into a plug then beat it into the rudder log with a hammer and screwdriver. We steered her to the hill by manipulating bed sheets tied to drag lines port and starboard. While the Smelta was on the railway being fitted with a new rudder, the Magician caught the Hunter writing down his LORAN numbers. They got into an argument.

"The Hunter took a hike and signed on as captain of a packing house boat. His first trip he caught two thousand pound in rough weather then went to the fort to get some rest before his long ride up the hill. His mate had never seen the fort so he tied up to the visitors' dock to let him take a look inside. As they were climbing on the dock two lobster boats came in and raced to the empty spot at the dock north of his boat. The winner reached the spot, jerked his throttle in reverse, backed down hard and laid the boat against the pilings. The loser wasn't quick enough backing down and slammed into the Hunter's starboard bow. The impact busted their cap rails, destroyed the Hunter's cabin and ripped the electronics from their mounts then flung them against the port bulkhead where they ricocheted onto the back deck.

"His next trip out he was crossing Rebecka when something happened with the shaft log and his only pump quit working. The boat sank in ninety feet. There was a small freighter anchored two miles away on a hump catching fish for dinner. He paddled over to it on his packing box lid and went back to selling insurance."

Snarly yelled, "Dragger coming in!" The dragger, which was named "Jagged Snags," dropped his anchor in the mud on the east side of the barrier reef.

Jolly said, "That's Hemanus the Heblew and Gay Swayed. They are tough guys in spite of their sexual preference. The chubby kid on the stern is some trick they hired to head and ice the shrimp while they fight over who gets to wear the strap-on dildo."

Snarly came down and said, "There's some more squalls coming at us."

Ruckus said, "You think?"

Snarly smirked as he said, "No, I try hard not to think. If I told people what I really think they would put me in an institution."

Hubbub said, "Tell us anyway. We know you're always right."

Snarly said, "Not so, but now that the environmentalists and the bureaucrats have given the fishery to the predators by protecting them, more people are going to be eaten if they are brave enough to get in the water. There's not just crazy shit going on out here. If I make it home without getting bitten by a shark, I won't be able to sleep past 4:30 in the morning because there will be a half dozen roosters crowing under the bedroom window because the conservationists have made Key West a bird sanctuary and turned the city into a chicken farm crapping salmonella and leaving bird flu in their wake while they attack children waiting for the school bus and old folks trying to get in the grocery store.

"So, idiotic ideology is still prevailing, and I can't feed it to the sharks with someone protecting it. I have to ASSume that most people will be happy with that until their feet are bitten off or they die from chicken shit. Maybe then they will reclassify the problems back to surf and turf. You may think that's alota' malarky, but just wait until you've got a dozen roosters in your back yard digging it to hell and leaving their stink all over everything. Forget about 'maybe' because that's what's going down. The city will only dump them on somebody else if you spend hundreds of dollars to trap them for relocation and everyone is happy with the way things are going. So, I'll stay pissed off, but I'll quit bitching about it until something else goes haywire in a glitchy clinch of silicon diodes while I pray for life without computers.

"Now that every anarchist teacher teaming with a course racist scheming has one, everything in the Middle East has escalated out of control and moved to our back yard while we are all being net-washed and online scammed like every new surfer in training, as we are being scanned by the overlords lounging in their glitzy suits. The whole mess leaves me feeling misinformed with illusions like a child who wanted a puppy, but didn't know he was going to be cleaning up alota' dog shit and suffer a serious shortage of lollipops because the pedigree of the little pooper cost too much."

I interrupted Snarly as I looked at Lead then said, "I heard it through the seaweed that the white man has chosen you as part of Key West's nautical history and immortalized you with a statue."

He said, "Aye, and if it were only so! Unfortunately the white man doesn't have such power. The best he could do was make a Kevlar mold of my head then paste it on a Kevlar dummy pulling on a dummy line running through a block and tackle then tied to a barrel of rum which I never smuggled and drank very little of.

"No! I won't be immortalized until my mangled meat has gone on down and my spirit is soaring in the body of a fish hawk, seeing what it's seeing. For fifty years I followed the osprey to the west. Now when it soars out of the trade winds it is hightailing to the hill telling me that fishing is over and it's time to become what I despise most."

I said, "Sad day and what might that be?"

He said, "A shiftless lubber."

"How so?" I asked.

He said, "While the white man was putting together the parts of my mock immortality his doctors were declaring me disabled. Now it's illegal for me to requalify for my restricted species endorsement, and I must settle for a Mickey Mouse retirement that I can survive on if I camp out while I poach alongside of the crocodiles. I have been conditioning myself between offshore trips for such an event. So far no one has followed me into my den of crocodiles to write me a ticket. I keep the crocodiles happy with fish carcasses so they don't have to work so hard to eat which allows them to appreciate the art of procrastination as I do. The tricky part of the challenge comes when I have to move the fillets through the long gauntlet from the back country to the fish house."

The squalls passed onto the northeast. The clear sky revealed man o' war birds gathering around the osprey as they glided in a circle over the fort.

Spiker asked, "What's for brunch?"

Snarly snickered, "I can whip you up some congo marine cuisine. Most of the ingredients crawled aboard in Trappers Cut. Have you ever tasted brazed scorpions and centipedes seasoned with shrimp heads and squid blood then topped off with a pile of poached roaches? If not, there's bread on the counter. There's also some baloney in the cooler made from horse cocks and pig nuts. Help yourself." He stood up and returned to his watch.

As we shuffled about the cabin making "Dagwood" sandwiches, Spiker asked Lead if he knew any of the shrimp boat captains.

He said, "Just Rebar who catches my bait. In the late sixties I met most of the captains while I was hauling their boats out of the water for repairs. I know very few from the recent generations. When I worked the boats the Tortugas pink shrimp fishery was in its youthful twenties like myself. Without the latest advancements in marine technology it was a lot more dangerous for greenhorns. Back then they didn't use dip tanks. They preserved the shrimp with a coffee can full of dip from a five gallon bucket sprinkled between the layers of iced shrimp. The captain of the "Widows Folly" hired a new greenhorn to help his rig man clean up the back deck between drags. The rig man was lazy and careless. Sometime in the past he had used up a bucket of dip until there was just a few coffee cans left in it. Instead of scraping out the bucket he put the lid on it and pushed it aside from the new bucket of dip that he opened. The boat used up many new buckets of dip during that year while the old bucket sat where the rig man left it.

"After they hauled back and headed the shrimp from the first drag, the rig man told the new greenhorn to get a can of dip from the bucket with the seal removed that was sitting with another bucket with the seal intact. Instead he opened the old bucket. The dip in it had deteriorated into a very powerful poison gas. He died instantly. The rig man saw him fall so he jumped into the hold to help him up. He died in the alley way.

"The captain stepped out of his chair with the autopilot on then walked to the stern, saw the baskets of shrimp still on deck and his crew laying on the concrete floor of the alley way. He got on his knees to get a closer look into the ice hold and fell dead on his side. The boat continued to drag to the west until the nets hooked up on the eighteen fathom rock pile.

"Murphy's Law dictates an abundance of ways to die on a dragger. Some just lose an arm or leg when they are guiding the main cable onto the drum and a strand of cable on the splice to the bridle hooks their cloths and pulls the limb under the cable then around the drum. Some fell overboard and drowned, too drunk to see what was going on."

Jolly interrupted and said, "The Cat Man died that way. Remember him?"

Lead said, "Aye, he was a big one-eyed Dutchman with a nasty attitude, always drunk and ready to pick a fight with anyone walking the deck. He spent his shrimp money on booze only. When he ran out of sea stores he ate the dogs, cats and rats that ventured onto the dock at night. One morning he was sitting on the back deck, drunk and getting drunker. The captain went aft and told him to get in his bunk and sleep it off because they were leaving the dock at noon to reach dragging ground at sunset.

"He laid in his bunk and continued to drink. He did his

job OK, setting out and hauling in the first drag. He retied the trip lines on the catch bags, picked up the catch bag and heavy chafing gear, heaved it over the cap rail then walked forward and tripped the pelican hook with his foot inside of the coil of lazy line. The forward movement of the boat and the weight of the catch bag pulled a bunch of coils tight around his boot then yanked him over the cap rail into a school of twelve-foot bull sharks that were following the boat to eat the bycatch."

Snarly came down frowning. He said, "There's nobody coming in or moving around. It's black over Loggerhead. The turkey buzzards that were eating the washed up carrion on the west side of the island have taken flight then joined the osprey and the man o' war birds."

He looked at Hubbub who was surfing and said, "How's the fishless net washing coming along?"

He said, "Up yours. I wish I could get away from you!"

Snarly growled, "You can hitch a ride back to the hill and hang with the disillusioned that are determined to domesticate the descendants of dinosaurs because they believe it's roosters that are being protected while they act like velociraptors and should be reclassified as wild historic game with a five dollar bounty on 'em to feed the hungry. I don't mind the hens, they're not so mean and loud unless the cats are after the chicks."

Lead interrupted and said, "The "Jagged Snags" looks like the Ground Pounder's boat. What happened to him?"

Jolly said, "Nobody really knows what went down except Batted and Ball- Peen. Every trip he had to hire a new crew because he worked his boat as if he was still a drill sergeant in boot camp. He hired Batted as rig man and Ball-Peen as boxman. The Ground Pounder always played nasty tricks on the Boxman, like piss in his coffee, drop the nets on him when setting out and hauling back, make him sleep on the bows next to the sampson post between drags and catch fish with a hand line until noon and then kept all the fish money. When they brought him to the dock dead with a gash on top of his head and water in his lungs, they said the towing cable on one of the rigs got jammed between the towing block wheel and the block casing. It was very rough and he wanted one of them to take a crowbar out to the end of the outrigger and pry the cable back onto the wheel. They wouldn't do it so he climbed out to the towing block and fell into the doors that spread the net which knocked him out. They pulled the rig in with the cable still wedged between the wheel and casing. After checking out the towing block the police let them go."

Lead said, "I haven't seen Batted around for a few years. Have you heard anything about him?"

Jolly said, "Instead of going home after his trip with the Ground Pounder he went to a bar and picked up a girl then took her to the boat. His wife saw him do it. When he got home later too drunk to stay up he passed out in bed and then she tied him up in the bed sheets and busted up his arms and legs with a baseball bat then hauled ass. After he could walk he took a fish house boat fishing. He was boarded by the Coast Guard for a safety inspection. They found a number of violations and wrote him a bunch of tickets. He was pissed off so he twisted the officer's nose brutally. Last I heard he's still serving time for that."

Snarly said, "The Greek treated his rig man like the Ground Pounder treated his box man. He wouldn't hire a box man to help clean up and ice shrimp. The rig man had to do it all while the Greek rode his ass and messed with his mind. His last trip he hired a rig man that gave him tit for tat with the verbal abuse. The Greek went mad and chased him around the cabin with a hammer. The rig man got tired of running around the cabin, grabbed a crow bar from the shrimp boat's tool shed – the "dog house" – then jumped on the cabin roof and busted open the Greek's head when he came around the corner of the cabin."

As weather conditions grew dark and thicker at the surface, the raptors soared above the trade winds. Jolly went to the stern then gazed up through the gray mist and said, "They are flying out of sight to the northeast." The wind shifted from sow'west to west and eased up to gale force.

Lead said, "If it holds out of the west for the next eight hours, it will trade out of the northwest and ease up to twenty knots, but we're not going to be that lucky while it's going around. It's time to tie loose ends and lower the antennas."

Spiker told The Dirt to make his way to the skiff then looked at me and said, "I've got to stay on my boat until I get a call about the mules' progress through the Yucatan Straits. The last aircraft surveillance report placed them headed for the center of the depression. They might have to change course to keep the rough stuff on their bows when they enter the gulf."

I faced Snarly then said, "Now that the raptors are riding the thermals to the jet stream, whatever is coming at us is high and wide, so you can stand down from your watch until after the shit hits the fan with Mariah's revenge."

I asked Jolly how the Magician was doing. He said, "I don't see him out here anymore. He played so many tricks with the fish that he isn't allowed to board any of his boats. He let some other fishermen work the Smelta. They tried to cross Rebecka in a nor'wester with the incoming tide bucking the wind because they were out of ice to recap their load of fish. When they reached the rip, the seas were twenty feet high and ten feet apart which filled her up and washed her under. I had a dream about it before it happened so I've tried to stay stoned beyond the dreaming zone most days and nights."

Another dragger named Toughy pulled his anchor at

East Key and moved south to the east side of the fort behind the barrier reef.

Jolly said, "He works those two ninety-foot rigs by his self." He gazed at Lead then said, "You hauled his boat out when he brought it to you upside down."

Lead said, "They brought me a bunch of boats that were upside down after they crashed together dragging illegally in the nursery after the twilight zone with no lights on. Some of them were split from the cap rail to the garboard and full of water with the fuel tanks holding them just under the surface. The Toughy's mishap occurred when he was steaming down northwest channel during the ebbing tide flowing to the southeast. The dog and the dog handle on the try net drum took that moment to break loose. The try net spooled off the drum then hooked up in a gully when the towing cable came tight, spun him sideways to the ripping tide as the cable pulled the cap rail underwater filling the hull and flipping it upside down."

Jolly asked, "Did you hear about Cowboy?" We shook our heads sideways. He said, "He was found floating dead on the south side. I haven't heard the official report yet, but the scuttle-butt over the radio says two refugees chartered his boat to fish, killed him then hauled ass to Rye Lee's Hump where they were caught. They said they needed the boat to go home to Cuba, but they went west by southwest instead of south which tells me they were there to pick up a load of dope."

After a long moment of remorseful silence we cursed and screamed obnoxious obscenities. The wind ceased to a brief lull foretelling the arrival of the major mass of squalls spiking off the tropical depression from every direction spawning water spouts as it hurried off to the northeast.

As swirling winds slammed us with sheets of rain, Lead asked, "What are you doing after this blow?"

I said, "We'll be fishing around Ryle Lee's Hump while

Spiker picks up his load."

He said, "There's plenty of fish around that hump to make a trip on, but I don't go there anymore. Too many bad things can happen with ships as well as the tugs and tows that cross it. It's not safe sleeping there and it's a long haul to anywhere that you won't get crashed into. Preacher George, Marty and Denie were longlining golden tile fish south of the hump. After a hard day's fishing they went to the hump then anchored up and went to sleep. A tug passed by with a greenhorn at the wheel. He passed west of them headed south. The tide was ripping to the southeast. The tug was towing two barges. They woke up with the first barge scraping past their portside. They could see the other barge coming at them. They had just enough time to heave the skiff over the side and dive in the water as the second barge crushed the boat under. They were rescued three days later by another tug and tow.

"Captain Wesley fell overboard and was carried away by the ripping tide. Fat Boy crashed into something then sank and some divers went down there to check out the big critters, but didn't come back.

"It's also a smugglers' convention. If you are looking for adventure, you may find it there or not if they see you coming and give you something else."

We sat or walked the deck observing the adverse weather as we thought of other Murphy's Law stories to tell, but the howling wind sealed our lips. Six hours later the tropical depression swirled into the Bay of Florida and dissipated into a tropical wave. The wind held steady at thirty knots out of the west by sow'west with a clear horizon. One hour later it shifted out of the west and increased to seventy knots for thirty minutes then traded out of the northwest and laid down to twenty knots.

Everyone's anchors held except the Merry Chaos. There wasn't anyone at the helm when their anchor pulled loose.

They drifted over the barrier reef bashing their running gear all to hell then the anchor hooked into a coral head for which they received a fine for reef restoration and a heavy repair bill for new running gear while Lead and Jolly grinned like possums eating sour persimmons.

While Snarly dug up the anchor and Ruckus raised the antennas, Spiker came over and said, "I'm headed to Run Aground Point to clear customs and wash the salt scum off the plastic wrap around the paper money and bullion so the Golden Viper can haul it back to the DEA."

I said, "What happened to the morp?"

He crunched his jaws and said, "They went down north of the Yucatan Straits in a cross sea when they tried to turn westward into the Lee of Campeachee. I'll give you a call when the vipers meet behind the barn so you can stand up for Jolly."

I said, "Jolly can do his own standing. I'm taking Spit Ball fishing while you're planning our future. Just let us know when it's time to follow your gloomy influence."

He said, "Fine, I'll see you at the barn or not." He boarded his skiff, returned to his boat then cranked his engine. After it warmed up he took in most of his anchor line because the water was only two fathoms and hitched it to the sampson post then tried to pull it out of the mud with the boat. After making four three-hundred-and-sixty degree turns with the engine roaring, the anchor refused to budge. He went forward and stared down at his anchor line then called to say that he couldn't see his chain, just the rope where it disappears into the mud."

I said, "Cut the rope and put a buoy on it so we can use it for a permanent mooring. We will be grouper digging the south side on the way to the fish house, and I'll be monitoring the sixes."

Captains Lead and Jolly followed us to the south side to top off their packing boxes.

CHAPTER 13
A Short Stay in the Boondocks And Looney Bins

After unloading our catch at the fish house, I looked at Snarly and said, "I'm not taking the boat home. I don't want anyone to know we are back. Take the boat to the fuel dock and the ice house and cap everything off then tie up in a slip behind the barn near Spiker. I'm taking a cab home. I'll be back in the morning with Bone Digger. Spitball and Dog Meat may show up before me."

Snarly asked, "Who's Dog Meat?"

"He's a friend and ex-mailman that's retired from mad dogs and loose cannons."

The cabby turned onto the government road then increased his speed to forty miles an hour through the jungle then took the turn to the west with his tires squealing and plowed into a flock of wild fighting cocks pecking at squashed lizards. The cab arrived at the boundary spattered with blood and feathers flying then let me out. The big birds were taking off from the Naval Air Station while the huge parrots in a cage next door imitated the shrill wine of the after burners.

Bone Digger came from behind the house and did pogo hops around me. The lady next door came out with her young son who was bent over and holding his rib cage. As they headed for their car I asked if I could help. She said, "No, he just needs some Lidocane for his busted rib because he thought it was OK to sucker punch Bayle Bruiser."

The Dinosaur stuck his head out of the door and smiled. Up until then it felt good to be home. As I entered the living room he said, "You have a lot of messages."

I asked, "Are any of them from lawyers or government personnel?"

He said, "No, they're mostly chuckles or apologies related to your greeting."

I said, "Bone Digger looks good and happy, thanks. Pretend I'm not here and go on about your bad self then roll me four hundred joints and put them in two bags."

Some draggers raced past the house headed for the crash and burn zone. I smoked a joint in bed then crashed into the zero zygotic zone without burning but well baked. I woke up from a brief dream of squally weather to the squawking and crowing of roosters fighting over hens before dawn. The Dinosaur placed a cup of strong espresso with heavy cream and brown sugar on the table while I brushed my teeth and lit a joint. After chugging the coffee I stuffed a bag of joints in each pocket then removed Bone Digger's leash from its hook. She pogoed about the room making me wait until her excitement settled down to wriggling so I could leash her then get her in the Dinosaur's truck. As we raced through the jungle we passed a pack of mangy mixed breed dogs chasing fighting cocks. Some of them carried large iguanas in their jaws dripping gore. On the way to the barn I noticed that most of the local commercial enterprises had a flock of chickens hanging out or digging up the grass around their parking lots. The only exceptions were the Quick Fried Chick stores. I suppose the roosters could smell their kinship boiling in hot grease and crowed for the hens to move up wind.

The Dinosaur stopped his truck at the stern of the boat. The dog and I stepped out. As he put it in gear to drive off, I said, "Park it at the end of the barn. I need you to make me some chum dough that will stay together and reach the bottom in fifty fathoms."

We boarded the boat then opened the galley door to the aroma of bacon and bucci. Spiker was sitting at the table with an expression of ruin on his face. I said, "Spit it out harbinger."

He said, "My engine won't crank for more than two seconds, then shuts off. When I was running the north side I hit something that bent my prop all to hell. The boat vibrates so bad that the spice bottles jump out of the rack. I've ordered a new prop from Miami. It will be here tomorrow afternoon."

I said, "If you are going to be balderdashing through Alexander's graveyard, you need the proper chart and a plotter for your semi-useless autopilot."

The Dinosaur returned from the bait and tackle store with a dozen fresh mullet and ran them through the grinder then mixed the ground flesh with silica sand to the consistency of firm dough. He put the tub in the stern packing box then went to the all-you-can-eat restaurant. Spitball and Dog Meat joined us for breakfast. Spiker asked Spitball if he could look at his engine?

"No way," he said, "It's my birthday and I want to catch a big grouper. Besides, I don't service or carry parts for Allison's. What's it doing?"

"It cranks then shuts off."

Spitball laughed then said, "Change your fuel filters and pull your injector screens then throw them in the trash. Don't bother cleaning 'em, you'll just make 'em worse because they're already ruined. "Crank" will open his shop at eight o'clock. He can sell you a set of screens. If you are going to be burning fuel around the Bahamas and the Caribbean islands you should buy a spare set."

As the light of dawn filled the hollows creating shadows an antique Rolls Royce followed by a nondescript armored vehicle turned onto the long road behind the barn. Spiker stood up then went to his stern. Three tall, elderly gentlemen with straight backs stepped out of the Rolls. The history of their achievements and their capabilities on the river are legends held in the upmost of respect while the expressions on their faces demanded it. One carried a satchel of paperwork for Spiker to sign. The others carried boxes of tricks for The Dirt to use on his scams.

As they boarded Spiker's boat, a four-man team of armed guards stepped out of their vehicles and loaded the million in hundred-dollar bills and one million in bullion into a safe in the back of their vehicle, leaving the other three million in bullion for The Dirt to set things in motion with the cartels. Fairel stuck his head out of his galley door in his slip next to Spiker, saw what was going down then quickly closed it.

I cranked the engines. After they warmed up I nodded at Snarly who cast off the dock lines. We headed south around Run Aground Point into Hawks Channel where I changed course to the west by sow'west for the fifthy-fathom rock pile, the home of massive warsaw groupers. As we skipped over the short choppy seas to our destination, Snarly removed the black grouper rigs from the one-armed bandits then attached leaders with ten hooks to the spreaders. He took four five-pound boxes of squid out of the freezer then put them in five-gallon buckets to thaw out.

Spitball asked, "How many warsaws can we keep?"

Instead of simply saying "One," I tried his patience by saying, "We can't do what we did thirty years ago when we brought young Black Heart with us to learn the ropes. They will lock us up as pirates and poachers. As I recall we hooked forty warsaws and boated twenty-two of them. Eighteen of them busted the three hundred and eighty-pound test wire leaders, but that was a good thing because the fish house only wanted the two- and three-hundred pounders and we didn't have room for a mess of five- or six-hundred pounders."

Spitball took the joint I was smoking from my fingers, sucked and slobbered on it then handed it back and asked, "How many?"

I tore off the wet end of the joint and threw it on the deck then puffed on the stub as I said, "Only one."

He asked, "What are you all going to eat?"

I said, "I'm allowed to catch all I can haul of other groupers. You can have the warsaw if you can catch it. There's two ways you can play him. You can put down one of the bandits with a large trash fish on it and hook one up within an hour, but he might be small, between a hundred and fifty to three hundred pounds. Or you can work the bandits catching yellow-eye snappers to pay the expenses for the trip. By the time it takes to put the stink of twenty pounds of squid on the bottom, you will chum up some of the five and six hundred pounders that hang out in sixty or seventy fathoms. Then you put down the big trash fish with an eight hundred pound leader on the bandit cable. There is also a landing law on the one warsaw."

Spitball chuckled then asked, "Does that mean I can catch and boat it, but not land it"

I said, "Precisely."

He reached for the stub of the joint so he could ruin that, too. I pulled my hand out of his reach. He pulled one from his shirt pocket then fired it up and asked, "So, what am I supposed to do with it? A five hundred pound grouper isn't going to fit on your boat grill?"

I said, "It can't be landed whole. It must be cut into

fillets then landed with the carcass."

He asked, "Why?"

I said, "So you can't sell it whole to a fish house. It's against the law. Conditions should be good when we get there. We are going to arrive at the end of the ebbing tide flowing to the southeast. This northwest wind has the gulfstream pushed off the rock pile far to the south which will create a lull in the incoming tide for six hours because it will be crashing into the south side of the gulfstream. The fishing is always best during the lull."

I focused on Snarly and said, "Use one strand of three hundred and sixty-five pound test line on the trip for the braced grapnel and play out five hundred feet of line when I tell you to drop it. The Magician put his grapnel down here when the stream was ripping on top of the rock pile during a south wind without a trip. He had to pull so hard on it that he broke two welds on the braces and bent the hooks, but before the welds broke he stretched the anchor chain so tight that each link in the chain was locked together as if they were welded, and it came up stiff as a construction rod. He cut it into four pieces, set them in concrete and mounted his mailbox on 'em."

When we were southeast of the rock pile I slowed down and changed course to the northwest, crossed the rocks to three hundred feet, then shifted into reverse, stopping the boat. Then I nodded to Snarly who lowered the anchor as the wind pushed us to the southeast over the rocks. The line came tight and we laid with the wind at the highest peak of rocks that stood seven fathoms off the bottom. The fish finder showed a large school of yellow-eye snappers with other larger fish scattered around the seamount and the reef that extends to the west.

While the five man crew took turns working the bandits, I put half a herring on my grouper hand line, wrapped a pancake of chum dough around it then sent it to the bottom. The mullet chum dough was so dense that I had to jerk the line to pull the herring out of it. A twenty-five pound red snapper ate it a few seconds later. While the crew pulled yellow-eyes, I pulled gag groupers along with cuberas mixed with the red snappers. Every now and then a large fish grabbed a snapper from the bottom hook on the bandit rigs.

By eleven o'clock the eight hundred pound chill barrel was full of mixed snapper and grouper. Suddenly a very large fish got hooked on the snapper rig. It bent the Kevlar leaf spring to its limit then pulled some cable off the spool with the drag set at a hundred and fifty pounds before it pulled loose from the hook. When Spitball cranked the rig to the surface it held seven snappers. Hooks number eight, nine and ten were fishless and bent.

I said, "That was your fish. He's still hungry and looking for something big to eat." I handed Spitball an eight hundred pound leader with an adequate hook. He removed the snapper rig from the spreader then attached the leader. I handed him a ten-pound almaco jack with the tail and part of the backbone removed. He stuck the hook through both lips then sent it to the bottom. Yellow-eye snappers began ripping chunks of flesh and skin from the jack. The Kevlar leaf spring stopped bouncing up and down then bent to its breaking point as the grouper inhaled the jack and hooked itself. Realizing it was in trouble, it headed for deeper water, pulling the cable from the bandit spool.

Spitball tightened the drag which slowed the fish causing it to swim in a circle as he cranked hard on the bandit to raise the fish off the bottom. The grouper fought with all its strength for the first hundred feet because its angle of ascent was too straight and it was being pulled through the pressure changes too fast. The quick release of pressure on the air bladder caused the compressed air it contained to expand into the stomach cavity forcing the stomach to balloon into the grouper's mouth as it rose to the surface quickly.

With no bend in the leaf spring and no strain on the cable, Spitball said, "He got off the hook."

I said, "Engage the motor and take up the slack. The fish is dead and rising faster than you are hand cranking." The fish broke the surface belly up fifty feet from the boat. Snarly and Spitball hooked gaffs in the grouper's lips then pulled him aboard.

I said, "Let's head for the barn and have lunch before we clean these fish. Put the grouper in the chill water." Hubbub measured the length and girth of the fish and guesstimated its weight at four hundred and sixty-five pounds.

When we arrived at the barn I noticed that Spiker had eighteen fifty-five gallon drums in the middle of his back deck. He was cursing and windmilling his arms in the air at Jolly, who had his face twisted into a nuclear meltdown. While the crew fried fish sandwiches Captain Lead left the hullabaloo between Spiker and Jolly then boarded our boat.

Snarly asked, "What are they yelling about?"

Lead said, "Spiker wants to carry enough fuel to do his tricks in the Caribbean without refueling anywhere except Great Inagua. On his way there he's going to pump the fuel from the drums into his main tanks after he's burned off enough then refill the empties before he heads to his next way point. He's trying to secure the drums in the middle of his deck with half-inch eye bolts through his gunwales and some Mickey Mouse straps with flimsy quarter-inch S-hooks.

"Jolly's in a rage because he's only happy with the half-inch eye bolts. He explained to Spiker that it's going to be a pain in the rectums trying to load the boat while climbing over a series of straps, and rough weather is going to bend the S-hooks then all the drums are going to helter-skelter."

Then he said, "Most everything you have done here is totally 'crowmag' thinking being executed by a stoned maladroit too many tokes over the line."

Then he said, "Put some one-inch line through the half-inch eye bolts and lash the drums to the bulwarks."

Spiker agreed to do it, but not without an eruption of hyperbole about who was giving orders.

Snarly said, "Aye, he tends to motor mouth a bit. We have dogs, we have dogma, but in Spiker's case we have dogmatism which is usually about as heart-warming as a pile of dog shit. However, it isn't a trait disturbance that can't be corrected with the help of a surgical hole-saw and some snippers. Or, you could approach his problem genetically, but don't look for hope."

Whenever we are in port, we put a gallon tin of tobacco and a case of rolling papers on the galley table. Snarly reached into the case, but it was empty of papers. To get out of cleaning fish he said, "I'm calling a cab and going to the head shop for a case of papers."

Dog Meat pulled out his keys and said, "Take my Vette."

Snarly said, "I'm not allowed to drive. Why not ask Dog Meat?"

Snarly growled, "Well, if I tell you the truth you might make some dogmatic statement about it that will force me to stuff you in a garbage can like the road whores did to me on the waterfront."

Seeing that he was a few tokes short of sanity, Dog Meat lit a joint then passed it to Snarly and said, "I'll be right back, don't call a cab, I could use a case of papers myself!"

While we cleaned and washed fish, Spiker and Jolly came over to look at Spitball's big grouper. Dog Meat returned with papers and Snarly gave him a large bag of fillets for his kindness. After cleaning up the boat and loading the fish on the Dinosaur's truck for market, we all walked to the tackle shop and sat on the patio. As we sipped cold beer, a fifty foot Viking throwing a six foot wake came in from the southeast and anchored south of Run Aground Point.

A minute later a call was made to the dockmaster's office. As the dockmaster answered the call, the U.S. Customs agent on duty to clear boats listened. The captain of the Viking wanted to know if there was a slip for rent in the marina. The dockmaster wrote up the paperwork and told the captain to pay at the office.

Then the captain did something extremely stupid. He defied the first rule of Murphy's Law, which is, put everything back in its place if you want it to function properly. Instead of hanging the mic on the radio he threw it on the console between the bulkhead and a case of Twinkies which rekeyed the mic. Then he said to his crew, "Break out that open bag of coke and let's snort some rails before we unload these bales of kilos."

The dockmaster came out of his office, looked at us, pointed at the Viking and said, "Watch this!"

A few minutes later the Viking was surrounded by boats and helicopters from all the local and government agencies. As we sat around the tackle shop watching the action, the fish doctor came in and tied up to the fuel dock for gas and oil. Then he motored around the south side of the barn to the public boat ramp to put his boat on its trailer. Two minutes later he came back, retied his boat up then jumped on the dock and sat at the table. The dockmaster walked over and asked him if he was all right because he was shaking.

He said, "There's a truck and trailer in the haul out and some guy trying to pull his boat up on the trailer, but it's stuck half way. It's too heavy and there's a plastic bale strap laying on his deck. His coffin box and his saddle boxes are full of something. One of the saddle boxes wasn't quite closed and I could see hot pink plastic wrap with white bands around it. It wasn't life jackets!"

The dockmaster stepped into his office. A minute later two boats left the crime scene at the Viking and raced to the haul out while local law enforcement blocked the exits from the marina. As it turned out, the load of coke on the small boat was fifteen hundred pounds heavier than the load on the big boat.

As a crowd of fishermen, local spectators and worried junkies gathered on the south side then flowed towards the tackle shop, Spiker stood up and said, "Let's go to my boat."

Upon entering his galley, Spiker said, "After I put the new prop on tomorrow afternoon I'm going to get some sleep, then leave at dawn the next morning. Our first waypoint from Great Inagua will be Pig Boat Shoals to pick up an air drop of five hundred kilos then put it aboard a cutter on standby when we shoot the windward passage on our way to the graveyard."

Lead stood up then said, "That's totally T.M.I. I'm going over to the reservation and find me a quiet squaw that likes to fish."

To prevent his friend from leaving, Snarly said, "Jolly told us you already have a new girlfriend."

Lead stared at the deck then said, "She doesn't like to fish so we haven't had sex yet, and I'm sure it's not going to happen."

To pry and try his patience, Snarly asked, "Why not?"

Not wanting to disappoint Snarly, he said, "After two days of conversation and observation I'm reasonably convinced that she's a bipolar Russian defector from something I couldn't understand and she suffers from a series of witless and alternating personalities that are caused by a handful of different kinds of pills she washes down with a case of beer while she burns up half an ounce of skunk weed."

As Lead reached for the door in pursuit of his fisher girl,

Fishing the Devil's Triangle...

I realized I had a day off from Spiker's demented hobgoblin hobby so I asked him what he was doing tomorrow.

He smiled then said, "I brought back a load of trash fish for the crocodiles. I'm going to haul them to ambush point in my bait skiff at dawn. My blue crab traps should be full. We can steam the big males and let the bitches go."

I said, "I'll see you there." I gazed at Spiker then asked, "Have you paid any attention to the weather?"

"Indeed I have. There's a tropical wave coming up the channel honking twenty-five to thirty and I'm going right through the middle of it where nobody can see me from the north or south. It's going to be too rough to pull my lobster traps south of Cay Sal on the edge of Nelson's Channel, but I would like to haul one for something to eat."

I said, "Well, you can run down the middle and get your ass kicked by the roguish waves in that deep water when the ebbing tide is bucking the wind and jamming them together eighteen feet high, but only ten feet apart. I'm going to haul ass across the stream and go on station at Dog Rocks. I've got a taste for a big bright orange dog snapper which are rare on this side of the stream, and I would like to eat my lunch somewhere it will stay on the table instead of flying into the galley sink. You can call me there after you pull your trap."

I smiled at the Rug Rats then said, "Enjoy your night and day off, but be aboard at dusk tomorrow night."

The Dirt looked at me then asked, "Cang jew take me fishing wheng dees messes are ober?"

Snarly intruded by saying, "If we take someone fishing they only have four options. Unfortunately you can't qualify for any of them."

The Dirt asked, "What's dees oxshuns?"

Snarly growled, "Fish, cut bait, sink or swim, we like to keep things simple. You don't know how to fish so you've never cut bait. You are hauling around too much butter so you can't sink even in rough weather and you will be bobbing so high on the surface with all that greasy fat you won't be able to reach the water with your arms. The best you will do is turn on your side and dog paddle with one arm which will only turn you three hundred and sixty degrees. There's a chance that might be helpful in locating something to crawl onto."

Spiker's landline rang. He picked up the cordless receiver and said, "Hello." A moment later he said, "I don't have any on board. I've got to clear customs tomorrow." Then he put the receiver back on its cradle upside down.

Snarly asked "Who was that?"

"It was Fairel," Spiker whined, "wanting some of my weed. Pass me that joint."

Fairel stuck his head out of his galley door and screamed, "Hang up your phone you lying bastard!"

Snarly frowned then said, "You should thank yourself and humanity for the fact that fuck ups never cease."

Spiker grumbled, "Why should I be thankful for that?"

Snarly muttered, "Because you wouldn't have anything to do except go fishing and hurt yourself, which is all I want to do, but with the hurting part on the other end of the string."

I chalked it up as another day in the Looney Bins of the insane last city. The Rug Rats cut out for the 'off the wall' bars. I try not to enter any doors except my own. I took a cab home and got the backcountry skiff ready to go at dawn. I stuffed my face on and off until six o'clock then I stoned myself into a twelve hour void. I woke to the essence of strongly brewed and condensed espresso doctored with heavy cream and brown sugar. The Dinosaur shuffled over with a sweet roll which I inhaled. I asked how things were in the park.

He said, "Mostly quiet except jets and draggers. Every now and then some crazy fucking shit goes down with the drunks and cheating wives that thought their husbands were out fishing. Once in awhile a wild dog or iguanas and roosters hop the fence and put Bone Digger into a snarly rage, so there aren't many dull moments with the boom boxers in between."

I walked down the hall sipping the hot coffee and puffing on a joint. Bone Digger wiggled past me then pogoed to the back door. I opened it and she ran to the floating dock then jumped in the skiff. I closed the door then turned off the very bright night light. I like to see whoever I might be shooting at before I work the action which lets them know that I am there and gives them a moment to get the fuck out of Dodge or make a bad move and suffer the consequences.

I cranked the skiff and headed south into Hawks Channel then changed course to the east until I was south of ambush point. I headed north to the apex. The point looked like any other arm of land and mangrove jungle extending off of lower U.S. 1. I put on my slicker with the hood over my head. I located the very small area of the bottom that didn't have any mangrove roots growing out of it. Only interlacing limbs covered the entrance. I told Bone Digger to go to the bow and lay down. I bent my head down then slowly motored through the limbs. About twenty feet in the limbs thinned out and revealed a small lagoon with mossy banks. To my right there was a white sign nailed to a four-by-four post driven into the ground to warn off nosey kayakers. The lettering was professionally applied with black cherry paint dripping red blood at the corners and curves. It said, 'Fuck Off Ass Wipe or Deal with a Dirty Ass Hole.'

At the northwest curve of the lagoon three saltwater crocodiles twelve to fourteen feet were laying in their slides. Only half grown, they looked fat and formidable. I looked in the water, and a school of mangrove snappers rose to the

192

surface. On the east side of the emerald green basin there was a twenty-by-fifty feet long platform built five feet off the ground with steps on hinges that could be raised with a rope to keep the crocs from climbing up. On the west end of the platform was a smaller platform with a table and chair. Sitting at the table was a young foxy squaw. She was gazing over the top of the mangroves to the southwest at the point, doing her job to see if I was followed. Lead was sitting next to his camp stove staring into a fish box that contained two dozen colossal male blue crabs.

Bone Digger jumped from the skiff and raced to the smaller platform then wiggled her body while wagging her tail at the squaw who began petting her vigorously. I climbed up the steps and sat not too close to Lead because of what he was about to do.

I noticed there were two dead roosters laying on the picnic table. I asked, "Why are you killing your roosters?" which is something I've never known him to do.

He said, "Got too many of 'em. Those two noisy bastards came too close to the house then woke the squaw up before dawn and ruined her beauty sleep, so I made some more noise when I shot 'em through the head with plastic pointed lead pellets then watched them hip hop and flip flop all over the back yard squirting their blood everywhere. After crabs, she's going to pluck 'em then boil us up a big pot of barley rooster soup."

As he reached into the fish box with a long set of tongs and clamped them around a crab from behind, I asked, "What's her name?"

He removed the massive crab from the box and held it on the deck between his feet then said, "Her birth name was "Fire on the Water," but she has come of age and is allowed to change it."

He placed the point of a fillet knife on the crab's shell just behind the eyes. The crab grabbed the blade in its claws.

He said, "Now she calls herself "Nine Moons."

He pushed the knife through the crab's shell. It quivered then died. He broke off its claws then laid them on a table to his left that had a rubber hammer on it. He ripped off the shell then threw it in the lagoon. Huge snappers charged the shell to eat the soft matter inside.

I asked, "Did she say why she chose such an introspective and uncompromising dock handle?"

He tore off the bottom half of the crab's face, pulled off the dead man, scooped out the guts, broke off the dick then heaved the mess at the fish then said, "Last night when we met by the creek we talked for three hours. She confessed at the end of our talk that she would like to have an annual relationship with me if she could take a three-month vacation."

To his right sat two large pots. One was topped with seawater. As he washed the crab and tossed it into the empty pot, he said, "I thought about it for a minute then agreed if she could take her leave during the spawning season when I don't like to fish."

While he removed another crab from the box, Nine Moons came down with Bone Digger. She took a heavy spinning rod from its rack and grabbed some chunks of squid from the trash fish cooler, baited her hook and quickly yanked and cranked three large snappers onto the platform. I could see that Lead was impressed. He said, "She's a meat fisherman, no sporty hook and release about her."

After cleaning the last crab, Lead kicked the box aside then picked up the table with the claws and sat it in front of his knees. He picked up the rubber hammer then lightly cracked each claw. As he did so, Nine Moons asked if she could help. He said, "Aye, loving help offered without a ruse is always appreciated. Bring me the fresh basil, oregano and minced garlic. Put a stick of butter in a sauce pan then melt

194

it slowly. Pour three cups of white wine and one-third cup of olive oil in another pan and warm it up until it is making vapors."

She placed the herbs on the table. He said, "Thank you Three Moons."

I asked, "Did she change her name again with sign language when I wasn't looking, which I don't remember."

He said, "No, but she's no dummy. She wants to spend her first vacation with me then get married on the fourth moon. In the meantime she wishes to be addressed in the proper lunar phase."

As he chopped the herbs he said, "She confessed that she wasn't too hot about fooling around and wanted some time to warm up because in her heart she was still "Fire on the Water."

I said, "She's a beautiful mystery."

He poured the butter over the crabs, sprinkled on the herbs then poured the hot wine and oil over the crabs. As he set the crabs on the fire he said, "All women are a mystery. They are the only thing on earth that can create a man. Most men don't know that they are 99.99.99 percent woman because dicks lead the blind. I don't know anything about the mysterious existence in the universe that blessed them with such a profound capability, but after reading history and living a little bit of life on land it seems they were also damned with it by the brutality of their creation. That's why I'm going to hang out here or ride out the hurricanes on the boat at the marina. The galley is stocked if we have to leave."

Three Moons emerged from their eighteen-man tent with a large box of assorted colorful talismans and went about hanging them on the limbs of the four towering black buttonwood trees that the platform was built around to hide it from the air and shade his surroundings.

I said, "There seems to be a lot of iguanas hanging out."

He said, "Yep, but they will scatter when I shoot the one

that's climbing up the back side of this tree we're sitting under. I don't want to shoot it, but I know it's going to be tasty. I like mine slow grilled with garlic rub, and it's going to make me pull the trigger."

I asked, "Why don't you want to shoot it?"

He said, "I've got plenty of other things to eat, but I'll put it on ice until I don't."

So I asked, "Why is it going to make you shoot it?"

He said, "Because it's arrogant and on its way to spoil our fun. It doesn't want us here. When it reaches the limb over us it's going to walk out above us and leave a crap on the table or us."

As the iguana headed our way Lead picked up his pellet gun and put one through its head. It fell on deck and he put it in a cooler. The other iguanas disappeared into the jungle. As they did so, Lead said, "They are also stupid with short-term memories. They always come back."

While the crabs steamed, Lead boiled a pot of angel hair and placed two bowls on the table. He put the angel hair in the bowls then poured the juices from the steaming crabs onto it. As we gorged on such a rare treat, Three Moons sat at the table with a power shake in one hand and an apple with an orange in the other. She confessed that the scavengers smelled delicious, but there was no track to run off the fat, which told me she hadn't been influenced by Black Heart.

After eating I told Lead that I liked his pets, climbed into the skiff with Bone Digger then pushed back through the mangroves into reality. When we pulled up to the dock, the Rug Rats were camping in the yard and trashing it so the Dinosaur would have something to do.

I said, "Get some rest. We are leaving for Dog Rocks in the twilight zone."

CHAPTER 14:
The Old Bahama Channel And the Puerto Rican Trench

We boarded the boat as the earth turned to the east in its northern quadrant and the edge of the sun touched the horizon to the west by sow'west. I unlocked the galley then went to the console and cranked the engines. The galley table and benches were stacked with boxes of sea stores. I gave the brats a hard look then walked to Spiker's boat. As I stepped aboard, a nondescript vehicle displaying a decal proclaiming the driver was a special agent for the sneak and peak investigative service from South Miami stopped at my boat and got out. He asked Snarly if he could board the boat. Snarly waved him aboard then offered him the stool freshly misted because he always expected interference before departure.

The Dirt and Jolly were sipping Crown Royal and lounging in fold-up beach chairs between the fuel drums. Spiker came out of his galley and said, "What's up?"

I said, "You need to get on your sideband and let your

home boys in the Bahamas know that we will be fishing Dog Rocks until late tomorrow morning catching fish for the Black Mamba. After you have crossed the stream and the tropical wave is kicking your ass in Nelson's Channel, we will be trolling the banks all the way to Great Inagua unless something unexpected happens. Give me a call when you are south of us.

"There's a private dick on my boat. What's that all about?"

"Don't know," he says, "I just got off the radio with the wife." He looked at Jolly and asked, "Has Sticker got someone watching you?"

Jolly curled his lips in a growl then said, "Most likely, she wants to stay stuck to me because she thinks we're road whoring."

I said, "See ya!" As I stepped on the dock the snoop rushed out of my galley and into his car with an irritated look on his face. I stepped aboard then twirled my left index finger above my head. The Rug Rats threw off the dock lines. I steered the boat around the barn and Run Aground Point then put her on a course to Dog Rocks. We skipped across the stream, dropped the anchor then began fishing the bandits. The water was calm, only ripples of current showing. There weren't any stars on the horizon to the southeast, foretelling a stormy sunrise.

The fishing was nonstop action which told me Dog Rocks was rarely worked on a commercial level. We quickly filled an eight-hundred pound chill barrel with mixed snappers and groupers. I told the Rug Rats to forget about gutting the fish.

"People on this side of the stream wash them then make fish tea soup out of what's left. Be sure to ice the fish heavy. The tropical wave that's coming at us may turn into a depression forcing us to seek shelter. Get some rest after you are finished, I'll stand watch until you've got to face your beating when Spiker calls."

I climbed to the flying bridge and smoked a joint to ease potential hostility and pain. There was ship traffic east and west of us moving north and south. Further to the east there was an unmoving light on the southwest corner of the bank. Maybe a local fisherman. There were no other lights on my side of the horizon to the southeast, but that didn't mean there wasn't something waiting now because Spiker would be crossing the stream.

The sky above shined bright with starlight. As the early morning hours wore away, the starlight faded into a misty gray shroud. The dawn came with gusty winds and swirling rain.

The Rug Rats recovered from their THC void to make bucci and breakfast while they passed a joint to get the munchies. I ignored my slime and grime to eat first then wash later.

After eating we pulled the anchor then put her on a course to the southwest corner of the bank. While the Rug Rats took turns working spoons on the bandits and helm, I went below to rest and wait for Spiker's call. I didn't bother to clean up because I was headed for a saltwater bath. The wind held steady at twenty knots standing up a three-to-five-foot chop. After spinning the spoons for four hours at eight knots I went on deck to see the catch. There were two yellowfin tuna in the forty pound range along with large dorado, kingfish, wahoo and cudas.

By now we could see the west end of the bank through the binoculars. Anchored on the bank in twenty feet of water was a house boat about fifty feet long and thirty feet wide. The poop deck of the boat was fenced off with animal pens lashed to it that contained pigs, goats and chickens. The stern half of the lower deck was open to the elements. The work area held packing boxes, tackle bins and eight brown men unloading a long boat lashed to her starboard side. The men were putting lobsters in live wells and splitting fish to be salted. We anchored the boat about fifty yards from the fishermen to wait for Spiker's call. While the Rug Rats were preparing lunch, some women came out of the forward half of their sea home with bowls of food for the men to eat. While we chewed grouper sandwiches and smoked weed.

Snarly asked if he could put the bait skiff over the side and go buy some lobsters. With only a three foot chop on top of the bank, I said, "Sure, get a dozen. Take those four cudas and that kingfish with you. Try to trade them for a six pack of Beck's beer to wash down the lobsters."

Soon after Snarly's return the eight fishermen jumped into the long boat. The captain sat at the stern and cranked his engine. He wasn't wearing any gear. The other seven fishermen were standing, facing forward with their hands on the shoulders of the man in front.

Each man had a catch bag, tickle stick, dip net and a triple banded speargun belted to their bodies. The captain threw off the stern line while the first standing threw off the bow line. The captain maneuvered the boat to the northwest two-hundred yards then slowed down and put the boat in a three-hundred and sixty degree turn. One after the other four divers dove on the coral patch. The boat raced eastward to a large sandy area surrounded by turtle grass. The divers jumped in then began putting queen and roller conchs in their catch bags. The captain tossed his anchor then leaned back in his chair and lit a long spliff of gunja. After choking on it he took another toke then opened a beer and gnawed on a conch. By the time he finished his meal and smoke I could see the conch divers waving their arms. He pulled his anchor and motored over then threw them three lines to tie around their catch bag handles. He went back to his seat. After the conch divers pulled in their catch he motored over to the other divers.

Jolly called on the side band. I laid down the binoculars then keyed the mic and asked him where he was. He said, "I'm south of Cay Sal laying side-to with the ebbing tide bucking the wind pushing this eight-foot chop close together and rattling my brains."

I asked, "You got more than one brain?"

He said, "Right now I could use three. The other two I'm working with are derailed."

I asked, "Is Spiker hurt?"

He said, "Not physically, but The Dirt's got a knot the size of a goose egg between his eyes."

I asked, "Did he piss you off already?"

He said, "Not yet. When we crossed over the stream Spiker made him get up and pull a lobster trap. He hooked the float and put the line in the snatch block as Spiker put the boat in reverse to stop it. At the same time the port stern slid into the trough and the prop picked up the line. The float jammed in the snatch block, the davit swung ninety degrees then the snatch block whacked him in the forehead."

"I asked, "What's Spiker doing?"

He laughed then said, "He's over the side cutting rope out of the prop and getting his hard head banged by this rocking and rolling bath tub. When he gets back in the boat he wants me to run south to the stream where the wind is blowing with the current and the waves are further apart. He doesn't care that it's going to take five knots off our progress forward which is half of what we are gaining now and he won't care about the freshwater he's going to waste taking a bath. I'll keep in touch, he's coming aboard."

We pulled the anchor, motored off the bank, put out the spoons and put her on a course to a small island of sand south of the Ragged Islands on the edge of the channel. There was usually a one-room shack with a coconut palm on it. Sometimes not because of hurricanes. As we trolled to the east we caught more tunas, mackerels and 'cudas. By the time we reached Santa Domingo the sun was touching the horizon to the west. I made a port turn to the north around the east side of the island to the northwest corner then anchored in the calm waters of the lee.

I told the Rugrats to rest and cook fish sandwiches. After chow, I said, "If we don't hear from Spiker at daylight, we'll run north and look over the fishery east of the Ragged Islands. The west side is mostly shallows and sand for miles, but the east side drops off fast and deep. Should be interesting, lots of big fish close to shore. Draw straws for the watch. If you see any lights to the north it will be Spiker's home boys and some of them won't be showing a light bigger than a cigarette, so don't be shooting at any red dots. They fish without a light because it draws predators."

I smoked myself into a dreamless sleep then awoke at dawn to the smell of bacon and bucci. While Snarly rolled joints, Ruckus put breakfast on the table and Hubbub came down from the flying bridge.

Shortly after eating I called Spiker. Jolly answered saying, "I need both hands to fight this wheel. I've lost the stream and the tide's bucking the wind that's increasing. Spiker and The Dirt are laying on the deck moaning and gagging with empty stomachs. Call me back if you need help."

I said, "That's a ten-four, I'll be on stand by for your SOS."

I puffed on a joint and cranked the engines. When their temperatures were up I twirled my finger and the anchor was pulled aboard. We headed north to the southernmost point of a long string of massive boulders that stretched over the horizon. The Ragged Islands. As we approached the first boulder the fish finder was showing schools of fish everywhere we turned.

I looked up at the top of the bluff before us. There was

a bare area of rock free of moss. I gazed at it through the binoculars. It appeared to be speckled gray and white granite. I wondered about the tectonic force that stood them there for all to see. They were too far west of the Mid-Atlantic Ridge nor did they seem to be volcanic. Perhaps they came smoldering down from above. Hurled here by a prodigious asteroid that entered the atmosphere from the southeast and exploded; blasting out the Gulf of Mexico, destroying most of Central America. Washing out the Puerto Rican Trench. Shaking loose the Baja Peninsula. Breaking away South America forming the Caribbean Sea. Leaving a divided erupting continent and the islands that were left behind scorched and blistered into an almost complete extinction, creating the brief reign of the dominant ground hogs that primates evolved from, which may explain why some primates are genetically and hereditarily overly piggish. Such a theory may shed some light on other mysteries.

Snarly wanted to fish. I said, "You will upset the local fishermen who own these fish." I put her on a course to the channel. The Rug Rats went to the bandits.

I punched the ON button to the autopilot, went aft then said, "We've got plenty of fish for the Mambas gang, unless you want to play at hook and release."

Snarly climbed to the flying bridge with the binoculars. Hubbub went to sleep. Ruckus put the covers on the bandits then joined me in the galley. I tossed him a bag of joints then said, "Help yourself." He put some in his coveralls, then lit one and passed it.

I said, "The NOAA says conditions are not favorable for development with this wave and the winds are going to stay at twenty-five knots out of the southeast. Spiker's not making more than five knots. At that rate he won't be south of Great Inagua until day after tomorrow. A hundred miles or so to the east there is a container ship laying on its starboard side against a sandbar. I'm going to kick her speed up to thirty knots. It will be a three and a half hour run so smoke all you want. The ebbing tide is in its final hour so conditions should be getting better for Jolly. I expect a call from him during the lull."

I put the boat on a plane, skipping across the shallows to the wreckage. A few minutes later I received a call from Jolly announcing that he had lost Spiker sometime in the last thirty minutes.

I asked, "What was he doing?"

He said, "He got up from his debilitating delirium then said he was going to the back deck to pump fuel from the drums into the main tank and he wanted me to slow down. I told him I couldn't slow down or speed up because she falls off to port or starboard at more or less than five knots. He twisted his face into a snarl and jerked the throttle back then went out of the galley and opened the port Bomar deck hatch cover. That's the last I saw of him because I had to increase her speed to bring her back on course to take the next wave on her stem and she was slow in responding to the helm so I took the next wave on her port bow which caused her to roll hard to starboard. I heard the hatch cover slam shut. I continued on course thinking he was pumping fuel. I told The Dirt to crawl to the galley door and see if he was back there but he wasn't.

"I'm going to try and turn around without rolling over. The waves on this deepwater are the largest I've ever seen in a twenty-five knot blow. I'm glad this doesn't happen around the fort and I hope I can find Spiker."

I said, "Don't bother to turn around. Have the seas layed down enough for you to lay side-to without broaching? That's a ten-four."

Then he asked, "Why would I want to do that?"

I said, "Because this isn't the first time somebody thought they lost Spiker."

A minute later he said, "I'm laying to, where is he?"

I said, "From what little evidence you have given me, my experienced guess would be, he's laying on his engine room deck with a big knot on top of his head caused by the slamming hatch cover. He was going down there to crank his generator so he could plug in his one-ten fuel pump. Go see if he's breathing then come back and let me know his condition."

Moments later he said, "He's down there and breathing well. What should I do?"

I asked, "Is he bleeding bad?"

He said, "No, it's stopped, but there's a large red ring around the top of his head with a huge purple knot in the center with a shallow cur across it. It's as big as the one The Dirt's wearing between his eyes. They both look like aliens from different planets in the cone head galaxy. I've got to make The Dirt get up and help me get him in a bunk."

I said, "Heave a deck bucket of seawater on him and make him climb out hisself. I'm headed for shelter behind the ruined derelict. Spiker knows where it is, tell him to call me when he's up and moving about."

We reached the unlit hulk at dusk. The wind was holding steady at twenty knots from the southeast. Snarly went below and came up with his thirty pound spinning buggy whip and said, "The last time we were here diving for lobsters there was big snook stacked up like cordwood around the wreck. I'd like to catch one for dinner."

I said, "Good luck. I've never fished for one, but I've eaten some Spiker netted. Hubbub is the expert at catching snook with a buggy whip."

While Ruckus made bucci and Hubbub fried dog snapper Snarly asked if he could shine the spotlight in the water fifty feet from the wreck to gather up a school of bait fish. I twirled my finger as I puffed on a joint then passed it. While we chewed on snapper with a fruit and vegetable salad, Snarly asked Hubbub what was the best lure to catch a snook.

He replied, "The rattling shad rap. I got some below."

It didn't take long for bait fish to gather in the light to eat plankton. The predators responded by rapidly streaking through the light in a flash. The bait would vanish then return to its feeding.

After a smoke and some bucci we went aft with Hubbub's tackle box. He gave Snarly a rattling shad rap. Snarly tied it to his line then said, "That should do it."

Hubbub said, "It might."

Snarly asked, "What do you mean by that?"

He said, "I noticed you tied your line to the slip ring they put on the screw-eye. Those slip rings are a trick. They don't work well with an acrobatic fish like the snook and you should be using at least three feet of wire because they have a tendency to fall on the mono when they jump and more often than not they cut you away with their razor sharp gill plates."

Snarly said, "No fish is that smart." He cast the lure past the pool of light then quickly cranked it through it with fast jerks. A twenty-pound snook streaked out of the darkness and hooked itself on the lure. It went airborne instantly, fell on Snarly's line and cut him away. He gave Hubbub a sulky look and asked for another lure. Hubbub handed him one along with a roll of thirty pound wire. Snarly put the end of the wire through the slip ring to make his haywire twist that wouldn't kink and break.

Hubbub said, "Wrong!"

Snarly said, "The slip ring is on there so I can remove the wire and fish it with mono. Have it your way when you're fishing." He made his cast at the light and hooked another snook that went airborne and landed on the wire then swiftly dashed at the boat as it did a three-hundred-sixty degree flip. Still hooked the fish rushed at the wreck doing a series of flips until the wire slipped around the inside of the ring.

Snarly sat on the caprail and shook his head. Hubbub

wired up a lure and passed it. Snarly thanked him then made his cast. A large cuda charged the lure and chewed it up as he worked it to the gaff. By the time he removed it from the cuda's mouth it was in pieces.

Hubbub gave him another lure then said, "You are zero for three and this is the last one."

The snook were surrounding the light. One grabbed the lure when it moved and put on a show equal to that of an acrobat as Snarly applied pressure to the drag, keeping the fish out of the wreck then to the gaff. He thanked Hubbub for his help and apologized for doubting his experience.

While he cleaned his fish, Ruckus and Hubbub went about casting lures with one barbless hook that the fish could easily dislodge by jumping then shaking their heads.

Spiker called and asked where I was. I said, "Just over the horizon from Great Inagua anchored in the lee of this rusting windbreak."

He said, "I'll be coming up from the south around sunset. Make your arrival from the west before me to get The Dirt's mule off his sailboat."

I asked, "How's your head?"

He said, "You should answer that question from your own mishaps. I'll see you tomorrow evening. At the moment I'm running blind, all my electronics have shut down. There's a crew coming over from a cutter to work on the wiring."

I said, "The Dirt must have let Fairel on your boat while you were sleeping."

He said, "That's a possibility I'll need to find out."

I asked, "You want some lobsters?"

He said, "I'm sure we would all like some!"

I said, "The Rug Rats will be in the water tomorrow. I'll save you a bucket of conchs, too."

"Thanks!" came the reply, "I'll be standing by on the sideband."

CHAPTER 15
Great Inagua

Spiker saw me anchored a mile to the west when he came up from the south. He called and asked, "Why haven't you taken care of the mule?"

I said, "Because we are going to do this my way."

We entered the mooring basin as the edge of the sun touched the horizon. I made a hundred and eighty degree turn then eased her against the seawall in the southwest corner of the basin, which left an open space between me and The Dirt's sailboat so the mailboat and Coast Guard could tie up. Spiker followed me in then tied up on the west side of the corner next to me. The Dirt's mule walked down his gangplank headed for Spiker's boat.

I looked at Snarly and said, "Get between him and Spiker. You don't need to be nice about it."

Snarly jumped on the dock in front of the mule, raised his arms then said, "Hold up dick stain before you get some seaman on you that don't wash off."

The mule said, "See here, you can't talk to me like that, I'll knock you on your ass!"

Snarly turned his head to port then said, "Damn that stinks. You need to change your mouthwash." A second later he placed his left ankle behind the mule's left ankle as he placed his left open hand on the mule's chest then shoved him on his ass.

The mule said, "I'll have the sheriff on you for this." By then, Snarly was flanked by his brothers.

Ruckus said, "You need to get up the road and do that."

The mule reached into his pocket and pulled out a cell phone. A small slip of paper fell to the asphalt. Ruckus quickly grabbed the phone and picked up the piece of paper. The mule stood up and headed to The Dirt's boat.

Ruckus moved around him then stood on the gangplank and said, "I'm impounding this boat. You can't board her."

He said, "I need my car keys."

Ruckus said, "Sorry, you must walk to the sheriff's office and spend the night there or take to the bush. There's plenty of pigs and flamingos to eat, but freshwater is hard to find even if it rains. You could pick up your pusher and take him with you. He probably knows a lot more about the bush if you're not afraid of the pit bulls that will be turned loose."

When the mule was up the road and out of sight Spiker and The Dirt came over. Ruckus handed The Dirt the mule's phone then said, "Tell anybody who calls that you are out of fix."

Snarly asked, "What's on that piece of paper?"

Ruckus pulled it out and read aloud, "Banana Boat, 16-K-H. The date is day after tomorrow."

Spiker intruded by taking the phone away from The Dirt and saying, "I don't want him talking to anyone." Then he said, "You've opened a can of worms with that piece of paper so you deal with it."

I said, "The Black Mamba will handle it and if he doesn't find it, I will." I asked, "What's in those ship containers over there?"

He said, "I don't know, but if I had to guess I would say heavy air-to-ground ordnance if things don't go as planned." He grabbed The Dirt by the arm and pulled him towards his sailboat to make the necessary calls that would set up an air drop at Pig Boat Shoals.

As darkness filled the basin, the wind ceased to a lull leaving silence. The street light at the top of the hill came on. There was a tall brown man standing under it. The silence was interrupted by the sound of a branch breaking.

Snarly growled, "There's something in the bush."

I said, "The Mamba's in his nest and that was a warning about that man on the hill."

I walked to the path that led into the jungle to some critter infested porta pottys. As I entered the path the jungle opened up and a long brown arm reached out then pulled me in. The Mamba pointed at the man under the light and said, "That's the mule's pusher. He's the last big problem here. Lately he's been intimidating poor people and ripping them off. He's a ballsy bastard. If you leave your boat open and go up the street to the Greek diner to eat he will board your boat to steal what he can. He's a ripe target for a few rounds from Betsy."

I said, "Snarly will set her up. I'll get everybody in a cab to the diner. Let me know the outcome at dinner."

He said, "Use game loads, dump out the rabbit shot and cut this into quarter-inch chunks." He handed me a piece of salted pork fat with some rind on it.

I returned to the boat and sat at the helm. I looked at Snarly and said, "Take Betsy, the ball-busting butt spreader, out of her cage and set her up on her tripod aimed at the port galley door at crotch level. Set the electronics to fire one shot per pass through the laser beam. With any luck he will take the first shot in the groin then turn around and take the other one up the ass."

I tossed the salted pork fat on the table then said, "Cut it in small pieces then pack it in game load shells. Don't use the buck loads, it might kill him."

Fishing the Devil's Triangle...

I sent Hubbub to tell Spiker that he needs to lock up their boats and call some cabs to go to eat dinner. As we stood around the parking lot waiting for the cabs, the pusher headed to a path in the jungle on the other side of the street. The cabs arrived then dropped us off at the restaurant. We entered and walked by the long bar to some tables in the back then ordered the special which was oxtails and land crab claws in curried rice with fried plantains.

While the food was being served, a tall husky drag queen strutted through the door dressed in a flashy outfit with pom-pom balls dangling. As he passed the bar hip-hopping he threw his arms over the shoulders of some of the men and pinched them on the ass.

Hubbub said, "It's SA-? It's SA-?"

Ruckus said, "It's an it's SA- for sure, No 'Bout a'Doubt it."

Snarly said, "You're both blind as a cave fish and daft as an unfortunate retard, for it's plain to see it's the Mamba doing his job tho' he be a'wearing his frills. Besides you shouldn't be talking that way about your half-brother."

The Mamba sat at the table across from me. I stared into the emerald green eyes of the most fierce-looking brown man I have ever seen. He looked at Snarly and said, "You were right on with the first blast, but it knocked him back through the laser so he took the other blast in the belly while he was falling backwards."

He asked, "Did you bring the keys to the trap house?"

Snarly replied, "Yes, what do you need them for?"

The Mamba said, "See those two men with turbans, they're the ones supplying The Dirt's mule. Shades from Hades and his horde of belly-dancers are on their way here to lure them into the trap house."

Snarly growled, "Why do we have to deal with him?"

The Mamba asked, "You got a problem with that?"

Snarly said, "I can't stand his grueling contempt, his

smirky intimidation and his hopeless self-fucking righteousness. It will only take a few seconds to walk over there and knock 'em in the head, pick up one under each arm then be out the door and throw them in the back of the Mamba's truck."

The Mamba smiled at Snarly, shook his head then said, "No rough stuff, just give me the keys."

I asked, "What's on your schedule for tomorrow?"

He said, "I don't have anything to do until the air drop."

I told him about the slip of paper and the banana boat.

He said, "That's something! I'll look it over. Tomorrow I'm going to the east side and run a pig out of the bush then spear some groupers and take a turtle. You can come along if you want."

As we stood to leave, Snarly headed toward the men's restroom. The Mamba said, "You don't want to go in there."

Snarly said, "It can't be that bad, I've got to wizz."

We waited for him then stopped at the bar to pay the tab. The greasy Greek at the cash register asked if we enjoyed the food. Snarly said, "Yea, it was OK, but it all turned to acid when I went into your restroom!"

The Greek asked, "Is the toilet stopped up again?"

Snarly growled, "Aye, and that ain't all. There's crap stains and dick stains everywhere on the floor, the sink and mirror ain't been scrubbed since they were installed decades ago, and I had to close my eyes while I was leaving a leak so I wouldn't read the historic and demonic literature written on your microbe crawling walls!"

As we headed back to the boats in the Mamba's truck I asked Spiker about the air drop. He said, "There will be four DEA agents here in three days with movie cameras to film what goes down. You might want to hang offshore until we leave, unless you want to smile for history!"

As Spiker and The Dirt went to their boats, the Mamba said, "I'll see you at sunrise."

Fishing the Devil's Triangle...

First light came with a cool breeze from the north. The Mamba tied his skiff to my starboard side. In the skiff were two very large female brindled pit bulls. Scattered around them were two baseball bats, dive gear, spearguns, a yo-yo with line and turtle hook plus a cooler full of snacks.

As I was climbing in, he informed Snarly that the crew from the salt plant would be coming soon to unload the fish. As the Mamba ran the skiff to the east side, I gazed with wonder at the amazing huge flocks of pink flamingos eating brine shrimp from the shallow salt ponds surrounding the miles of bush that are infested with wild hogs. The Mamba beached the skiff near a pig run that snaked through the jungle. The pit bulls jumped from the skiff and raced into the pig run.

The Mamba picked up the bats then handed me one. He said, "Stand on the side of the path and knock the hog in the head when he makes a run for the water to get away from the dogs."

While we listened to the pit bulls braying on the trail of a hog, the Mamba asked, "Why did you offer to help Spiker after what he did the last time around?"

I said, "Because he's unarmed and we don't have to be, tho' it may not help, since I don't want to start popping caps unless we're pushed into a corner."

He asked, "Why don't you get out of this drug mess and get into politics?"

I said, "Not enough exercise. I'd go pot belly and shiftless. Besides, what I'm doing now ain't much different than politics. In either case you must force your will on something that can bite back. I'd rather take my chances with the real sharks. If they start taking too many fish off my hook, I can hook a buoy on them and let 'em fight that or I can just blow them away without dodging bullets and suffering the bureaucratic flack that comes with them if I come out on top!"

The braying of the pit bulls was closer. "Hog coming," the Mamba said. "By the way it's pounding the ground I'd say it's a big one." The 300-pound boar rushed out of the bush headed for the water. The Mamba clubbed it then I clubbed it as the pit bulls grabbed it by its hind legs. The boar arched its body, trying to gore the dogs. The Mamba gave it a few more whacks that ended the struggle. As the boar convulsed while dying he grabbed a knife from the skiff then slit the boar's throat. After it bled out he dragged it on to a canvas tarp and wrapped it before we hauled in into the skiff.

We headed for the north side to some coral patches where he speared some large grouper and snapper. There was a green turtle resting in a coral cave. He swam it to the surface and laid it on its back under the stern seat. We had lunch and a slow ride back to the basin. Men from the salt plant hauled away the catch. Having nothing to do until the banana boat arrived in the morning, we smoked ourselves asleep.

Just before sunset we awoke to the sound of men from the salt plant putting seafood on the counter and galley table. We feasted and guzzled beer until we passed out.

Snarly woke me from my hangover at sunrise with breakfast on the table. I smoked a joint to remove the hangover pain.

As we sat around stuffing our faces, the Mamba came down from the flying bridge then said, "Banana boat coming in."

The captain of the banana boat eased his starboard side against the seawall between my stern and The Dirt's sailboat. I climbed to the flying bridge. The Mamba, the sheriff and the deputy inspected the cases of assorted tropical fruits and bananas that were being loaded on trucks. After all the cargo was unloaded, the Mamba asked the captain and crew to stand on the seawall so a search for contraband could be held. As the sheriff and deputy went below, the Mamba searched the wheelhouse. After completing his inspection he turned on the radar. It didn't light up on the display. He stepped out of the wheelhouse then looked up to see if the turret was turning. It wasn't. He gave the captain a suspicious look.

The captain said, "I've got parts below to fix it when I have time." The Mamba went below to talk with the sheriff.

After completing what they said was a thorough search the Mamba looked up at me then said, "We can't find anything, I guess I'll have to let them go."

I said, "You need to finish your search."

He asked, "What did I miss?"

I said, "All of it!"

He said, "Then you climb down and show me!"

He followed me below in the banana boat. All the large storage drawers were removed from their frame and the contents dumped out on the work tables except for the one containing the box of radar parts. I opened the box and saw a complete set of components for the guts of the turret box and display cabinet on the console. I removed the box of parts from the drawer then put it in one of the empty drawers so I could inspect the bottom.

The box of parts set three inches lower into the empty drawer. Under the false bottom of the first drawer was four kilos of heroin.

I said, "Go put the captain and crew in cuffs then take the radar boxes apart. There should be two kilos in each one. I'll look for the other eight."

I couldn't see anything in the packing room large enough to contain eight kilos. I entered the small engine room. There was a large block of rough cut wood three feet square and five inches thick bolted to the engine bed aft of the engine. It was butted against the bulkhead that separates the engine from the lazarette. Mounted to the block of wood was a large one-ten generator. Between the engine and generator there was some scrapes and scratches on top of the engine bed beams, as if the block of wood had been slid forward many times.

To confirm my suspicions I grabbed a small hammer from a tool box and tapped on the front end of the block of wood which produced a solid thud sound. As I tapped towards the back end of the block the sound changed to a hollow thunk foretelling possible cavities.

The Mamba entered the engine room then said, "There's eight kilos top side." He asked, "Anything down here?"

I said, "Unbolt the generator from the engine bed and slide it forward. The dope is in the aft end of the mounting block."

As he picked up a socket wrench he said, "I've been a friend of the banana man for years, and for that reason I believed his lie. Sorry, I won't fall for that trick again."

I said, "Don't worry about it, it's OK to believe a friend until something happens to create doubt. Gather up your friends from the salt plant then we'll get the boat ready to go fishing so the Coast Guard can use this spot to tie up and deal with Spiker."

When everyone was aboard we headed north to some coral patches. We fished until the evening of the next day when Spiker appeared on the horizon headed south for the cutter on station north of the windward passage.

We pulled the anchor and headed for the mooring basin where we unloaded the fish along with the crew from the salt plant then headed south in Spiker's wake.

CHAPTER 16
Gitmo Bay to Aruba

When we arrived at the cutter on station north of the windward passage crews and boats were launched to transfer the drugs and agents along with their cameras that showed Spiker receiving the drugs and giving the pilot of the air boat the ten small boxes of bullion valued at one million dollars.

As we headed south through the center of the passage Spiker called on the side band to confess that his oil pump had blown its seal and he was turning southwest to Gitmo for a replacement that was being flown in.

He went on to say, "When we get closer there will be a long line of Cuban gunboats flashing white strobe lights displaying our course into Gitmo."

I said, "I'll follow in case you need a tow but I won't throw you a line. You must throw it to me so I don't have to be responsible for your decisions."

We made it into Gitmo without towing then tied up to a low dock in the northeast corner of the bay. The west side of the bay was mostly massive high docks built to accommodate battleships. The entire bay is surrounded by mountains crawling with lizards. The oil pump arrived the next morning then one hour later we were underway on a course to Aruba. The wind was calm and the air humid all

219

the way there. We tied to a seawall in a large bay that contained hundreds of sixty to ninety foot boats loading up with whiskey and cigarettes imported on large container ships, then exported to places in South America by the motley crews of the smaller boats.

We climbed up the seawall then walked north up the road where we encountered numerous streets lined on both sides with bars to slack the thirst of thousands of sailors and dock workers. At each end of each bar was a legal whore that saw the doctor twice a week. Spiker and The Dirt checked into a hotel to meet with a cartel employee that arranged for four hundred and fifty kilos to be loaded on his boat in the graveyard on the north coast of South America. We hailed a cab to tour the island and have our laundry cleaned.

The next morning we headed west before sunrise. Overnight the wind had increased to gale force out of the north, forcing us to run in a deep trough with battering waves pounding her starboard side. When we reached the graveyard towering waves were crashing on the eroded hills that surrounded it. Scattered on the beach and in the water were wrecks of all shapes and sizes that tried to pick up drugs in foul weather. The water was deep right up to the beach. If your engine stalled or you moved too close in a northerly gale, that's where you stayed.

At the entrance to the bay there was an exhaust funnel on a large freighter sticking out of the water. The freighter was sunk on the south side of a windbreak that created a calm area.

Snarly lassoed the funnel and we laid with the wind. Spiker rigged a grapnel with a trip then hooked it on the freighter's railing. We caught some fish for dinner as the sun moved to the twilight zone. As we munched on the wreck grouper a launch entered the bay from a creek on the south side. The transfer of drugs and bullion went quickly and Spiker headed north as darkness hid his boat with all lights off except the compass.

I called him and asked, "What's your next way point?"

He said, "There's a large rock sticking out of the water two hundred miles south of Hispaniola. There's an air boat waiting for a call from The Dirt when we get there. It's loaded with another four hundred and fifty kilos."

I said, "When you're over my horizon give me a call if you don't like what you see. We will hang here for awhile and let you know if any go-fast boats leave the bay on your trail." I fired up my last joint then told the rug rats that I was going straight until we get home.

When Spiker could no longer see the coast, he called to say someone was shooting off distress flares from the southeast.

I said, "I see them, stay on your course, we are on our way." As we headed north I found it hard to believe that no one was trying to take Spiker's load. I guess they were misinformed and didn't know he was virtually unarmed.

We reached our way point south of Hispaniola then The Dirt made his call on Spiker's side band. Four hours later the air boat arrived with Spiker's dope then flew away with the bullion.

We caught some fish to eat then Snarly fried 'em up crispy. As we munched and crunched I asked Spiker what our next way point was.

He said, "I've got to take The Dirt and this nine hundred kilos to Montego Bay where they will be transported to a warehouse at the base of mount Valhalla where the other four hundred and fifty kilos have been stored. In order for The Dirt to win his stay at a halfway house, he must get the Mussarana in front of a camera with the pay off money and the bales containing the thirteen-hundred and fifty-kilos.

"Now that me and The Dirt are out of the danger zones, your next way point is Key West or wherever you choose and you can take Jolly with you unless you want to see this through to the end and meet the Mussarana while you look upon the effects of his disease with its stink. I don't know if its leprosy or kuru, it could be both or just a lot of pusy boils."

I said, "We will leave you to it. I'm headed back to the Black Mamba's shack to refuel and get some rest while I try to find some gunja for the ride home. When I get there I'm going fishing with the porgy master. We will be hauling ass in his "panga" fishing one spot then another in the inshore bays and harbors catching a few large porgies here and there while we piss off the blow boaters who don't care for the wakes.

"After that it won't be possible to reach me or the rug rats for comment because we will be catching fish for a hungry tribe of mad cannibals somewhere along the Ivory Coast."